Lizzie

By Sarah Price

Copyright © 2020 Price Productions, LLC.

All rights reserved.

No part of this book may be reproduced in any form, stored in any retrieval system, or transmitted in any form by any means—electronic, mechanical, photocopy, recording, or otherwise—without prior written permission of the publisher, except as provided by United States of America copyright law.

Published by Price Productions, LLC, Archer, Florida

Disclaimer

Out of respect for the Amish families who have accepted me into their homes and hearts, I honor their wishes to center my novels on major towns such as Shipshewana in Indiana, Berlin in Ohio, or Intercourse in Pennsylvania. Otherwise, the more rural communities may risk having tourists disrupt their tranquil lives.

Therefore, this novel takes place in a fictitious area of Indiana: Blue Mill in Lower Austen County and Clearwater in Upper Austen County. The names of the towns were created in my imagination. The people in this novel are also fictional and bear no resemblance to anyone that I've met in my travels.

Chapter One

Lizzie hurried down the driveway, her bare feet kicking up dust as she waved the plain white envelope in the air. "Letter for you, Daed!" she called out as she approached the barn.

With the sun overhead, the faded siding on the two-story building appeared even more bleached than she remembered from previous days. It seemed that there was always something on the farm that was in dire need of a fresh coat of paint. Now that spring was only weeks away, Lizzie suspected that painting the barn would be one of the projects they'd tackle first, after the crops were planted, of course.

Then again, she knew that her father, Amos Bender, didn't always put much stock in making the farm look well cared for. After all, he'd grown up in a family that hadn't focused on the appearance of a property but, rather, on the functionality of the farm and its occupants. Lizzie suspected it had something to do with both of her father's grandparents having been raised by Swartzentrubers, one of the most conservative groups within the Amish faith.

Thankfully, when Amos's father reached the age to become a baptized member of the church, he'd left the strict church district run by the Swartzentrubers and moved to a nearby and less strict Amish community, bringing his future wife with him. Understandably, however, just because Amos's parents were baptized in a less strict church district hadn't meant that they gave up all the practices learned from their childhood. Those lessons were often the hardest to forget, it seemed, and had been passed along to Lizzie's father.

Amos was one of the older Bender sons. When he married Lizzie's mother, Susan, Amos had purchased his own farm, close enough to help his parents, if needed but still far enough away to gain some independence. The family always thought that Amos's younger brother, Samuel, would inherit the family farm. But, to their surprise, Samuel had taken up carpentry instead and, a few years before his parents passed away, moved to a new Amish community in Westcliffe, Colorado, where he helped build houses and barns for other families who had relocated to that area.

And so, the family farm had somehow passed to Amos, instead.

Whenever Lizzie had visited with her grandparents, she'd wondered why they rarely cleaned their house and was always taken aback by the heaps of garbage that piled up behind the shed. They seemed to grow larger with each passing year.

"It's the Swartzentruber way," her father had explained to her during one of their visits. "To tend to the yard or remove the garbage or even to clean the house is thought to be prideful."

Not only did Lizzie disagree, but she also couldn't fathom living that way. She knew she would've disliked having been raised in such a strict manner. While her mother wasn't from such a background, she also wasn't one to fuss too much over the condition of the yard or cleanliness of the house, though she always kept a tidy kitchen. Fortunately, Jane and Lizzie felt otherwise and did what they could to stay on top of the household chores when their mother failed to do so.

"A letter?" a deep voice called out from the hayloft. "Bring it here, Dochder."

As soon as she heard her father's command, Lizzie made her way toward the handmade ladder against the side of the barn. It was nailed securely to the building and led upward to the double doors of the hayloft. Today, the doors were hanging wide open and two sparrows were perched on the edge. As she began climbing higher, the birds grew nervous and flew away once she reached the top rungs.

As she climbed, her view of the farm changed. Ever since she was old enough to climb the ladder alone, she would sneak off to the hayloft to lean against one of the windows and gaze out over the fields. She loved to watch the black Angus cows as they meandered up the hill and through the back pasture near her grandparents' old farm. No one lived there now; its vacancy was a constant thorn in her father's side.

Toward the rear of the property, there was a small spring-fed pond where the cows often paused for a long sip of fresh water. Even during the hottest days in August, the spring fed water was always cool. The pond was another of Lizzie's favorite places, especially on hot summer nights when the air stilled, and no breeze could be found. Quite often, after her chores were finished, she'd escape to the pond with her older brother, Jacob. There was nothing she liked better than to sit beside him with their feet dangling in the water, surrounded by the silence of nature while they tossed fishing lines into the pond.

Today, however, was neither hot nor summer so she thought it odd that she was thinking about the pond and her brother Jacob. Besides, it had been a long time since they'd gone fishing together. That thought gave her a pang in her chest. Why *hadn't* they gone fishing as of late? Perhaps it was because her brother was too busy with all the animals that needed tending and field work that needed to be completed. And, on those rare occasions when he had a free moment, it felt as if he preferred visiting friends in neighboring towns to hanging out with one of his younger sisters.

Of course, Lizzie didn't always mind when he wasn't working or hanging around the farm, because it meant that she had her father all to herself. And today, Lizzie was especially grateful that he had finished up early and gone to visit with friends.

It was no secret that Amos Bender favored his firstborn—and only—son. But, of the three daughters that followed Jacob's birth, Lizzie knew she held a special place in her father's heart.

When Lizzie reached the top, she climbed through the open doors and stood, pausing for a second to brush off her rich burgundy dress. She wore no shoes and the remnants of hay on the rough strewn floorboards tickled the bottoms of her feet.

"Where are you, Daed?" she called out.

She heard a shuffling sound coming from the far end of the loft. "Here, Lizzie."

Quietly, she made her way toward the bales of hay that were stacked ten high at the back of the loft.

"Ah, sweet Lizzie," her father said with a long sigh. He sat on a chair; his feet propped against the sill of the small open window. It was their secret, this hiding place of her father's. Long ago, he had built a makeshift desk in the back of the hayloft. Shortly thereafter, Lizzie had helped him move an old chair up there, one that swiveled so he could look out the window and gaze upon his fields.

Lizzie had never asked why her father hid himself away from the rest of the family. She already knew the answer without having to ask the question. Like her, Amos Bender relished his time alone to reflect and ponder life without disruption. Up here, in the dusty hayloft with cobwebs filling the corners and exposed beams hanging low overhead, there was no fear of having his thoughts interrupted. Her younger sister, Katie, was terrified of heights—or, perhaps it was just her fear of hard work, Lizzie often wondered—so she rarely ventured into the barn. As for Lizzie's older sister, Jane, she mostly stayed inside the house, helping their mother. Lizzie was sure that she knew nothing about the secret hiding spot. But, even if Jane had discovered her father's favorite hiding place, she would never have told their mother about it. Even though Jane was not as close to their father as Lizzie, she wasn't one to share secrets.

After all, anyone who knew their mother and her trying ways, would certainly understand the need for their father to steal a few minutes of peace from time to time.

As Lizzie approached him, he reached out his hand to take the envelope. "Is it from my cousin, then?"

Lizzie gave a little laugh. "Now Daed, you know I'd no sooner open your mail than Maem wouldn't hesitate to do so!"

His eyes brightened and his weathered face lit up at Lizzie's playful jest. "That's quite true, my girl," he laughed, the deep baritone of his voice resonating in the hayloft. "Quite true, indeed." Taking the letter from her, he reached into his pocket for a pair of reading glasses. "Let's see now," he said with a soft sigh, sliding the glasses onto the bridge of his nose so that he could read the return address. "Why, indeed! This *is* the letter I've been waiting for!"

Plopping down on a nearby haybale, Lizzie leaned her back against the wall, swatting at a small spider that dangled from the low-hanging rafters, while watching her father open the letter.

She knew that he had been waiting for this letter for some time and she also knew that her mother had no idea it was due to arrive. If there was one thing the entire church district recognized about the Bender family, it was that the matriarch, Susan Bender, was the nosiest women in all Blue Mill. Perhaps in all Lower Austen County!

And Amos Bender did not want his wife to spread gossip if there was none to be shared. So, he hadn't shared the fact that something was brewing with anyone except Lizzie, that is. She had long ago earned the role of confidant to her father. Of course, even if there *was* something to share with Susan and even if her father *could* trust his wife, Lizzie suspected that Amos enjoyed the thought that he alone could savor the knowledge of deliciously wonderful news before his wife caught wind of it.

"What's it say, Daed?" Lizzie watched his face as he slid a finger along the back of the envelope and pulled out a single sheet of lined paper, both sides covered in neat handwriting.

Her father's tired blue eyes peered over the rim of his glasses. "The Lord might know everything, Lizzie, but, my dear *dochder*, I can assure you *I* do not."

She smiled at his teasing words.

"You'll have to wait until I actually read it." He winked at her. "Which, if you don't mind, I'll do right now. Your *muder* will certainly want to hear of the news the moment I tell her a letter has arrived."

Lizzie settled onto the hay bale and watched her father as his eyes scanned the paper. "That's quite true, I'm sure."

It was also true that Amos Bender—and Lizzie, for that matter—were anxiously awaiting news regarding his parent's old family farm, located less than a mile from the Bender's property. Last autumn, their long-term tenants had suddenly moved. They'd decided to try their hand at farming in Westcliffe, Colorado where land was more readily available, and a farm was far cheaper to acquire. Westcliff had attracted a small Amish community and word was that they were flourishing as families relocated, now able to purchase their own land instead of farming someone else's. Their tenants were not the only family to abandon Austen County where the land was scarce and very dear. When they left, Amos had written to his cousin, informing him about the sudden vacancy.

"*Ach vell*," her father finally said, removing his reading glasses and setting them atop his head. "Seems he knows of another family that's interested in renting the farm." Amos smiled. "I knew that Thomas would come through."

Lizzie had never met this cousin of her father's. In fact, she hadn't met much of her extended family. They were scattered about the United States, most of them in Austen and Holmes County, but many in Indiana and Pennsylvania, too. One branch of the family even lived as far south as Tennessee. But if there was one thing about the Benders, it was that no matter the distance, they always kept in touch with each other.

"Which family, Daed? Anyone you know?"

Amos shook his head, his eyes still scanning the letter. Suddenly, he smiled. "Ah, the nephew of his *fraa*. A man named Christopher Burkholder."

Lizzie breathed a sigh of relief. "That's *gut* news!" To keep the old farm rented meant that the income it generated would help ease some of the burden her father always felt around this time of the year. After winter, money seemed to dry up and, as every farmer knew, springtime meant a lot of bills in order to prep for new crops.

He glanced up, pausing for effect. "And there's more."

Lizzie leaned forward on the hay bale, resting her elbows on her knees and her chin on her hands as she peered at her father. "What's that, Daed?" she asked, eager to hear. She loved the way he told stories, dragging out details and creating an air of suspense rather than just telling her everything all at once. Her mother was the complete opposite. She couldn't stomach the strain of anticipation which, Lizzie suspected, was probably why her father had mastered the skill.

"Promise you won't tell this little tidbit to your *maem*? It was shared in confidence."

Lizzie laughed. As if her father needed to ask her that. "Not unless you want the entire *g'may* to learn the news before the roosters are up." Her mother loved to share news with the church district, that was for sure and certain.

13

Lowering his voice, her father scanned the letter as if to confirm what he wanted to share with her one more time. "Well, it seems this Christopher Burkholder isn't yet married."

Immediately, Lizzie rolled her eyes. She knew exactly what *that* meant. "Oh help!"

Her father laughed. "If your *maem* finds out, we're all in big trouble."

That was an understatement. "Trust me, for Jane's sake, I'd never tell." The last thing Lizzie wanted was for her sister to be paraded around this Christopher fellow like a prize cow at auction. And, knowing her mother as well as any daughter could, Lizzie knew that would be *exactly* what she would do. With four unmarried children—and three of them daughters—Susan Bender was eager to marry off any and all of her children. Her greatest hope was that one or two future sons-in-law, would take over the bulk of the work on their farm so she and Amos could spend their winters in Pinecraft, Florida with the other Amish folks who were fortunate enough to do so.

But Amos Bender hated that idea, almost as much as Lizzie did.

Even though Lizzie suspected that her father was tired...tired of working so hard and not having very much help, he surely hated the idea of wintering in Pinecraft.

Unlike many of the other farmers in Blue Mill, Amos was blessed with only one son and, therefore, he was accustomed to working hard to make up for the lost manpower on the farm. Sometimes his daughters helped in the fields, but, as a rule, Katie was far too lazy and Jane far too ladylike to make a dent in the heavy field work. So, the task of helping with spring planting and fall harvesting often fell upon Lizzie's shoulders, chores she didn't particularly mind since it kept her out of the house and away from her mother. As of late, the topic of discussion almost always focused on Susan's desperation to get her three daughters married, so Lizzie welcomed the farm chores even more than ever these days.

There were few prospects in Blue Mill for the Bender sisters. Or, at least, not prospects that suited the *needs* of the Bender family. After all, with land being so expensive and the Amish families so large, most of the young men who wouldn't inherit their family's farms, focused on developing other skills to earn a living. Skills such as carpentry, cabinet making, shed building, and even landscaping. Many moved far away, venturing to new Amish communities that were springing up in places like Colorado or Montana. A few even traveled across oceans, settling in in even more isolated communities in Belize and Costa Rica, a prospect that didn't appeal to anyone in the Bender family.

Even more unfortunate, particularly in their small church district, most of the farmers were either already married or nearing retirement, preparing to pass their farms down to one or two of their sons. Their *married* sons, as Susan often lamented to anyone who would listen. With an older son and two of her daughters of marrying age---and so few potential suitors in the community!--the matriarch of the Bender family spent far too many sleepless nights worrying about the future prospects of her children. And, to make matters worse, it seemed that she was becoming more and more vocal about her concerns.

More than she cared to admit, Lizzie often overheard her mother as she sat with the other women after worship service, scheming about how to marry off her daughters before they became old spinsters. It was quite the joke among the other Amish women in the church district that Susan Bender would do just about anything to lure a young Amish man to her house for Sunday supper. And, because of that, most young men avoided the Bender girls all together.

Lizzie didn't really care though. Usually her mother's attention centered on Jane because she was not only the eldest but appeared to be the "perfect" Amish woman. Quiet and kind, Jane had large green eyes and shiny blond hair. She was also very pretty—although everyone knew that Amish people aren't supposed to care about such prideful things like beauty.

Unfortunately, though, Lizzie knew that many Amish *did.* And she couldn't compete with Jane's beauty. After all, she had inherited her mother's mousy brown hair and almond shaped chocolate eyes. Sometimes, late at night when she lay in bed trying to find sleep, she would wonder what it would feel like to have such a pretty face instead of such a plain one.

But it didn't bother Lizzie one bit. In fact, she was grateful that *her* name wasn't mentioned often in her mother's matchmaking plans. Frankly, she was content to remain at home, working alongside her father even if it meant that she would never marry. As far as she was concerned, if that was part of God's plan for her, then so be it. Besides, even though she had committed to the Amish way of life and worship when she was nineteen, Lizzie never favored a single one of the young men in her church district or any of the neighboring ones either, for that matter. She wasn't about to marry a man simply for the sake of getting married—she'd leave *that* to her two sisters, Katie and Jane. While she didn't approve of marrying unless it was a right match, Lizzie knew her sisters wouldn't be the only ones that might make compromises. Many Amish couples *did* marry for the sake of being married. Undoubtedly, there were economical and financial advantages to being married. But, for Lizzie, she viewed marriage in a very different light all together.

To her, marriage was about love and respect. Perhaps it was all the romance books she devoured—usually in secret so that she wouldn't have to listen to her mother reprimand her for reading romantic fiction instead of inspirational or devotional books. *No one married for love*, her mother always said, as if doing so was one of the most absurd thoughts she'd ever heard.

Still, Lizzie didn't care. Conformity was one thing. Two years ago, she had made *that* choice, quite willingly, when she took her kneeling vow before the church congregation, officially being baptized into the Amish faith. She couldn't imagine leaving the Amish community. However, as much as she didn't mind committing to following a plain life, she drew the line at committing to a marriage that was void of love.

Chapter Two

"My word, Christopher!"

Phineas stood on the edge of the field closest to the barn, holding his hand to his brow as he scanned the overgrown pastures and broken fences. The sun lingered overhead, blinding his blue eyes. The rim of his straw hat was not wide enough to block the harsh light.

"Truly, we must be in a different country, never mind state," he grumbled. "I've never seen such an impoverished Amish community in my entire life."

Just the day before, they had arrived in Blue Mill and already Phineas missed Clearwater. The town of Blue Mill was small, the farms built close together, and most of the buildings edged the road. It was so unlike Clearwater where the farms were spread out and long driveways meandered through pastures and fields that led to hidden farmhouses and barns nestled between pastures. And, to Phineas's disdain, many of the outbuildings were in terrible shape. Dirty, broken windowpanes in the barn, chipped paint, and rotting boards, heaps of trash piled three feet high behind dilapidated sheds, all caught his eye and made him long for home. It certainly did not leave a good first impression on a visitor, that was for sure and certain.

His friend, Christopher, walked up behind him and clapped him on the back in a good-natured way. "Oh Phineas, please!" He opened his arm and gestured around the property. "You see poverty and I see opportunity." He glanced over his shoulder at his friend. "Not all of us are fortunate enough to be born the sole male child to a wealthy farmer."

Knowing that Christopher was referencing his own situation, Phineas scoffed. "Being fortunate has nothing to do with it." He took a few steps and knelt, his hand immediately sinking into the dirt. "Clearly no one has fertilized this soil in years. How will you ever grow *any* crops worthy of selling?" As he stood up, he slapped his hands together creating a small cloud of dust. "I make my offer to you again, Christopher. Abandon this notion you have and return to Clearwater and continue to help me farm my land."

But, as usual, Christopher shook his head. "*Nee*, I won't do that, Phineas." He took a deep breath, his eyes scanning the pastures one last time. "I rented this place already and I intend to farm it. You know that."

"But you know no one here!"

Christopher took a deep breath and exhaled. "I prayed long and hard about this. I feel as if God wants to see what I can do here." He smiled at Phineas, his dark eyes sparkling. "Surely you can understand a man wanting to build something for himself."

Phineas wanted to tell him that the comment was unfair. It wasn't *his* fault that his father had inherited everything from *his* father and so forth.

Back when Phineas's grandfather first acquired the farm in Clearwater, land had been dirt cheap. They'd moved from Pennsylvania, a place where land was increasingly hard to come by anymore. He'd had five sons and bought as much land as he could to provide for each of them. But two of them didn't join the church, one died, and the other never married. That had left Phineas's father to inherit everything. And *he* had been blessed with just two children, one son and, many years later, a daughter. Upon his untimely death, Phineas had been the sole heir to the large homestead in Clearwater.

In truth, he hadn't *built* anything. He'd been handed *everything*. Of course, what he'd done with the land since then was another matter entirely.

"Besides," Christopher continued, "Blue Mill strikes me as a quaint town—"

"With quaint people, too, I imagine."

Unsurprisingly to Phineas, Christopher laughed. His positive attitude always seemed to prevail, even in the grimmest of situations. Clearly that was true even in regard to Blue Mill. "I find old fashion values to be rather attractive."

Phineas scoffed. "Old fashioned or lazy? Half of the farms around here have broken fences and overgrown fields. And more than a few have piles of garbage that need to be hauled away. You know how I detest unkempt farms!"

It was true. Phineas always worked from before sun-up until well after sun-down just to ensure that his farm was kept in the most meticulous of manners. Even though he was a bachelor, he paid a neighbor's daughter to help with the household chores. Five days a week, Ruth would arrive in the morning to do the cleaning, washing, canning, and weeding. He knew that the day was coming when Ruth would soon settle down—and it appeared that John Esh might be the man to steal her heart. He only hoped that his only sister, Grace Ann, had learned enough about housekeeping to manage the chores alone. But before that day came a hired hand would have to do. She was, after all, only fourteen-years-old and still in school.

In the meantime, Phineas spent his days tending to his cows and crops. But, every morning right after breakfast and just before he saw his little sister off to school, he took the time to walk his entire property to make sure that no fence board was broken. Twice a week—usually on Mondays and Fridays—he carried along a gasoline powered weed whacker to trim the fence line where need be.

"Now, now," Christopher chided gently. "My *daed* told me that many of these families were raised Swartzentruber."

Inwardly, Phineas groaned. Swartzentrubers! *That* explained a lot about the unkempt farms. The most conservative branch of the Amish, the Swartzentrubers lived as plain and simply as possible. Most of their homes didn't have running water while others shunned propane appliances and other conveniences that were permitted in other Amish communities.

It seemed to Phineas that the Swartzentrubers carried the weight of the world on their shoulders and, with the few that he knew, it showed in more ways than one. By the age of forty, most women walked with hunched over shoulders and appeared to be twice their age. Being in Blue Mill felt almost as though he had stepped back in time. It was hard for him to grasp that the Swartzentrubers felt that taking care of their property was a sign of vanity and pride. As a result, garbage often piled up in rear yards and rarely were the fences or houses painted.

"If that's so," Phineas said, "I reckon that's why things are so disorderly."

"Disorderly?" Christopher made a scoffing noise, his dark chocolate eyes scanning the horizon. There was something serene about his expression and, for the first time, Phineas found himself envious of his friend. Would he ever find such inner peace? Probably not for, as a child, Phineas's father had drilled work, work, work into his brain. "Just look around you, my friend. See how beautiful this place is. See what God created. I give thanks to his plan, for it has landed in my hands so that I may tend to it as he sees fit."

Sighing, Phineas followed his friend's eye. In truth, he had to admit that it *was* picturesque and, with such great potential for improvement, opportunity abounded for Christopher. It wasn't as flat as Clearwater and there were more tall trees to provide shade from the sun in the pastures. The white farmhouse—which looked as if it hadn't been painted in decades—had two large oak trees on the south and west side to help keep it cool during the hot summer months.

And yet, as Phineas looked around, he also recognized the tremendous amount of work and effort that needed to be put into the farm. Fencing had to be repaired; most of it was rotted and needed to be replaced entirely. The smaller barn had two broken windows and a missing door to the hayloft. He hadn't even entered the dairy barn yet, but he was certain the milk containment system would need to be overhauled.

There was much to do, that was for sure and certain. And not much time to do it. Phineas needed to return to Clearwater in no less than one month. After all, he had his *own* farm to manage and a sister to care for. Despite having Ruth help with the chores and a hired young man to tend to his animals, Phineas knew that the least amount of time away from his farm, the better. And, having sent Grace Ann to stay with their relatives in a neighboring town, Phineas knew he'd have to return soon for her sake, as well. Surely Grace Ann shouldn't spend more than a few weeks with her cousins and miss so much schooling. That would be taking advantage of their kindness and setting her behind with her schoolwork, he told himself.

As they stood there, each man lost in his own thoughts, Phineas heard Christopher take a deep breath and slowly exhale. It was a pleasant sound, one that spoke of happiness and contentment.

"Isn't this just grand, Phineas? I finally have my own farm!"

Giving into his friend's determination to make this work, Phineas managed to smile back at him. He'd never been one to take his own fortune for granted. He knew how hard good land was to find in the area. Christopher, indeed, was quite fortunate to have found this farm to lease even if it was in such poor condition.

"Indeed," Phineas said, reaching out to place his hand on his friend's shoulder. "But before you get too comfortable, we've much work to do in order to make it livable for both man and beast alike."

Christopher groaned.

Ignoring him, Phineas started walking back toward the house. "I suggest we make a list of what needs to be done first and another list of supplies we will need to get the work done. Your *schweister* will tackle the *haus*, I imagine, while we start mending fencing and the barn and the—"

Christopher laughed. "It took God six days to create the world, Phineas. I imagine we'll need much more than that to fix this farm."

"You can be sure about that, my friend." Phineas clapped him on the back before repeating, "You can be sure about that."

Chapter Three

Almost two weeks passed before Lizzie heard any news about the young Burkholder man who was leasing the farm. To be truthful, with all the work to be done preparing the fields for planting, she'd completely forgotten about the impending arrival of their new neighbor. Gossip was always the furthest thing from her mind because she had much more important things to do such as helping her father and Jacob with the milking and field work.

There was nothing she loved more than being outdoors, especially when winter gave way to spring. Lizzie enjoyed the longer days and warmer weather almost as much as she enjoyed the changes to the landscape. Trees began to bare little buds that, within a few weeks, would slowly open to reveal a sea of green, new leaves that would provide shade all summer long. Flowers would begin to poke through the soil, the crocus's and daffodils the first to paint the beds with pretty shades of purple and yellow. And the birds would return from their migration south, sharing their cheerful wake-up songs while Lizzie tended to the dairy cows as the sun was rising.

This morning, being a church Sunday, Lizzie worked quickly as she milked the cows alongside her brother. Unlike other farms that used milking machines, Amos insisted on hand-milking their herd. Lizzie suspected that was a throw-back to his upbringing. His parents had not favored installing a modern milking setup for the cows, even rejecting something as simple as a side opening parlor which permitted individual attention to each cow.

Without such a system, each cow needed to be milked by hand, each teat squeeze manually, the milk streaming into the metal buckets. Once filled, Lizzie carried each bucket to the milk cooler located in the back room. Despite their reluctance for modernization, neither her grandparents nor her father could fight the government regulations for installing a modern method for maintaining the temperature of the milk until the hauler came to fetch it, usually twice a week on Tuesdays and Fridays.

Today, as Lizzie carried the buckets to the back room, she barely noticed the humming of the diesel generator, which kept the bulk milk tank cool. As Lizzie poured the milk from each bucket into the tank, she glanced around the dark room. Someone had left three buckets in the large plastic sink under the window. She suspected that her father had left them for her to clean and sterilize. She didn't mind because that was one of her jobs. The men milked the cows and she cleaned the buckets. Lizzie set about sterilizing them, along with the two she'd just brought in from Jacob. Everything had to be sterilized after each use. Occasionally they were inspected by the agricultural department. Not once had they been issued a warning or citation for uncleanliness and Lizzie wanted to keep it that way.

When she finished with the buckets, she set three of them on the roughhewn bench by the sink—ready for the afternoon milking—and then she carried the others to her brother who sat on a three-legged stool, his shoulders hunched over and his cheek pressed against the cow's flank.

"Here you go." She set down the empty buckets and started to pick up the full one that needed to be emptied.

"I'll take that one, Lizzie. I'm almost finished," Jacob said, his attention on the cows, not his sister. "Go on inside and get washed up. I'll clean the last bucket for you." He turned his head and glanced at her, a mischievous smile on his lips. "You know how Maem gets when you aren't ready for worship on time."

Lizzie nodded, knowing he was right. Jacob had always been thoughtful like that.

Quietly, she hurried out of the barn. As soon as she entered the mudroom, she kicked off her old, battered work boots, and dashed through the kitchen toward the staircase.

Her mother's first floor bedroom door, located along the back wall of the kitchen, was still shut but she heard her call out, "Now don't you be dawdling, Elizabeth! You hurry now!"

"I will, Maem," Lizzie replied as she hurried upstairs.

Her mother always liked arriving for worship early, preferring to be one of the first women to get there. Lizzie suspected that she wanted to appear devout, but, in truth, she knew her mother only wanted to make sure she caught all of the gossip.

Upstairs, Lizzie washed her face and neck before donning her Sunday clothing: a dark navy dress, fastened together with tiny straight pins instead of buttons. Over it, she wore a crisp, white cape and apron, both made from organdy and both freshly laundered. The previous evening, she'd made certain everything was ready, inspecting her clothing to make sure there were no wrinkles. If there were, she'd have heard about it for days from her mother.

Finally dressed, Lizzie turned to the small oval mirror that hung from a rusty nail by the dresser. Earlier that morning, she'd hastily pinned her hair into a messy bun and put a simple scarf over her head. Now, however, she unpinned her hair, letting it fall down the length of her back, the long, loose waves almost reaching her waist.

Quickly, Lizzie ran a brush through her hair wishing, not for the first time, that she had been blessed with light, flaxen-colored curls like her sister Jane. But she knew that was foolishness. God had given her and Katie straight, brown hair while Jacob had inherited the curls but not the color. No amount of wishing would change it.

In truth, Lizzie didn't really mind. Blond or brunette. Straight or curly. God had made her special just the way she was and something as silly as her hair wouldn't change who she was.

"Lizzie?" Her mother hollered up the staircase. "You ready yet?"

"Coming." Quickly, Lizzie twisted her hair into a neat, slick bun and pinned it at the nape of her neck. Only then did she place her black prayer *kapp* on her head. Because she was a baptized member of the Amish church—and unmarried—she wore the black head covering on Sundays. One day, if she married, she would return to wearing a traditional white *kapp*. But until then, the black *kapp* was what she was required to wear on Sundays, a sign to the young men of the area that she was both baptized and available to be courted.

By the time she got downstairs, her brother was standing at the sink, washing his hands. Her sisters and father were already seated at the table, waiting for Lizzie and Jacob to join them. Breakfast on church Sundays was a quiet and modest affair for the Bender family. Amos and Susan might exchange a few pleasantries while their children tried to brace themselves for the upcoming three-hour long church service that faced them. Of course, afterward would be the fellowship meal and, for all of them, their favorite part of Sunday: a time to socialize with their friends. That evening, as was the norm, they'd attend a singing with the other young adults in their district. But first, they had to get through those three, long hours, seated on hard, wooden benches. It wasn't any wonder that not one of the children appeared to be enthusiastic about the morning's activities.

"Heard we might have some guests attending worship service today," Amos said, breaking the silence.

Everyone looked up, a silence blanketing the room. It wasn't unusual for guests to attend church service. What *was* unusual, however, was for their father to know in advance and, even more importantly, to mention it at all.

Every pair of eyes focused on him, although Susan tried to appear uninterested. Lizzie, however, clearly noticed the gleam of curiosity shining from behind her mother's eyes. If their father had intended to capture his wife's attention, he had achieved his objective.

"Oh?" Susan said casually. "And who might this guest be? Anyone we know?"

Amos reached for a slice of toast and began to spread it with homemade jam. He took his time, moving the knife slowly across the surface. Lizzie watched her mother's expression change from curiosity to irritation. Clearly, she was getting anxious because her husband was taking his sweet time to disclose the information she longed to hear. As for Jane and Katie, they fully expected that they would be learning some wonderful news as their father was putting on quite the performance. "Seems we've a new neighbor." he replied once he was finished with the jam.

The news created a wave of excitement around the table, but each for different reasons. Katie glanced at Jane and they exchanged a look of delighted curiosity. Lizzie's eyes scanned the table, amused by her sister's reactions, both of whom could barely contain their excitement. However, being that it was Sunday, they had no choice but to reign in their enthusiasm—as well as their ravenous appetite for more information about their new neighbor.

Susan's mouth opened as she stared at her husband. "How do you know such a thing?"

"A few weeks back, I received a letter from Thomas—"

Gasping, Susan leaned back in her chair. For a moment, Lizzie feared she'd tip over backwards. "Your cousin? From Clearwater?"

"Distant cousin," Lizzie corrected.

Susan shot her daughter a dark look before turning her attention back to her husband. "And you never told me?"

"—writing me that he knew someone who was interested in renting our old farm."

Susan let the chair legs fall onto the floor with a loud clap. "Amos Bender!"

He ignored her tone. "Appears they've arrived. Just two days ago, I met him at the feed store yesterday."

"Him?" Susan's eyes widened. "A man?"

To Lizzie's delight, Amos gave a little shrug as if what he was telling her was of no great importance. "Indeed. In fact, a young man—"

Another gasp.

"—and his *schweister*."

Immediately Susan looked at her son who promptly dropped his knife into the jelly bowl.

33

"Also, a friend of his, another young man, who is here to help our new neighbor, although from what I can gather he won't be staying very long."

"And none of them married?" Susan laughed out loud, clearly delighted. She clapped her hands together and beamed across the table at Jacob and Jane. "Oh, joyous day! Such news! And on a Sunday, nonetheless!"

Chapter Four

On Sunday morning, Phineas couldn't believe that Christopher had left the house without them. In his eagerness to get to the worship service, he hadn't waited for his younger sister, Cynthia, either. Again.

As usual, Cynthia was taking far too long to get ready and that meant that Phineas was stuck in the kitchen, waiting for her to come down the stairs so that he, and not her brother, could escort her to the Yoders' farm for Sunday worship.

Phineas scowled. He didn't even know *where* the Yoders' farm was!

Staring at the clock on the wall by the kitchen cupboard, Phineas tapped the tip of his freshly polished black shoe against the floor. Why on earth do women always take so long? he wondered. Phineas knew well enough from his own sister that getting ready for church service was a chore, but Christopher's sister was taking it to a new level altogether. Now, they were surely going to be late.

And he detested being late to anything.

Getting more frustrated by the minute, he walked to the bottom of the staircase and called up, "Cynthia? What's taking so long? The cows will be ready for their second milking if you don't hurry up!"

"Coming!"

Still, it was another two minutes before hearing her shoes on the hardwood floor above. *Finally,* he thought. No, if there was one thing Phineas couldn't tolerate, it was being late. And *especially* for Sunday worship. To him, it smacked of disrespect for God, the church, and the congregation. It certainly would create a bad first impression if they arrived tardy for their first worship service in Blue Mill. Phineas would be quite unhappy if they had to walk in after the first hymn had begun. Surely everyone would stare at them and speculate about not just who they were but why they couldn't get to worship on time.

Cynthia hurried down the stairs, pausing to give him a warm smile.

It was not returned.

"Do you know where we're going?" he asked her.

His question was met with a blank stare. "To worship."

He raised an eyebrow at her and gave her an exasperated look. "I know that, Cynthia. I meant *where* is it being held?"

"Didn't Christopher tell you?"

Phineas took a deep breath and exhaled slowly. She was always one to answer a question with another question, another trait of hers that irritated him beyond measure. "If he had, surely, I would not be asking you, would I?"

The smile faded from Cynthia's face, replaced with a dark scowl that mirrored his own. "Why on earth was he in such a hurry this morning?"

Phineas suspected he knew the answer but wasn't about to share it with Cynthia. Just the other day, Phineas and Christopher had been at the hardware store in town. As they were paying for their items, they'd been introduced by the store's owner to another man who was standing behind them: Amos Bender. Besides the fact that Amos owned the farm that Christopher now leased, apparently, he was also a neighbor. It seemed that the northeastern tip of his property aligned with the far edge of the Bender farm. After they'd exchanged pleasantries and Amos had left, the store owner leaned forward, whispering that Amos had a pretty young daughter or two and neither one of them were spoken for.

That had been enough to set Christopher into a dreamy state for the next twenty-four hours.

"I'm sure I don't know," Phineas said drily. "We'll just have to head down the road and look for a house or farm with lots of buggies parked out front."

Cynthia's scowl disappeared. It was clear that the thought of spending time alone in a buggy with Phineas did not displease her. Phineas, however, felt differently. He was more than annoyed at the prospect of being lost in Blue Mill with his best friend's sister who was pining after him.

Phineas had first met Christopher in school when they were young boys, even though Phineas was almost four years his senior. They hadn't become friends until Christopher turned sixteen. Because of his height, he always appeared older than his age. During his rumschpringe, Phineas often hung out with Christopher who preferred to talk about farming than fast cars and transistor radios like the other boys his age. The fact that Christopher pursued knowledge instead of worldly folly had impressed Phineas. A few years later, after Phineas had taken his baptism—something he'd done at a much younger age than most of the other young men in his district—and after he'd taken charge of his father's farm, he'd run into Christopher at the feed store. They talked briefly, the younger man asking Phineas about crop rotation and the benefit of sacrifice paddocks for dairy herds and horses. Phineas had been impressed yet again by Christopher's thirst for knowledge and, after learning that he wished to become a farmer but hadn't the means to do so, Phineas had invited him to come work his property.

From that point forward, they'd been fast friends. For several years, Christopher and Phineas worked side by side, the two men plowing and planting, hoeing and harvesting. Phineas was generous in sharing the profits from his farm for, in truth, what did *he* need so much money for when he had no wife or children and already owned more land than one man could farm. Land that was paid for and unencumbered except for the taxes.

For that reason, Christopher had worked hard and saved enough money, his objective clear: to find his *own* farm to cultivate.

Yet, not once during those years of friendship, despite their close relationship, had Phineas ever paid *any* attention to Christopher's sister. Not then and not now.

But the same could not be said in reverse.

It would take a blind man to not see that Cynthia held hopes of courting Phineas, a sentiment that was most certainly not shared by him. However, being a proper and righteous man, he remained as pleasant and respectful as he could without ever letting down his guard. As far as he was concerned, she was just the annoying little sister of his best friend and boss and nothing more.

Perhaps, he thought, she'd eventually meet a nice young man from Blue Mill and settle down. As soon as he was finished helping his friend get the farm in working order, he would be heading back to Clearwater and wouldn't have to deal with her exasperating tendencies again. What a welcome journey that will be, he thought wryly.

Chapter Five

"I wonder what the new family is like," Katie questioned as she walked between Jane and Lizzie. They'd left the house just ten minutes earlier, their parents having taken the horse and buggy. Their brother would follow with his own buggy after he cleaned up from the morning chores, but the three girls preferred to walk today due to the fine spring weather.

"I don't think that it's a family," Lizzie stated. "Daed said it was a man and his younger sister."

Katie wrapped her arms around herself and spun around. "Perhaps the sister will suit Jacob's fancy. I'd love to have a niece or nephew to coddle."

"I'm sure they are nice enough," Jane said, clearly attempting to temper Katie's excitement.

"And perhaps the brother will take to one of you!" Katie clapped her hands in delight, spinning around in the road. "Wouldn't that be grand? You'd move just next door."

Jane blushed, but Lizzie scolded her younger sister. "Oh hush, Katie. You're putting the buggy before the horse. Again."

Katie stuck her tongue out at Lizzie then jogged ahead. Jane laughed and linked her elbow with her sister's. "Oh, Lizzie. Don't scold her. We were like that once, too, don't you reckon?"

Lizzie gave her a sideways glance. "Mayhaps you, but I'm quite certain I was never as silly as that girl."

At this comment, Jane laughed again. Her laughter was light and carefree, pure in nature and kind in delivery. "I'd think you'd appreciate her a bit more. She's just a hopeless romantic, Lizzie. Like you."

Lizzie scoffed. "Such childishness. And I'm most certainly *not* a hopeless romantic"

"Spoken from my *schweister* who devours those romance books!" Jane teased. "If you're *not* a romantic, I'd have a hard time imagining someone who was."

"Just because I read those books doesn't make me a romantic," Lizzie shot back, feeling especially saucy. "I like to think of myself as practical. A true romantic would jump at any chance to court someone just for the sake of courting and that's not me." Lizzie didn't need to remind her sister that she wasn't as eager as other young women to marry. She was perfectly content at home and did not feel the same level of excitement as her sister regarding the arrival of a new and unmarried neighbor. "And that's most certainly not why I read those books."

Behind them, the all too familiar sound of an approaching horse was heard. Without looking back, Jane and Lizzie moved to the side of the road, giving the oncoming buggy enough room to pass. On church Sunday, there were usually many buggies on the road, all headed in the same direction. Sometimes one of them would even stop to offer them a ride.

"Books!" Katie scoffed from up ahead. "You always have your nose buried in a book!" She twirled around in front of Lizzie. "I'd rather have a dozen *bopplin* than spend my nights with a dusty old book filled with trivial words!"

Lizzie frowned. "There's a lot to be said for reading, Katie. You might try it sometime. You might find you actually learn something and, even better, you might enjoy it."

"Like how you constantly read *Martyrs Mirror?*" Katie was clearly not impressed, and no amount of convincing would change her opinion. "Reading about dead martyrs will never land you a husband!"

Lizzie pressed her lips together. How dare her young, sister mock a great novel about their ancestors! "That's very disrespectful. They sacrificed their lives for their faith. Because of them, we are here to worship freely."

"What. Ever!" Katie replied with a dismissive wave of her hand. "You speak like the old spinster you will surely become!"

"Katie!" Jane gasped, a horrified look on her face.

There was no further time for reproach as another horse and buggy drew near.

"Pardon me," a voice called out.

Still angry with her youngest sister, Lizzie picked up her pace. However, she noticed that Jane had slowed down and had turned to greet the stranger who wore a sunny bright smile and had beautiful eyes, the color of which matched the sky.

"You wouldn't by any chance be headed to Yoders' farm? For worship?"

It was a male voice. A *young* male voice.

Lizzie couldn't help but to peer over her shoulder. Katie jogged back to Jane's side and they both stood before the open-top buggy—a courting buggy!--that had pulled up beside them. The driver, a young man, greeted them with a smile, and eyes crinkled into tiny half-moons. His accent was a tad unusual and his manner of dress clearly told them that he was not from Blue Mill. But he was Amish. That was for sure and certain.

Forgetting about their previous argument, Katie giggled, standing behind Jane and placing her chin on her sister's shoulder.

It was Jane, however, who finally spoke up. "*Ja*, indeed. Church is to be held there today," she responded, her voice soft and modest.

The man removed his hat and ran his fingers through his blond curls. "Might you direct me, then? I'm not familiar, you see." He paused for a second, plopping his hat back on his head. "Christopher Burkholder's my name," he said, flashing another bright smile at the girls, though his eyes had settled on Jane. He hesitated long enough for Lizzie to nudge her older sister.

"Jane Bender," she responded, looking down, aware of his evident attention. "These are my sisters, Lizzie and Katie." When she glanced up and saw that he had nodded to the other girls but had returned his gaze to her, she added with a simple gesture, "We live over that hill there."

"Bender, eh?" He grinned in a secretive sort of way. "I reckon that makes us neighbors, then."

Jane gave a little gasp that Lizzie hoped he hadn't heard.

"And relatives, too," he continued. "Well, by marriage, I reckon. Anyway, mayhaps you'd show me the way to Yoders, then? I'd hate to be late for my first worship service."

Lizzie watched, amused to see the color flooding to her sister's cheeks. When she realized that Jane was too flustered to respond, she stepped forward. "I don't reckon the three of us would fit in your buggy." She thought she felt Jane's shoe tap the back of her foot. Ignoring her, Lizzie pointed further down the road. "Besides, Yoders' farm is just four driveways ahead. It's a long gravel one on the left. You can't miss it. You'll see all the buggies."

He nodded at Lizzie. "Very well," he said pleasantly. "Mayhaps I'll see you later, then? At the singing tonight?" He addressed the question to no one in particular, but, once again, his eyes found Janes. "Unless of course," he continued, sparing a quick glance in Lizzie's direction, "Blue Mill Amish don't believe in singings?"

The good-natured tone of his question caught Lizzie off-guard and immediately she knew that she liked this young man. Clearly their new neighbor Christopher Burkholder held no hard feelings toward Lizzie for having declined his offer to have Jane ride in his buggy. She'd known he had asked Jane specifically, but it would be quite improper for her to arrive at worship alone with a man she didn't know.

"Oh, we believe in singings," Lizzie teased back. "And volleyball games, too. We're progressive like that."

He laughed, a pleasant and joyful sound, before he slapped the reins against the back of his horse, clicking his tongue to urge the horse to pick up its speed.

Katie barely waited until the buggy pulled away before she clutched Jane's arm. "Have you ever seen such a handsome man?" she gushed. "Oh, why am I not old enough to go to singings yet!"

Lizzie picked up her pace. If it wouldn't do for Christopher Burkholder to be late for worship, it would be even less acceptable for *them* to arrive late. "Even if you went, Katie, I highly doubt he'd have any interest in you," she said. "You're far too young for a man like that."

A few minutes later, another buggy pulled up behind them just as they were turning down the driveway. As they moved to the side, Lizzie glanced over her shoulder, surprised to see a second unfamiliar buggy. Unlike Christopher's two-seater buggy, this one was a typical black topped buggy. At the reins was another young man she didn't recognize. As the buggy neared, Lizzie noticed a young woman seated by his side. If it weren't for their solemn expressions and the fact that the man wore no beard, Lizzie might have thought that they were a married couple. Unhappily married, she thought. At best, she figured they might be courting, but there was something about the way they sat that made her doubt that very much.

When they passed, Lizzie's eyes met the drivers.

For the briefest of moments, the buggy slowed. It was easy for her to see that the man was giving them a quick study, an obvious look of disdain crossed his face. Perhaps it was because they walked barefoot, carrying their shoes instead of wearing them.

Lizzie didn't care.

It didn't bother her, either, that he didn't even lift his hand to wave to them as he drove past. Instead, his dark eyes flashed from beneath a wave of black hair. With a tilt of his chin, he looked away and then urged the horse to trot faster.

Lizzie didn't need to be told that the man in *that* buggy wasn't from Blue Mill either. Perhaps he was the friend that her father had spoken of at breakfast. However, he appeared as different from Christopher Burkholder as day was to night. Stern, serious, and snobby. That's how she would describe him if anyone cared to ask for her opinion.

"Did you see her odd prayer *kapp*?" Katie whispered. "She's clearly not from around here."

"She must be from Clearwater, too!" Jane replied. "I bet she's the sister!"

Katie made a face. "Forget Jacob fancying her, then. She looked plain miserable! I don't think I'd like her for a *schweister.*"

Lizzie leaned forward and whispered into Jane's ear. "And that man. Why, he didn't even nod or wave! He appeared most unpleasant; don't you think?"

Katie had clearly overheard. "Do you think all people from Clearwater are unfriendly?"

Lizzie couldn't help but give a little laugh. "I don't think it's a prerequisite for living there, so no. Besides, Christopher seemed nice enough," she added. "And, with eyes only for you, Jane, perhaps there's a match to be made one of us."

Chapter Six

"My word!"

Phineas took a deep breath, preparing himself for what would surely be a long-winded, criticism of the young women they'd just passed.

Long ago, Phineas had learned better than to engage in small talk with Cynthia. He hadn't wanted to take her to the Yoders' farm for Sunday worship in the first place. But, in his eagerness to get to the worship service on time, Christopher had left earlier--and without any warning!--so Phineas had little choice in the matter. Still, that didn't mean he was required to spend his morning engaging with her. Knowing that she was smitten with him, the last thing he wanted to do was encourage her.

Cynthia, however, did not appear to notice that he hadn't acknowledged her remark.

"Did you see those three women walking to worship?"

He refused to look at her, instead focusing on steering the horse and buggy down the road. He wasn't used to this horse—it had only arrived the previous week and he hadn't much time to get used to its nature. Even still, he wouldn't have looked at her anyway. Cynthia Burkholder needed no encouragement from him. If she sensed that he was even remotely interested in her as anything more than his friend's sister, it would surely cause angst for him.

"Did you hear me?" she continued.

Phineas sighed. Obviously, she wasn't going to give up.

"What about them?" he finally relented.

She clucked her tongue as if cross that she needed to explain what *she* clearly knew was obvious. "They weren't wearing shoes!"

Phineas sighed again.

"No shoes to worship!" Cynthia shook her head in a disapproving way. "What type of place is this Blue Mill, after all? So country." She emphasized the word *country* as if it left a sour taste in her mouth.

"Nothing wrong with country," Phineas said just to be a bit argumentative. He, too, had been a bit taken aback by the three girls who carried their shoes, swinging them by their sides as they walked. "Some might consider Clearwater to be rural, too."

"But not like this!" she insisted. "In Clearwater, *no one* would attend a worship service barefoot!"

"Well, they carried their shoes with them. I'm sure they intend to put them on once they arrive at the farm for worship."

But, no sooner had those words left his mouth did he think she had a point. Surely their feet would be dirty from the long walk and cleanliness was next to godliness as far as worship service was concerned. It was one of the reasons that Cynthia had taken so long to get ready that morning. Still, he'd visited other Amish communities over the years and knew that Blue Mill was not alone in having such a casual attitude toward proper etiquette when it came to Sunday worship.

Cynthia, however, wasn't about to give up. Clearly her sensibilities were bothered. "Can you imagine our bishop's reaction to such a thing?"

For once, he almost chuckled. Oh, he most certainly *could* imagine their bishop's reaction and the thought of it made him wish that someone would actually do such a thing. Bishop Wegner was as staunch and strict as they came, even for Phineas's taste.

"Surely the Bible does not mention clean feet as being necessary to worship God," he pointed out. "Why, even Jesus walked barefoot."

"You're teasing!"

"Never about Jesus!"

Indignant, Cynthia crossed her arms over her chest. "Seriously, Phineas. You must admit that this Blue Mill is about as backward as can be."

It wasn't just *that* she said it, but *how* she said it. Even more telling was the fact that he was bothered by her statement. Wasn't it just a week ago that he, too, had commented about Blue Mill? Why did it sound so condescending coming from Cynthia, then?

He clenched his teeth. Had he sounded superior when he'd made the same remark to Christopher?

The truth was that, after having spent a week in Blue Mill, he did not find it backward at all. Yes, the farms were smaller and more unkempt than in Clearwater, even if he did not compare them to his own place. And the people did dress a little less conservatively; he'd noticed that the women's dresses were hemmed higher than those in Clearwater. Still, that didn't make the place *backward*. Just different. Was it to his liking? Not at all. Most places weren't. He much preferred living in Clearwater and, to be quite specific, on his own farm.

However, he did not want sound anything like Cynthia Burkholder and the similarities of their statements bothered him more than he wanted to admit.

He'd known her for as long as he'd been friends with Christopher. As a young teenager, she'd always struck him as a little pretentious. And nothing changed when she grew into a young woman, if anything, she became even more self-righteous. Nothing was good enough for Cynthia Burkholder...including the young men in their church district. Phineas had never encouraged her attentions, although he knew that Christopher and Christopher's father would have liked nothing more than to hear wedding banns announced between Cynthia and Phineas at a Sunday service.

Phineas, however, knew *that* would never happen.

To date, he'd never met a young woman that he came remotely close to consider courting. Not that he didn't want to settle down one day. No, that wasn't it at all. However, he'd had no time to think about courting and, if he had, he certainly wouldn't have considered any of the women from Clearwater. They were all far too eager to catch his attention. As far as Phineas's preferences, there were two traits that he required in a future wife: righteousness and humility. While Cynthia claimed to have the former, she most certainly lacked the latter.

Looking ahead, Phineas saw that the driveway was lined with black buggies. "I suppose we're at Yoders' farm," he mumbled.

"My word!" she said again as she lifted her hand and pressed it against her chest as if in distress.

Phineas didn't need to inquire about what had caught her attention. He was sure it was a myriad of things. There were chickens running through the yard and barefoot children chasing them around in circles. The farmhouse was desperately in need of a fresh coat of paint and there were rusty bicycles strewn about the front yard. Weeds were everywhere too, appearing as if the flower beds hadn't been tended in years. The only building on the property that look well cared for was the barn. It was quite different from Clearwater, that was for certain.

Ignoring her theatrical reaction, Phineas tugged gently on the reins and guided the horse further down the driveway. At least twenty buggies were already parked near the far side of the barn, the horses tied to a rope that was stretched between two trees. Covered by the shade, it was a nice set up for the horses while they rested, still harnessed but not hitched to the buggies.

Slowly, Phineas stopped the buggy. Now was his chance to send Cynthia inside while he unhitched the horse.

"You go on ahead."

Cynthia frowned. "I'll wait for you."

"The women are all inside."

"I know no one."

So that's how this is going to be, he thought. "Suit yourself then."

He began to unhitch the horse from the buggy, purposefully taking his time in the hopes that she might wander into the house. But she didn't. *It'll be quite a long day,* he thought, *if I'm supposed to babysit Cynthia.*

After tying his horse to the rope, he paused to pat its neck before heading over to where Cynthia waited for him.

"Best get going. I hear them singing already."

He took longer strides than necessary, not caring that she couldn't keep up with him. At least inside she'd be seated with the other women and he'd have some respite from her company.

Chapter Seven

By the time the Bender sisters arrived at the Yoders' farm, the driveway was lined with buggies and the horses were tied to a long line fastened between two trees in the yard.

Lizzie headed toward the horse stable, careful to avoid the cluster of young men standing by the open barn doors. She couldn't help but notice, however, that Christopher Burkholder was among them. As the three Bender sisters walked by, he smiled, his face lighting up.

"Come on, Katie," Lizzie whispered when she noticed that her younger sister was lingering behind.

The barn was a new building, the Yoders having raised it just two years prior. The ground floor, where the young men were standing, housed eight stalls and a large feed room in the back. There was a second floor which was comprised of a large, empty room. This trend was increasingly popular among the Amish of Blue Mill as their houses were usually too small to comfortably accommodate the bi-weekly worship services and, even more so, the weddings that were held mostly in the fall.

Lizzie was glad that their house had been built in the traditional style with a large first floor gathering room that, once the furniture was removed, could easily hold up to two hundred people. She didn't particularly care for the new, modern looking two-story barns with windows lining the second floor and a staircase against the outer wall that led to the gathering room above.

After climbing the staircase, the sisters entered the room and paused, just for a moment. Lizzie scanned the room and saw the long line of women standing together, some of them talking in hushed voices, as they waited to greet newcomers to worship.

It was like this before every service. As the newcomers passed through the line, they were greeted by each woman with a shake of the hand and simple kiss on the lips, a gesture that signified faith and friendship. Then, they would take their position at the end of the line where they, too, would greet the next woman who entered the room.

It was a tradition as old as the Amish and one that Lizzie never quite understood. But, like many things about the Amish, she never questioned it. Instead, she merely accepted it as the way things had always been done and would continue to be done for generations to come. Sometimes, however, she slipped to the side so that she didn't have to greet everyone and could enjoy a moment or two of solitude before the service started.

A few minutes after eight, loud footsteps could be heard on the staircase beyond the open door. Lizzie looked up in time to see the bishop and ministers entering. As always, their expressions were solemn as they, too, approached each of the women, extending their hand in friendship and giving a simple nod as a way of greeting. When they reached the end of the line, the bishop led the rest of the church leaders—preachers and deacons and the host, Matthew Yoder—to the front of the room where two rows of benches had been set, facing each other. The church leaders would take their place in the front while the rest of the congregation would sit on the benches behind the leaders: the men on the left of the room, and the women on the right.

As soon as the church leaders were seated, it was time for the women to take their places. As always, the oldest woman led the way for the other elderly and married women with their children who sat according to their age. Next, the unmarried baptized women entered the room. These young women always sat together in the rear of the room. Lizzie was glad to be among them, preferring to sit in the back where she could escape the watchful eye of her mother and the other critical women who loved to pinch misbehaving children or scowl at the girls who whispered too much.

The same process was followed for the men with the elderly leading the way to their benches followed by the married men, sometimes with a child in hand. Last to be seated were the unmarried, baptized men. The entire procession assembled quietly, except for the shuffling of feet and occasional cough that would echo through the cavernous space. After everyone was seated, there was a long moment of silence. Not even the young children could be heard fussing. And then, without any cue that Lizzie had ever been able to notice, the men reached up and swept their black felt hats from their heads in unison. In a single movement, they bent down and slid their hats under their bench.

Church had now begun.

The Amish worship service followed the same structure each time they met. It started with a hymn from the *Ausbund,* an old hymnal that had travelled to America with the Amish when they migrated in the 1700s. Lizzie knew most of the hymns by heart so she didn't need to look at the chunky black book that had been placed on the benches. Instead, she listened attentively to the singing, by far her favorite part of the service.

One of the men would start the hymn, singing the first syllable of the song. Then the rest of the congregation would join in, slowly singing each syllable in a long, slow, rhythmic tune. One hymn that could take Lizzie one minute to read might take twenty minutes to sing. But the drawn-out nature of the song gave her time to reflect on the meaning of each and every word.

By the time the congregation started the second verse of the hymn, the bishop and preachers stood up and left the room. As a child, Lizzie had always wondered what they talked about once they were gone, fearful that they were discussing the sins of certain members of the church district. One time when she was eight years old, she'd almost cried in anticipation of being scolded for having avoided chores that week by faking a stomachache.

When she'd confessed to her father later that afternoon—the stress having been too much for her to handle—he'd laughed at her and told her that the bishop and preachers were only men and didn't know what she did when they weren't around, though God did. That was the day she learned that the church leaders left the room to discuss which of them would present the two sermons of the day.

She'd breathed a bit easier after that, but she'd also never again faked a stomachache in order to skip out on her chores for fear of God being disappointed in her.

When the bishop and preachers left the congregation, Lizzie took a moment to scan the faces across the room. In particular, she sought out that young man who had offered a ride to them earlier that morning. Usually the guests sat in the front, directly behind the church leaders. But Christopher Burkholder wasn't seated there. Instead, Lizzie found him in the back of the room with the other unmarried baptized men.

She found that curious. Could it be that he already joined the church district? When exactly had he arrived? It must have been within the past two weeks for he'd have to present a letter to the bishop before he was accepted as a new member of the congregation. Lizzie realized he must have arrived within days of her father receiving the letter from Thomas. This surprised her because no one had made mention of newcomers, although, to be fair, Lizzie hadn't done much socializing in the past week or so.

As she studied the young man, she noticed that he, too, was not paying attention to the singing. Instead, he was looking in Lizzie's direction. Or, perhaps more correctly, further down the bench from where Lizzie sat. He was staring at Jane.

Suppressing a smile, Lizzie leaned forward—just a little—and glanced down the row where her sister was seated. Because the women sat in order of age, three young women were between them: Fannie, Rachel, and Emma. Lizzie wasn't surprised to see Emma staring in the direction where Christopher Burkholder was seated—she'd always been rather nosy!—but, as she'd expected, Jane was singing along with the other women, her eyes staring at the front of the room where the bishop and preachers normally stood to deliver their sermons.

Surprisingly, Jane had no idea that she was the object of Christopher's attention.

Lizzie glanced once more, in his direction and her eyes caught upon another figure. The stranger sitting at the end of the last bench was far too old to be seated among the other young men. His dark hair hung in loose waves over his forehead, casting a shadow that shielded his solemn eyes from view. She recognized him at once as the second man who'd driven past them in the buggy, not even pausing to smile, nod, or lift his hand to wave hello.

The stranger sat there, his lips moving in tandem with the long, drawn out hymn—but Lizzie suspected he wasn't really singing at all.

She narrowed her eyes, trying to discern whether she was correct or not. It was almost impossible to tell. Just as she was about to look away, she focused not on his mouth but his eyes and realized that he'd caught her staring at him.

Mortified, Lizzie quickly averted her gaze and focused on the hymn, not the man. She could feel the rise of heat to her face and prayed that her cheeks did not mirror the embarrassment she felt at having been caught.

Beside her, Fannie poked Lizzie's ribs with her elbow. "Behave," she whispered.

Lizzie made a face at her friend then did as she had been told, too self-conscious to look up to see if he was still watching her.

The three-hour service felt extra-long on this particular Sunday. Lizzie couldn't help but fidget as she sat there, listening to the bishop give the lengthier of the two sermons. But she could barely concentrate on his words as he spoke. His sermons were her least favorite of the church leaders. He spoke in such a clipped manner, his high German difficult to understand, so she often caught herself dozing when he was chosen to preach.

Finally, he finished his sermon and the congregation knelt for a silent prayer, their foreheads pressed against their folded hands which rested on the benches. Lizzie barely listened when he bestowed a prayer upon the congregation and was quick to bend her knee for the genuflection that officially ended the worship service.

"What had you so preoccupied earlier?" Fannie asked as everyone began to scatter.

"The newcomers," she whispered back. Then, as Jane joined them, Lizzie gave her a mischievous smile. "Seems a certain young man was quick to seek out where you were seated today."

Jane blushed. "Behave yourself!"

Laughing, Lizzie glanced around the room which, unlike the orderly processional before the service, was now in complete organized chaos. The men were busy moving the benches, sliding the legs into trusses to convert them into dining tables. The younger boys scurried around the room collecting the *Ausbunds*, eager to see which of them could carry the most. And the women hurried to the back of the large room where the food had been set earlier.

Discretely—or so she hoped—Lizzie eyed the crowd until she spotted the two gentlemen. They stood near an open window, talking with several older men. Lizzie noticed her father was one of them and she could hardly wait to pull him aside to find out what they were talking about. The companion of Christopher Burkholder, however, once again caught her attention. She'd never seen a man look so awkward. His shoulders were stiff, and his hands were clasped behind his back as if he didn't know what to do with them. Unlike his friend, Phineas didn't smile or nod his head when the others talked. Instead, he merely stood there as if he were completely out of his element. There was an air of self-regard about him that Lizzie found both pleasant and distasteful at the same time. Never had she witnessed an Amish man behave in such a stand-offish manner.

"Lizzie," Jane said, interrupting her thoughts. "Maem told us to help serve the men's table."

Barely had she acknowledged her sister when she felt a pitcher of water being thrust into her hands. Lizzie looked at Jane, hardly surprised that she, too, carried a pitcher and was already headed toward the men's table. Leave it to Jane, Lizzie thought, to not even question the demand from their mother. She, however, saw it for what it truly was: a way to get her two oldest daughters in front of the newcomers in the hopes that they might notice one—or both!—of them.

Jane started at the one side and Lizzie headed toward the opposite side. Slowly, they made their way down the length of the table, filling the men's water cups. Unlike the worship service, the men sat anywhere they preferred. As luck had it, Lizzie noticed that Christopher and his friend sat toward the end of the table near the preachers. Even more fortunate, Christopher was on the side that Jane was serving.

Lizzie paused when she found herself standing beside his friend who was seated directly across from Christopher. She watched as Jane reached for his cup. When he said something, Jane leaned in closer as if to hear him better.

Then she smiled and pressed her lips together, giving a slight nod.

If only Lizzie could hear what he'd said to her sister! She felt the pressure of something against her arm and, when she looked, saw it was a cup. Once again, Christopher's friend had been watching her only this time, he'd caught her observing Jane's exchange with Christopher.

"If you don't mind," he said flatly, lifting his cup for her to fill.

Jane flushed. "I'm sorry," she managed to mumble then tilted the pitcher. But, as she was filling his cup, the water splashed out too quickly and soaked his sleeve. Flustered, she gasped then reached for a napkin, but not before several of the other men began chuckling.

"Phineas!" Christopher said, a big smile on his face, "You've always been one to make a splash wherever we go!"

More laughter erupted from that section of the table. Embarrassed, Lizzie hurried away, passing the pitcher to Emma when she passed her.

"Go finish filling the men's water," she snapped before retreating to the far side of the room and slipping out the door. She couldn't get down the stairs fast enough. Once on the driveway, she began to jog toward the road, tears stinging the corners of her eyes. What was it about that man? That made three times in one day where she'd been made to feel like a fool in his presence. Oh, she knew that she didn't like him and she certainly didn't like the way he made her feel. She'd rather go home, alone and hungry, than remain in that fellowship room with the likes of him for one second longer than necessary.

Chapter Eight

"Phineas, did you see that Jane Bender?" Christopher sighed for what felt like the dozenth time in an hour. If the distant glazed look on his friend's face wasn't irritating enough, so were his repetitive comments about Jane. "Surely such beauty must radiate from the inside out."

Phineas took a deep breath and exhaled slowly. How much longer would he have to listen to his friend gushing about the pretty blond woman who'd served him his water? While he knew that Thomas Burkholder had great hopes that his son Christopher might settled down with a young Amish woman from Blue Mill, Phineas certainly hadn't thought that his friend would fall so quickly. After all, they had plenty of work to do in the upcoming weeks. Becoming smitten with the first young Amish woman that crossed his path was not on Christopher's to-do list!

"At least twenty times," Phineas complained. "Perhaps more."

Christopher laughed. "As always, you exaggerate."

"Indeed."

The two men sat on the front porch, watching as the sun slowly descended behind the west field. In the ten days they'd been in Blue Mill, they'd managed to get quite a bit of work finished, including fertilizing the neglected fields. It was too late to plant corn for the upcoming season, but Phineas had managed to talk Christopher into planting hay. Even if he managed to get just two cuttings, it would save him money on food for his livestock during the first winter of his tenancy.

But Christopher certainly had something other than farming on his mind.

"I simply can't wait until tonight," Christopher said. His eyes practically glowed. "She said she'd ride home with me. Did I tell you that, Phineas?"

Inwardly, Phineas groaned. He would have much preferred to talk about their plans for the farm for the upcoming week than to listen to his friend point out the many virtues of one Jane Bender. "At least twenty *more* times since we left Yoders' farm."

Clearly ignoring his friend's lack of enthusiasm, Christopher stared at Phineas, a new sense of eagerness in his eyes. "You will come with me, won't you?"

"Come where?"

"The singing."

Phineas shut his eyes and moistened his lips, trying to weigh in on how he should reply. When he'd agreed to accompany Christopher to help set up the farm, Phineas had zero intentions of socializing with the good people of Blue Mill. And surely, they *were* good people, although Phineas felt there was little to entice him to *want* to find out. He had enough on his plate in Clearwater and he hardly ever socialized *there* so why should he socialize here?

As far as Phineas was concerned, he'd volunteered to accompany his friend—at the request of Christopher's father, of course—because he cared deeply for the young man. He also knew that Christopher needed help getting things organized and *that* was something Phineas could do in his sleep.

Three weeks. Maybe four, Phineas had thought. Then he would have to return to Clearwater and fetch his little sister Gracie Anne, from relatives. It was a three-hour drive, not too far for a short stay, but it *was* far enough that he could not travel back and forth too frequently.

"I can assure you," Phineas replied slowly, enunciating each word, "that I have no intentions of attending *any* such thing."

Christopher stopped rocking his chair, his feet planted firmly on the floorboards, and gaped at him. "You'd have me attend a singing alone?"

Phineas raised an eyebrow. "If you intend to drive Jane Bender home, then you would undoubtedly be leaving *me* there alone. I don't see how that would be any different."

Christopher made a face. "But Phineas, you're much more confident than I am. You'll be absolutely fine by yourself." He paused. "Well, with Cynthia, anyway."

Phineas scoffed. So that was what this was about! If Phineas went to the singing, he'd be able to ensure that Christopher's sister, Cynthia, arrived back at the farm safely. Otherwise, Christopher wouldn't be able to escort Jane home in his buggy. At least not alone.

"Cynthia, eh? You're truly enticing me now."

"Oh, come now, Phineas! She's quite fond of you."

"Too fond," he admitted. "And it's not returned."

Laughing, Christopher began rocking again, the runners of the chair pressing against the warped floorboards and making creaking noises. "Then you'll be happy to know that when you return to Clearwater, my dear sister will be remaining here with me."

"Something to look forward to, indeed!"

"Now, now," Christopher said in a light-hearted tone. "I was just as surprised as you were when my Daed said she was to come with us. But I must admit that it sure is nice having a woman in the house. Without her, one of us would have to do the cooking and cleaning."

"I reckon there's merit to that." Truth be told, Phineas knew far too well what it was like living alone in a house. His father had unexpectedly passed away four years ago, and in the prime of his life, too. At fifty years of age, he should've had many more seasons of planting and harvesting. Just as disconcerting was how Phineas, just twenty-four years old, had been thrust into a solemn life, that included taking care of his younger sister, the house *and* the large farm.

There'd been plenty of pressure for him to marry. Phineas, however, refused. He was quite happy to live with Gracie Anne. He certainly would never marry just for the sake of *being* married or finding someone to take on the maternal responsibility of raising his sister and keeping a home. Besides, the women of Clearwater did not appeal to him, that was for sure and certain. They were young and silly, he thought, and not one of them had a fraction of his work ethic.

And that included Christopher's sister.

Still, Phineas knew that it was the right choice for her to stay behind with Christopher. He'd need to have someone to cook his meals and clean the house while he farmed the land. At least until he was properly settled.

"Cynthia will prove her worth, I'm sure," Phineas admitted. "I don't know what I'd do without my hired girl, Ruth. Especially with Gracie Anne being so young still."

"See?" Christopher leaned forward and slapped Phineas's knee. "There's always a bright side to every dark cloud if you look hard enough. Just like tonight—"

Phineas groaned.

"You might actually have a good time...for once."

"Don't count on it." Phineas pressed his lips together and scowled. "You know that fun is not a part of my everyday vocabulary."

"Well, then, consider it a good deed. I need your moral support."

Phineas pressed his head back against the rocking chair and stared up at the bright sky. *Moral support.* How could he argue with Christopher on that front? After all, hadn't his friend been there for him when his father had passed, and *he* had needed moral support?

"Fine, Christopher," he said at last. "I will attend your 'youth singing', but I can assure you that I will *not* enjoy even one second of it!"

Chapter Nine

Outside, on the front yard of Yoders' farm, several young Amish men stood in small groups near the barn while the women sat together on the front porch of the house.

It was Sunday evening and, as expected, the youth had returned to the farm where worship had been held earlier that morning. The host and hostess from the service always held the youth gathering that same night. They'd serve pretzels and potato chips, water and lemonade, and sweet treats would be laid out toward the end of the evening signaling that it would soon be time for them to make their way home.

At the beginning of the gathering, the youth would linger outside, catching up on the weekly gossip or making plans for the upcoming weeks. Later, they'd return to the barn for the singing and refreshments.

Lizzie hadn't wanted to go, but after learning that Jane had promised to meet Christopher, she knew she had little choice. She'd never allow her sister to attend the gathering alone.

Now, as she waited for the singing to begin, Lizzie leaned against the doorframe, uninterested in the chattering groups of young women who laughed and cast furtive glances in the direction of the men. Most of them wondering which, if any, of the young men might offer to bring them home that evening.

Lizzie let her eyes sweep the front yard. To her, the young men of her church district were just that: young. They didn't understand farming, not the way Lizzie did. Her father had taught her so much about soil and field rotation, planting and harvesting, that, whenever a young man *did* talk to her, Lizzie immediately steered the conversation to farming. But, she soon learned that this was a turnoff to would-be suitors as once they realized how well versed she was on the subject, they soon lost interest in speaking with her. After all, what Amish man wanted a wife who knew more than *they* did on the subject matter?

Instead, they wanted to talk about who won a volleyball game or who had a faster horse. In fact, as far as Lizzie was concerned, the area between the ears of the unmarried men in her church district was devoid of anything interesting.

"Oh look!" Lizzie said to her sister. "Seems your Christopher Burkholder has arrived at last!"

Jane grabbed her arm. "He's not *my* Christopher Burkholder," she whispered.

"We'll see about that."

However, when another figure emerged from the other side of the buggy, Lizzie knew the color must surely have drained from her cheeks. She hadn't thought his friend—Phineas—would attend. He was certainly a good four or five years older than Christopher, much older than any of the other boys at the gathering. By her calculations he had to be at least twenty-four! More a man than a boy.

What on earth was Phineas doing at a youth gathering, she wondered.

Emma leaned over and, in a low voice, whispered, "That's Christopher Burkholder," she said, clearly not aware that Jane and Lizzie had already met him. "He's the man renting your daed's family farm."

Neither Jane nor Lizzie spoke up to tell her that they already knew this.

"And, I learned from my daed that the tall fellow with him—the surly looking one—he's a well-to-do farmer from Upper Austen County. Came to help his friend Christopher get situated."

"A friend?" Lizzie gasped and returned her gaze to the sullen looking man. "Why, the two seem about as opposite in character as a baby foal to an old long faced mule!"

Emma laughed. "*Nee*, Lizzie," she confided. "Apparently Thomas Burkholder asked this man to accompany Christopher and his sister. His name is Phineas." She paused as if thinking. "Phineas Denner, I believe. And he comes from quite a line of farmers. My *daed* said that Phineas's *daed* passed on a few years back.

All the land passed down to Phineas—one of the largest farms in Upper Austen County. I heard it covers half of the county!"

Lizzie made a face. "I'm sure that's an exaggeration. Besides, he appears like a man too vain to get his own hands dirty!"

Emma rolled her eyes.

Jane placed her hand on her sister's arm. "You mustn't judge him so, Lizzie. We haven't even gotten to know this young man."

"He's not that young," Lizzie quipped. "He must be almost thirty."

Jane ignored her. "You know nothing about him. Mayhaps he is kind and righteous. Surely he is a good Amish man; he did come to help his friend and to our worship service today."

Lizzie highly doubted that this Phineas Denner was any of those things. Just one look at him and she could tell that he was everything he appeared to be: arrogant, disagreeable, and certainly condescending.

"Enough about him," Emma whispered, making a casual gesture toward a young woman standing alone near the refreshment table. She appeared uncomfortable standing by herself, not knowing anyone with whom to talk. "That's Christopher's sister, Cynthia. Mayhaps we should go visit with her. She looks a bit lonely."

Despite Lizzie wanting nothing to do with the sour-faced Cynthia, she followed Jane and Emma as they headed toward the lone girl.

"You're Christopher's sister, *ja?*"

Leave it to Emma, Lizzie thought with a smile. Despite being an only child, Emma was one of the most out-going young women in Blue Mill. Her mother had died when she was a mere child and her father doted on her ever since. Emma, however, didn't seem to notice as she went about her daily routine, visiting with the elderly Amish men and women, often bringing them homemade soup and bread. Lizzie had always suspected she did it more for the gossip than the charitable act itself. But still, she was a kind-hearted young woman who appeared to be headed straight toward spinsterhood as she'd never once expressed any interest in courting a young man.

Slowly, Cynthia looked at the three women. She wore an expression of complete disinterest. Clearly, she had no desire to be at the singing either. Her eyes narrowed, just ever so slightly, which did not go unnoticed by Lizzie. "I'm Cynthia Burkholder, ja" she finally said.

Jane introduced herself and immediately began to ask questions about when the Burkholder party had arrived and how Cynthia liked Blue Mill so far. With her soft, gentle voice and bright blue eyes, Jane was easy to talk to and even easier to like. Lizzie watched the exchange, half amused and half envious of her sister's ease with strangers, even one who seemed to look down her nose at their too-short dresses, bare feet, and untied prayer *kapps*.

Only once did Cynthia let her eyes drift in Lizzie's direction. It was evident that she found her unsuitable. Lizzie was quick to take notice of this and lifted her chin in defiance.

"I find it interesting that you accompanied your *bruder*," Lizzie ventured, trying to change the air of disdain that was directed her way.

"*Bruder* and his friend," Cynthia was quick to correct, her gaze trailing to where Phineas stood with Christopher and some of the other local young men. Lizzie observed him turn, ever so slightly. Clearly, he noticed that Cynthia was talking about him because he nodded, but then turned his back to them and focused his attention on the men before him.

"Will you be staying a while, then?" Jane asked, oblivious to the cold exchange between the two girls.

"That depends," Cynthia sighed. "*Daed* wishes for me to stay until Christopher is more settled here." She smiled at Jane, the first truly genuine act that Lizzie saw from the girl. "Land is getting expensive in Lower Austen, and since Christopher wants to farm his own land, it only made sense to lease something more affordable."

There was no time for further questioning, although Lizzie certainly had quite a few more questions that she would have loved to ask. Why would their father send his son so far away? Why had Cynthia been sent along with her brother? And why was this disagreeable-looking Phineas here? To chaperone the others, or was there a courtship established between him and Cynthia? The questions floated through her mind, and to say that her curiosity was piqued would have been an understatement. But she knew better than to pry into someone else's business, even if she was curious to know the answers.

Once the singing was about to start, the youths began to move to the benches, the women on one side and the men on the other. Lizzie noticed that Christopher made certain to accidentally bump into Jane, reaching out to steady her with a strong hand that spoke of hard work but also gentle care. He smiled at her and leaned down, whispering into her ear words that Lizzie couldn't hear, but which effect could easily be observed. The color flooded to Jane's cheeks and her dazzling blue eyes sparkled in a way that Lizzie had never before seen. Jane bit her lower lip and glanced away, but it was clear that her heart was pitter-patting deep in her chest. Indeed, Lizzie could see that her sister was starting to become *ferhoodled*.

"Pardon me," a voice said.

Lizzie looked up, surprised to see Phineas standing behind her. She hadn't realized she was blocking his way.

"Oh," she gasped. "I'm sorry." Quickly, she stepped to the side so that he could pass. "I'm sorry about spilling the water on you earlier."

He stared at her. "That was you?"

For some reason, Lizzie had the suspicion that he *knew* that and, for the life of her, she couldn't figure out why he was pretending that he didn't. Instead of stating as much, she changed the subject to something less combative. "You're visiting here with Christopher Burkholder, *ja*?"

He nodded but made no effort to introduce himself.

Despite still finding him to be rather self-absorbed, Lizzie decided to follow Jane's advice and give him a chance. "Do you attend singings frequently, then?" she asked.

"As infrequently as possible," came the sharp reply.

It took Lizzie a moment to realize that he was being sarcastic. She narrowed her eyes, digesting his words. If he had meant to leave an unfavorable first impression, he had truly succeeded. Between his stance and his words, there was nothing left to the imagination about this Phineas Denner from Upper Austen County. Clearly, he thought himself to be far superior to others. Without doubt, her first impression had been correct. She knew that she did not care for him one bit nor would she ever, for that matter.

There was nothing left to say so she merely nodded and moved on, her mind trying to understand how any one individual could be so rude. *No wonder*, she thought, *that he wears no beard. What woman would want to pair with such an unlikable man?*

She took her place beside her sister Jane and feigned indifference.

Katie was still too young to attend the singings, a fact that created great strife and tension in the house every other

Sunday. While Lizzie felt sorry for her younger sister, she was also relieved to have a few hours away from her silliness. She dreaded the day when Katie would turn sixteen and join them at the singings. With her overly enthusiastic giggles and often embarrassing comments, Katie was eager for attention when it was more proper to remain silent.

"What did that Christopher Burkholder whisper to you?" Lizzie demanded, her eyes searching Jane's.

"Oh," Jane replied, her hand rising to her chest as she flushed. "He's just so kind, isn't he? And quite handsome, *ja?*"

Lizzie lightly pinched her sister's leg. "You didn't tell me what he said!"

Jane covered her mouth to stifle her giggle. "He reminded me of my promise to ride home with him and said he had been looking forward to it all day."

While the youths around them sang from the hymnal, Lizzie felt her own heart flutter. She looked over to where Christopher Burkholder was seated and a warm premonition washed over her. Handsome, charming, hardworking, and lively: *What a fortuitous match for Jane*, she thought. Lizzie barely heard the words that were being sung from inside the building as she lifted her heart to God and thanked Him. If anyone deserved a chance at happiness, Jane was that very person.

During a break in the singing, Lizzie slipped away to use the facilities in the main house. She also needed a break from listening to the idle chitchat of the other women who, at times, seemed to talk about the silliest of things. Just once, Lizzie thought with a sigh, she wished she could find someone who shared her interest in more important issues, like the conversations she often had with her father.

It was dark in the driveway. The moon was out, a crescent that graced the path with a gentle blue light. As she returned to the barn, she spotted two men standing in the doorway and quickly realized that it was Christopher and Phineas. As she approached, Lizzie saw that they had yet to notice her so she stepped behind a tree and waited, hoping they would go inside before they noticed her. The last thing she wanted was another uncomfortable exchange with that Phineas character. As she waited in the shadows, she could hear them talking amongst themselves. Normally, she would never eavesdrop on a private conversation, but their words were too difficult to ignore.

"You have already won the heart of the prettiest girl here, I reckon," she heard Phineas say.

Christopher laughed. "You always have such a way with words, Phineas." There was a hint of sarcasm attached to his words. "You might see her as being just a pretty face, but I can see that she's so much more. Kind, righteous, and pure at heart."

"You can see all that, can you?"

"It's easy to see," Christopher said. "You just have to know how to look beyond the exterior."

Phineas made a "hm" noise but did not respond further, a fact that made Lizzie press her lips together and bite her tongue.

"Why, Phineas, I think you should consider practicing on Jane's *schweister* Lizzie," Christopher added. "She's rather pretty and has a bit of a sparkle in her eye. From what I heard from Amos, she has a quickness of tongue that would suit your temperament! And, did I mention she possesses quite the knowledge of farming?"

Lizzie's eyes widened as she waited for Phineas to respond.

To her surprise, he scoffed. "My sort of temperament, indeed! You must think me quite shallow if I'd fall for a sparkling eye or quick-witted tongue. Besides," he added with a long, drawn out pause, "I've already met her and find her tolerable, at best."

"Oh, Phineas!" Christopher laughed. "Now you're being ridiculous! You haven't even had a chance to get to know her, or anyone else for that matter. Spend some time with her and mayhaps you will feel differently."

"Doubtful." From where she stood, Lizzie could see Phineas straighten his shoulders and jut out his chin as if he were digging his heels in. "In fact, I see nothing special about these Blue Mill girls that can't be found back in Clearwater." He tugged at his sleeve. "If I were so inclined, that is. Anyway, lest you forget, I have to take your *schweister* home."

Lizzie pressed her back against the tree trunk, hoping that the shadows would hide her from their view. Her heart was pounding, and she felt her cheeks flushing red. So, he had noticed her after all. Yet his opinion of her appeared to be poor and unfair. How dare he, she thought, trying hard not to let the emotions she was feeling get the best of her. Tolerable! What an ugly word! She felt a soft rage rising inside and realized that it was the devil's insidious attempt at worming his way into her soul. Pride, she thought. He has hurt my pride, and that will not be permitted! Taking a few deep breaths, she did her best to gain her composure. She would not let a man such as Phineas Denner, with his fancy farm and airs of superiority, ruin her night. She would never accept a ride home in his buggy even if he begged her. A man like that, she told herself, was destined to a lonely life or a mousy wife.

Lifting her chin, she stepped from the shadows and hurried into the barn, barely giving them a glance as she passed. When she got inside, her ears still smarted from the rude comment and it was all she could do to avoid glaring at him. She hurried over to where Jane was waiting for her. Under normal circumstances, she'd have told her sister about what she'd overheard, but tonight she held back. She wasn't sure if it was because she was humiliated that he considered her 'barely tolerable' or if she didn't want to ruin Jane's good mood. Either way, she managed to swallow her anger and make the best of the unfortunate situation.

"I see you have a cup of meadow tea," she teased her sister, reaching for her hand and giving it a squeeze. "I wonder how you managed to get that..."

From the soft glow on Jane's cheeks, Lizzie knew that her suspicion had been correct. Christopher Burkholder had offered the refreshment to her sister. A true gentleman and a good Amish man, that was for sure and certain. Her sister's happiness was all that mattered to Lizzie, so he pushed Phineas's ugly words from her thoughts, though she knew they would remain etched in her memory for quite some time.

Chapter Ten

"Have you ever seen *such* a gathering before?"

Phineas grunted. Clearly, Cynthia was expressing her displeasure. He held the reins as he guided the horse and buggy down the road that led to the Burkholder farm. The ride was far too long for his taste, mostly because she kept trying to inch closer to him in the buggy.

"Such silliness from all those *girls*. Just standing around, giggling and gossiping while gawking at the men. And in those short dresses too!" She scoffed as if such things never happened in Clearwater, although Phineas knew that she was a frequent participant at the youth gatherings there. "But I do like that Bender girl," she added.

"Which one?"

"The one that Christopher insisted on driving home. Not the other one."

From the corner of his eye, he saw her reach her hand up to tug at the white ribbon that hung from her stiff cup-like prayer *kapp*. It was a gesture he knew all too well as she often played with the ribbons when donning an air of superiority.

"Such a country girl that one is."

In the darkness of the buggy, Phineas raised an eyebrow. If he felt like arguing—which he didn't—he'd have pointed out that she, now, was a country girl, too. Just like those *Bender* girls. In fact, Cynthia Burkholder had been raised in the country, only not on a dairy farm. Her father had focused on crops, not livestock. And since her brother, Christopher, had leased the old farm in Blue Mill, that made him a country *boy*, too.

But Phineas knew better than to respond. Antagonizing her with logic would only draw them deeper into conversation. And that was the last thing he wanted. No, what he really wanted was nothing more than to get back to the farm and go to sleep. Engaging with Cynthia further would only delay his longing to retire for the evening.

"I noticed you speaking to her," Cynthia continued. "The brown-haired Bender girl."

Phineas stiffened. Clearly, she was referring to Lizzie Bender. Why! He'd barely talked to her at all. He'd been too irritated with himself for allowing Christopher to convince him to go the gathering in the first place. At twenty-eight years of age, he was far too old to be attending a *youth* singing anyway!

Cynthia, however, must have been watching him like a hawk all night because she had apparently witnessed the short conversation he had with that girl. "What's her name, anyway?"

"Lizzie." He paused. "And she's hardly a girl, Cynthia."

"Now tell me, Phineas," she said in a sweet tone that sounded as though she were teasing him. "Whatever would *you* might possibly have in common with *her*?"

"It was a short exchange, Cynthia. I don't even recall what we talked about."

"Oh?"

He refused to respond further.

Satisfied, Cynthia settled back into the seat, her arm brushing against his every time the buggy wheel hit a rut in the road.

Phineas moved closer to the door.

For well over a year, he'd known that Christopher's sister had set her sights upon him. She'd have liked nothing more than to court him. Truth be told, Phineas wondered if that wasn't part of the reason that Aaron Burkholder had asked that he accompany Christopher on the journey in the first place. Perhaps that had been his intention all along! Perhaps he'd known from the beginning that he would encourage Cynthia to go with her brother in the hopes that spending some time together might soften Phineas's heart toward his only daughter.

Phineas, however, knew that was simply *not* part of God's plan. Not for him, anyway.

Despite his age, he had no desire to marry. He'd never met a young woman who met his standards. He needed a woman who challenged him. A woman who was more of a partner than anything else, an equal in more ways than one. Too many girls in Clearwater batted their eyes and smiled at him, hoping to catch his attention because of *what* he had instead of *who* he was.

And *that* did not interest him one bit.

Having so much land and, therefore, opportunity for his future off-springs was a challenge for Phineas. He knew that many young women saw him merely as means to an end. So many farmers struggled these days. But not Phineas Denner. If he ever married, the woman who stole his heart would never have to worry about money.

And, without doubt, Phineas knew that Cynthia Burkholder certainly hoped that *she* might become that woman.

"Perhaps this week the weather will be pleasant enough for a picnic," she said, breaking the silence.

The long pause after she spoke indicated that she expected an answer. The change in topic caught him off-guard. But he knew better than to answer her without thinking first. A picnic? There was too much work to be done to make time for a picnic. At least for him and Christopher, anyway. "If that sort of thing suits your pleasure," he said at last. "Unfortunately, your *bruder* and I must seed that back pasture if he's to get at least two hay cuttings in before winter."

"Work, work, work." She gave a light laugh. "That's all you do, Phineas. Don't you know that all work and no play—"

"I've no interest in play," he interrupted. "I'm here to work and *that's* all. The sooner we see to what needs to be done, the sooner I can return to Clearwater and my own farm."

She sighed. "You're no fun at all."

"I never professed to be."

"Well, if I invite Jane Bender," Cynthia said slowly, each word drawn out and calculated, "then surely Christopher will go, too. And then I know *you* will have no choice but to attend my picnic as well."

Phineas didn't need to see her face to know that a smug smile played on her lips. She was correct. If Christopher agreed to a picnic, Phineas would have to pause his work—most of the chores that needed tending to in the late afternoon required two people.

Silence filled the buggy for the remainder of the ride. Inwardly, Phineas fumed at the thought of spending even one second of a good workday frolicking around a picnic basket. *Work before pleasure,* his father had always said. That was how he had been raised and thus how he lived his life. Truthfully it worried Phineas that Cynthia was so intent on diverting her brother from his farm work. In another two or three weeks, Phineas would be heading home and Christopher would have to make do on his own, relying only on his own sound decisions and work ethic.

What on earth would happen to Christopher's dream of farming his own land if he allowed his attentions to be swayed by a pretty girl?

Chapter Eleven

On Monday morning, the sun had barely risen as the Bender family sat around the kitchen table eating breakfast. Their plates were filled with scrambled eggs and sausage, toast and cooked potatoes and the scent of freshly baked bread filled the room. Lizzie loved nothing more than smelling the yeasty aroma that greeted her as soon as she opened her eyes. It would always remind her of early mornings with her family gathered around the table, her father detailing the chores he intended to tackle while her mother hustled about the kitchen, making certain that everyone's coffee cup was filled and the platters full.

Today, however, was different.

While everyone else ate, Susan played with her food, absentmindedly moving it from one side of her plate to the other. She was far too distracted to focus on eating; instead, she wanted to hear how the previous evening's singing had gone. She prodded and asked questions but, to her dismay, typical for young women, both Lizzie and Jane provided vague answers. Katie merely pouted, her elbow resting on the table and her hand pressed against her cheek.

"So unfair," she muttered.

"Now, now." Susan pushed the bowl of scrambled eggs toward her youngest daughter. "Your time will come, Katie. And sooner than you think." She glanced at her husband. "Isn't that so, *Daed*?"

Amos looked up, not having paid attention to the conversation. "What?"

"Weren't you listening? I was talking about Katie!" Susan snapped. "Her time for singings will come, I said."

"I reckon that's true," he replied, nodding his head indifferently.

Susan scowled and Lizzie had to hide her smile, knowing full well that her father had merely answered with what he thought would appease his wife or, better yet, put an end to the exchange. But after almost twenty-five years together, such a response was transparent. "It'll do no good to have three *dochders* vying for young men, I say," Susan fussed, glancing at Jane.

"No one is *vying* for anyone, Maem," Lizzie volunteered, a lightness to her tone that justified forgiveness for any perceived back talk. "You just happen to have three *dochders* quite close together in age, ain't so?"

That answer caused Susan to cluck her tongue. "You have no idea of the burden I bear from such a predicament!" she exclaimed.

"A predicament?" Lizzie laughed, her eyes sparkling as she glanced at Jane. "Three *dochders*? I fail to see how 'three *dochders*' creates a predicament. Or a burden either! Why! I should think that you'd be *relieved* to have six extra hands to help with all the house chores. Just be lucky you don't have eight *dochders* like some of the women in our district!" She laughed. "Burdens, indeed."

Her mother waved her hand, dismissing Lizzie's statement. "Oh, Elizabeth!" she scoffed, which immediately made Katie giggle. Their mother only used Lizzie's full birth name when she was exasperated with her second oldest daughter. "What would *you* know of the burdens I bear, what for having not one married child among the lot of you!"

Amos cleared his throat, setting his coffee cup down and raising an eyebrow. His greying beard was resting on the edge of the table as he leaned forward. "Ah, your burdens," he said, a teasing smirk on his face. "Your burdens are so many, indeed. My familiarity with them is great, for they've been my constant companion for so many years."

Susan's mouth dropped open and her fork fell from her hand. Katie broke into giggles while Jane and Lizzie clasped hands under the table, an unspoken camaraderie to stifle their own giggles.

"Oh help!" Maem cried. I should think the burden would be yours, too, Amos." She dabbed at her eyes with the corner of her apron. "To think that your *Grossdawdi* put so much effort into keeping this farm and for what? We've no grandchildren to pass it down to."

Lizzie's eyes widened and she looked across the table at her brother. She saw him take a deep breath, exhaling slowly. "I suppose I'll marry one day, Maem, and solve that problem."

Susan waved her hand at him. "One day. One day. That's all I hear from you, Jacob. Why, you're practically an old man!"

Jane squeezed Lizzie's hand again.

"He's not even twenty-five!" Lizzie laughed. "I hardly think that qualifies as an old man!"

A knock at the door interrupted the conversation.

At first, Lizzie thought that she had imagined the sound. But everyone else seemed to have heard it, too. "Now, who could that be at this hour?" Amos pushed his chair back from the table and stood then walked toward the mudroom, too aware that five pairs of eyes were watching his back.

Immediately, Susan began wringing her hands. "Something must've happened!"

Lizzie frowned. "Why do you always think the worst, Maem?"

"You'll understand if you ever have children."

At this, Lizzie let out an amused laugh. "But Maem, all of your children are here in this room!"

Susan waved her hand at her. "Hush now, Elizabeth!"

Lizzie glanced around the table, intrigued by the silence and the variety of expressions on her siblings' faces. From the mudroom, they heard the squeak of the screen door and

Daed's low voice. Another male voice joined his, followed by friendly laughter shared by the two men.

Only a few short seconds passed before Amos sauntered back into the kitchen, a piece of paper in his hand. "*Ach vell,*" he said, glancing down at his hand. "Seems someone has already made a new friend."

Immediately, Susan lit up, the weight of her 'burdens' miraculously forgotten. "Oh! You must share! Don't delay the news!"

Lizzie rolled her eyes good-naturedly as Jane poked her leg under the table. Katie's eyes were as large as their mother's while Jacob did a complete one eighty and was suddenly disinterested. Lizzie's reaction was somewhere in the middle: she couldn't deny feeling mildly curious but, if her father crumpled up that letter and tossed it in the rubbish bin, she doubted she'd give the matter a second of thought!

"Someone has dropped off a letter." Amos held it in the air as he glanced around the room.

"Who?" Susan cried out, practically jumping from her seat.

Amos suppressed a smile. "A young man."

Jane sat up straighter as Katie blurted out, "Christopher?"

Susan sat up even straighter, her eyes wide. "The Burkholder boy?"

"He's a man, Maem," Lizzie corrected saucily. "He's here to work his own farm. That would make him a *man*, not a 'boy.'"

She scowled at Lizzie. "Sassiness is not becoming of a young woman."

"*Nee*, not Christopher," Amos said, turning the paper over in his hand. "The other one."

Lizzie caught her breath, instinctively knowing that her father meant Christopher's friend, Phineas. *Barely tolerable.* Wasn't that how he had described her? For a moment, she felt a wave of anger wash over her. How dare that man—a complete stranger!—judge her so?

For different reasons, a collective gasp went around the table and, without asking for permission, Katie jumped up from the bench where she had been seated and raced to the window, hoping to catch a glimpse of Phineas Denner. But, to her dismay, his buggy was already nearing the end of the lane by the time she peered through the glass.

"Oh, bother!" Katie pouted. "I didn't get to see him."

"He wasn't at the singing last night?" Jacob asked.

"Ja, he was," Lizzie mumbled, but they hadn't heard because they were too busy chattering to each other, wondering why this Phineas Denner had showed up on their doorstep in the first place.

Ignoring them, Susan clutched her hands together. "The letter, Amos. Who is the letter for?" She reached out for it.

His eyes scanned the front of the envelope. "It's addressed to Jane." He looked up, outstretching his hand so that Jane could take it. "Best to let her open it, don't you think?"

With all eyes upon her, Jane took the letter. For a long second, she held it in her hand. Lizzie could sense her sister's disappointment that the letter—had not been delivered by Christopher.

Lizzie nudged her. "Open it," she urged quietly. "Put their curious minds out of misery."

Jane's lashes fluttered upward, and she scanned the room. All eyes were upon her. A blush covered her cheeks and she focused on doing what Lizzie had asked. Without a word, she tore open the envelope and pulled out a single piece of paper, her eyes darting back and forth as she read the note. And then she smiled, a soft and kind smile.

"It's from Cynthia Burkholder," she started.

Susan sank back in her chair, unable to hide her disappointment but still intrigued as to why she would be writing her daughter.

"She's invited me to join her on a picnic." Jane looked up. "She asked if I'd join her tomorrow. What a lovely gesture of friendship!"

"A picnic?" Susan scoffed, shaking her head. "I'd be much more excited if it was her *bruder* who invited you on a picnic."

"Mayhaps he'll be there, Maem," Katie said.

Susan's disappointment immediately returned to enthusiasm as she brightened at this thought. "Oh Amos!" She turned toward her husband. "Do you think he might?"

"I can assure you that I think nothing of the matter at all."

Susan, however, acted as if she hadn't heard him. "Of course! That's why she invited you! For company. Why would she wish to picnic with just her brother when she could enjoy our dear Jane's company?"

"Don't forget about that miserable Denner fellow," Lizzie added drily, still smarting from his comment the previous night. "Even Katie would be better company than Denner!"

"Hey!"

Lizzie stuck her tongue out at Katie.

"That's enough, girls." Amos stood up, clearly finished with both his breakfast and their conversation. Taking his battered straw hat from the hook near the door, he glanced over his shoulder. "Lizzie, Jacob and I will need your help outside getting ready for baling the hay we cut last week."

She nodded, happy to help him. There was nothing she loved more than working outside. Satisfied, her father glanced at Katie and Jane. "And you two can come help with stacking the bales when we're ready."

Katie groaned, but Amos ignored her.

"Oh hush," Lizzie whispered. "You barely help outside at all!"

"Maem!" Katie whined. "I'll freckle!"

"Nothing wrong with a few freckles," Amos said, rubbing at his nose which, like Lizzie's, was dotted with tiny brown spots. "Come along, Lizzie."

Grateful to escape the confines of the house, Lizzie hurried after him.

Baling hay was almost as wonderful as cutting it. She loved watching as the tall fields were slowly shorn and the smell of fresh cut grass that filed the air.. Today, however, everyone would rake the lines of hay, ensuring that most of the cut grass was ready for the baler. She would drive the mules along the rows, the great big baler scooping up the dried grass and compressing it into square blocks. Her father would stack them on the back of the wagon. It would be a full day of work, but she was ready for it. Nothing made her feel closer to God than working in the fields.

After helping her father harness the mules to the baler, Lizzie took the reins and drove it into the fields. No sooner had she driven the mules toward the far end of the pasture when she saw Katie and Jane slowly making their way from the house. Standing behind the mules, Lizzie waited patiently and stared down the long rows of raked hay. By the end of the afternoon, all of it would be pulled through the mule-pulled windrow, baled, and stacked on the wagon. She knew that her arms would ache, and her face would burn, but it was a feeling she anticipated with joy.

The sound of a horse and buggy approaching from the road behind the field caught her attention. She turned to see who was approaching from the narrow, winding road. A large pond and towering oak trees separated the Bender farm from their neighbors. In fact, there were only a few farms further down the way, one of which was the Burkholders.

Squinting in the sun, Lizzie lifted her hand to shield her eyes. Who could possibly be driving down the road?

And then she saw him.

Phineas Denner.

She'd have recognized that long, sour face anywhere. Beside him sat none other than Cynthia Burkholder and Lizzie found herself wondering if she was, indeed, courting Phineas. Surely *that* would explain his dull personality and lacking manners, she thought.

Uninterested, she was about to turn away, but something caught her eye. As the buggy approached, Phineas appeared to deliberately slow it down as he passed by her. There was an odd expression on his face, his dark eyes widening but the hint of a smile on his lips. For the briefest of moments, Lizzie lost her breath. Why was he staring at her like that? And why had she suddenly noticed that, when not scowling, Phineas Denner was a rather attractive man indeed!

Chapter Twelve

When Phineas saw the farmer waving from up ahead, he pulled on the reins and slowed down the buggy. Cynthia exhaled loudly, clearly annoyed at this unexpected delay. Phineas, however, didn't particularly care.

Somehow, she'd convinced him to let her accompany him to town for seed. Besides, she'd claimed, she needed to shop for their picnic. Christopher had been busy painting the barn—something that was *not* the first or even second thing on Phineas's priority list—and, being covered in white paint, hadn't been able to take his sister to the market.

Phineas had refused at first, but after listening to Cynthia beg and plead for five solid minutes, he finally gave in. He suspected that it would be faster to take her and return than to get her to stop following him around with her repetitive requests to accompany him.

Now, however, as the buggy headed toward the intersection that would lead to Main Street, Phineas felt that not stopping to say hello to the man would be ill-mannered.

Besides, he recognized him from earlier that morning. It was Amos Bender, the same man who had opened the door when he'd dropped off Cynthia's picnic invitation.

"Hello there!" Amos called out as he approached the fence that separated the pasture from the road. He wore a plain straw hat that covered his head, his wiry gray hair jutting out from beneath the tattered rim. The weathered texture to his face spoke of years working outside in all kinds of weather but the leanness of his body suggested he was not as successful a farmer as others.

Phineas glanced over Amos's head at the farm toward the bottom of the slight hill. No wonder he appeared less successful than others. His was a smaller farm with a large pasture behind the dairy barn for the cows. Upon closer inspection, he could see that it had been overgrazed. There wasn't much grass left for grazing and by this time of year there should have been signs of regrowth. The few cows that meandered about, their heads tilted to the ground as if looking for something to nibble on, were thin, their hip bones sticking out far too much for Phineas's liking.

"Amos Bender," the man said. "We met this morning. Well, you dropped off the invitation, anyway, for my *dochder*, Jane. We didn't formally meet, did we now? Your friend is leasing the farm that borders ours."

Phineas frowned and studied the man. He hadn't realized that the Bender farm extended so far east toward the top of the hill. He forced a thin smile as he quickly introduced himself. "Phineas Denner. I don't quite have my bearings around here yet, I fear."

Leaning against the fence post, Amos tilted his hat backward so that it hid less of his face. "I understand you're the fellow who's helping Christopher ready his farm then, ja?"

Phineas nodded. But he was far too aware of the young woman standing behind the mules to speak. She looked quite different working in the pasture than she did at the singing. Her hair was covered with a plain blue handkerchief and her skin shone in the mid-morning sun. Why hadn't he noticed that her skin was so tanned the previous evening? Probably because of the lighting.

"That's correct." Without realizing it, Phineas's eyes remained focused on Lizzie. She hadn't smiled at him nor had she acknowledged having met him the previous evening. In fact, she looked annoyed, irritated at the disruption in her work.

Amos followed his gaze. "That's my other *dochder*, Lizzie."

Phineas paused and then nodded just once.

She merely stared at him, no expression on her face.

"We met," Phineas said. "Last evening."

Amos raised an eyebrow. "I see." He glanced down the row of hay and pointed toward the young man and woman raking the hay. "My *sohn*, Jacob, and youngest *dochder*, Katie."

Phineas lifted his hand and waved in their direction, his eyes lingering on Jacob. The young man hadn't attended the youth gathering the previous evening. He appeared to be the oldest of the Bender children. A tall young man with broad shoulders, who gave a big smile and waved back before returning his attention to his work.

Suddenly, Phineas had an idea.

Cynthia cleared her throat and leaned around him, peering through the open door at the man. "We're heading into Blue Mill. I'm hoping that Jane has agreed to attend our picnic—"

Phineas cringed at the word 'our' as if he had something to do with it!

"—as we'll be buying food and I'll be making a large thermos of tea."

Amos ran his hand over his beard, hesitating for a moment. His eyes scanned the sky for a moment. "Might rain tomorrow afternoon. Mayhaps it'll ruin your picnic."

Cynthia gave a carefree laugh. "Nonsense. The sky's as blue and clear as any perfect May day! There's no hint of any approaching storms. Not today and surely not tomorrow."

Phineas noticed that Jane's father raised an eyebrow. Surely, he, too, had picked up on the condescending tone in Cynthia's voice.

"Storms can sneak up rather quick in these parts," Amos said slowly. "Different than in Upper Austen County."

"You speak as if it's a thousand miles away!" Cynthia looked down her nose. "But if she doesn't want to attend..."

There was something about the way Amos regarded his travel companion that made Phineas hold the man in higher regard than he had just a few moments prior.

His thoughts were interrupted when Lizzie spoke up. "She's attending." He noticed that she wore a forced smile when she addressed Cynthia. "She was rather pleased with the invitation."

If Cynthia felt any embarrassment about not including Lizzie, it didn't show on her face. Instead, she raised an eyebrow and nodded. "We'll pick her up in early afternoon. Tell her we'll be here by two o'clock."

We'll. Phineas clenched his teeth. Certainly, Cynthia was deliberately making it appear as if they were a couple. Nothing could have been further from the truth. In fact, he'd almost refused to accompany Christopher when he'd learned that his sister would be traveling to Blue Mill with them. Her interest in him was more than apparent and, for that reason—among many—he had no desire to spend weeks in her company. The last thing he wanted to do was to feed her fantasy that he might return her favor.

"I'll let her know," Lizzie said at last then backed away from the fencing.

Phineas knew that if he didn't speak up now, he'd lose his chance. "Mayhaps you and your *bruder* would be interested in attending, too."

He thought he heard Cynthia catch her breath and he knew he felt her nudge him with her elbow. But he chose to ignore her. Instead, his eyes locked on Lizzie's, hoping that both she and her brother would say yes.

She appeared to be taken aback by the invitation and, for the briefest of moments, it sounded as if she might decline. "I don't—"

Her brother, however, had overheard and jogged over to where they stood. "A picnic?" He looked from Phineas to Lizzie and then directly at Cynthia. "Sounds *wunderbarr.*"

Lizzie shot him a dark look.

"Being new neighbors and all," Jacob added sheepishly. "I can bring Jane and Lizzie, save you the trip."

Phineas nodded, his appreciation of the offer apparent by the smile on his face. But, before he could agree, he noticed Lizzie had turned away. "*Kum,* Daed," she said. "Let's get back to work."

Amos sighed and shook his head. "Forgive her eagerness, Phineas. Gotta give my Lizzie credit though. She has the work ethic and drive of four *sohns*!"

Surprised, Phineas's eyes darted from Amos to Lizzie. She was tapping her fingers against the railing, a distant expression on her face.

"My apologies for the interruption," he managed to mumble.

"No worries," Amos said. "Enjoy your trip into town, anyway. "

Jacob stood beside him. "We'll see you tomorrow, then."

There was nothing left to say so Phineas nodded once again before urging the horse forward. As the buggy continued down the road, his eyes traveled to the small side mirror, watching as the willowy figure of Lizzie Bender disappeared from his view.

Chapter Thirteen

At ten-thirty on Tuesday morning, Lizzie and Katie were helping their father load the last of the baled hay onto the wagon when the wind picked up. It brushed across the back of her neck. One glance toward the heavens and Lizzie saw that the crystal-clear skies had started to darken.

As her father had predicted the previous day, a storm was brewing. And, Jacob had already left with Jane to go to Christopher's farm. Lizzie had begged off, claiming that, if she stayed to finish the chores, Jacob would then be free to attend. After all, they needed to get the rest of the hay under cover just in case bad weather set in.

Lizzie looked at her father and he gestured toward the barn. She knew that they had to get the hay under cover before the first drops of rain fell. The hay had to be completely dry before it could be stored. Any moisture could wreak havoc as well as the potential to smolder should the temperature rise. And smoldering hay has been known to catch fire.

"Hurry Katie." Lizzie reached down and grabbed a hay bale, lifting it onto the wagon.

"They're so heavy!"

Lizzie fought the urge to snap at her sister. There was always an excuse. Instead, she walked over, grabbed a hay bale from her sister and tossed it on top of the previous one. "See? It's not so hard?"

Katie rubbed her arm. "You're just stronger than me."

"That's because I help Daed more."

"See?" Katie let her lower lip stick out, pouting. "I just can't do this like you can."

Sighing, Lizzie motioned for her to lift one end of a bale. At least, if they worked together, *something* would get done.

Twenty minutes later, Lizzie walked along side Katie as their father drove the wagon toward the barn.

"Do we really have to unload it *all* now?" Katie whined.

"Katie Bender!" As usual, her younger sister wanted to cut corners and escape more work. "Leaving work unfinished is just a sign of laziness!"

"Well, it *is* going to storm." Her sister looked at her sheepishly. "Besides, I'm hungry. Can't we just leave the wagon in the barn and unload it later when Jacob gets back."

But Lizzie would hear none of that. "This hay will feed our horses and mules and cows. They get hungry, too, Katie. And we need those animals healthy in order to work the fields and sell milk. Putting off stacking the hay in the barn is just *schtinkichi!*"

Katie gasped.

Before her sister could refute the charge, Lizzie held up her hand. "Don't try to defend yourself. Now, with both of us working, we'll be finished in no time. I'll toss down the bales and you stack them."

Begrudgingly, Katie stood near the edge of the wagon, waiting for Lizzie to begin tossing them over the side of the wagon.

By the time they'd managed to transfer the baled hay into storage, it was just after three o'clock. The sky was almost black. The wind had picked up, something fierce, too. In the distance, trees swayed, and the sound of heavy rain could be heard as it approached from the west.

"Get inside," Amos yelled over the wind. "I'll see to the mules and milk the cows."

Katie hadn't needed to be told twice. She ran across the driveway and disappeared inside. But Lizzie remained at her father's side, helping him unharness the mules and get them settled into their stalls. She brushed their coats with a curry brush while her father hurried to fetch grain and hay to sustain them through the evening.

"This storm," he said, shaking his head.

"Came on awful fast, don't you think?"

Amos stood inside, peering out the open door. "Reckon it cut short your *schweister's* picnic." He sighed and removed his battered straw hat, wiping the sweat from his brow. "But at least that hay is stacked." Plopping the hat back on his head, he started to walk toward the dairy. "You go on, now, Lizzie. I'll see that the cows are tended to."

Lizzie would no sooner have abandoned her father than she'd have taken the Lord's name in vain. So, she followed him. He didn't say anything as she worked alongside him, opening gates so that the cows could escape from the storm. Then, she made certain their water troughs were filled while her father fetched them hay. It would hold them over until later that evening.

By the time Lizzie and her father walked into the kitchen, it was almost five o'clock.

"Land's sake, Lizzie!" Her mother's eyes practically bulged. "Look at you, child! You're drenched through and through."

"And dripping water on the floor I just cleaned," Katie grumbled.

Susan ignored Katie; her attention focused on Lizzie. She gestured toward the stairs. "Go change before you catch your death from cold! Then come sit for some warm dinner." Impatiently, she clapped her hands. "Quick now. You and your *daed* must be starving!"

Katie plopped down at the table. "What about me? I worked out there, too."

Susan dismissed her youngest daughter with a wave of her hand. "Oh, Katie. You're *always* starving!"

A few minutes later, Lizzie returned to the kitchen. The room seemed empty without Jacob and Jane, but Susan had plenty to talk about and that more than made up for their

110

absence. Lizzie only half listened as she sat at the table, her mind wandering. She wondered if her sister and brother were okay. How strange it must be for them to be stuck at the Burkholders' farm. Lizzie wondered if they were anxious for the storm to let up so they could make their way home.

After a few minutes, she tuned out her thoughts, as well as her mother, for she was too eager to fill her stomach with the warm slices of ham, cold applesauce, green beans, and mounds of whipped potatoes. Working in the fields always gave her a hearty appetite.

"Here comes Daed," Katie announced.

Sure enough, the sound of his heavy boots on the porch followed her words. When he walked inside, water poured from the brim of his hat.

Susan fussed over him, hurrying him into the first-floor master bedroom so that he, too, could change into dry clothing. When he finally emerged, the food was set on the table and the girls were seated, waiting for him to take his place at the head of the table.

After the silent prayer, Amos reached for the platter of ham and speared two thick slabs which he plopped on his plate. He glanced at the window as he passed the platter to Lizzie. "Still raining hard and I think I saw some lightning over the ridge. Glad we did the baling yesterday and finished stacking this morning."

"I've never seen such a fast-moving storm!" Susan sighed, an irritated look on her face as her eyes flickering toward the window above the sink. "Makes for a gloomy night. And my laundry is soaked through and through! I had to move it to the basement. It'll take hours to dry, if at all."

Lizzie gave a little laugh. Leave it to her mother to worry about such nonsensical things. "Eventually it will dry, Maem," she quipped. "It's not as if it'll be damp forever."

Her mother gave her a sharp look. "I know that, Elizabeth," she snapped. "But it's not quite the same as drying on the line under the sun, now is it?" Her mother poked at her ham with her fork. "It always smells musty when it dries downstairs anyway."

Looking at her father, Lizzie suppressed a smile. If there was one thing that they could count on, it was Susan always pointing out the negative aspects of every situation.

Amos winked at Lizzie then turned his attention to his wife. "While unfortunate about your laundry," he said solemnly which made Lizzie cover her mouth to hide her amusement, "I just hope Jane and Jacob have enough sense to stay at the Burkholders until the storm passes."

"Goodness gracious!" Susan cast a dark look in Lizzie's direction. "For the life of me, I've no idea why you'd have turned down the invitation. How will you ever get married—"

Suddenly Lizzie sat up straight. "Married? To whom?"

Susan's mouth hung open as she struggled to find words to respond to her daughter.

"It seems you're already planning to plant celery for Jane and Christopher as well as Jacob and Cynthia. So, who exactly are you intending *me* to be coupled with?"

Susan shut her mouth, pressing her lips into a tight line as she reached for the mashed potatoes. "There's nothing wrong with that man who dropped off the invitation yesterday, I'm sure."

Lizzie gave a short laugh. "You can't be serious, Maem! Not only didn't you see him, you haven't even met him, and I can tell you that he is the most conceited man I've ever laid eyes on."

"You mean Denner?" Amos said.

Lizzie scoffed. "You might as well ship me off as a mail order bride to some stranger in an Amish community in Missouri!"

Susan shook her finger at her daughter. "That's enough, Elizabeth. Don't be sassing me, now."

Turning toward her father, Lizzie changed the subject. "What about Jane and Jacob, *Daed*? Will they have to stay there overnight if the storm doesn't pass?"

A dark cloud passed over his face. Lizzie knew that it was not unheard of. When fierce storms hit suddenly, visitors often stayed put until the weather cleared. In this situation, however, it was clear that her father did not favor such an idea. "Unless the lightning stops, I don't think they would dare to take the buggy home."

Maem dropped the spoon into the bowl of potatoes. "Surely they wouldn't risk taking the buggy out with thunder and lightning" she said, the sentence more of a question than an actual statement.

Lizzie watched as her father got up and walked to the window, quietly peering outside. He tugged at his white beard and assessed the situation. "Hm," he said under his breath. "I doubt they'd try it. I'm sure the incident last year is still fresh in their minds." He sighed and turned toward his wife. "That horse that was spooked by the thunder surely must have taught them a lesson."

Lizzie remembered that incident far too well. In fact, the whole community had been shaken when Old Man Jebson lost control of his buggy last year. He'd been travelling home in a storm when his horse was spooked by the thunder. It had been a sad day when they learned of the accident that took his life. A runaway horse can be dangerous, but when it's pulling a buggy it's almost impossible to regain control."

"Oh help!" Suddenly with something new to worry about, Susan began wringing her hands and pacing the floor. "My dear Jacob! And sweet Jane! I hope they have the sense to remain where they are—"

Amos took a step toward her and laid his hand upon her arm. "—they are smart enough to stay put, Susan."

"Oh Amos." She stared up at her husband, her eyes wide with fright. "I'll never survive if something happened to either of them."

Lizzie rolled her eyes at the melodramatic way her mother clung to him. "It isn't as if this storm Is your fault, Maem," she pointed out only to receive a stern look and a sharp, "Hush now!"

Fortunately, the meal ended shortly thereafter. Lizzie waited for her father to say the after-prayer before she stood up and began collecting the dishes. With great sighs and dragging feet, Katie followed her example and carried the remaining plates to the sink where Lizzie began to wash them.

After the dishes were cleaned and the table wiped off, Susan put on a pot of coffee. Amos stayed at the kitchen table, pouring over the newspaper from the previous week. Lizzie wondered if her father had memorized it, for surely he'd read it countless times since it had arrived. But she knew that it made him happy; his eye lit up and sometimes his lips curled in the hint of a smile as he read about the happenings in other Amish communities around the country.

Meanwhile, Susan stood by the stove, waiting for the coffee to perk. She tapped her bare foot against the linoleum floor, her arms crossed over her chest as she kept gazing out the window and lamenting the situation.

Quietly, Lizzie retreated to the sofa where, by the light from a kerosene lantern, she picked up a book and began to read. Her mother lived for drama, whether real or imaginary. While Lizzie knew that the storm was bad, the melodramatic way that her mother was acting was not only expected but tolerated. If she didn't have something to worry about, her mother simply wasn't happy. But that didn't mean that Lizzie had to pander to her theatrics.

Chapter Fourteen

Phineas shook the rain from his hat before hanging it on the hook by the back door. He glanced over his shoulder and took in the sight of Cynthia and Jane who were seated at the kitchen table, talking as they pored over recipes. The lantern that hung from the ceiling hissed as the propane hit the flame, creating a bright white light that filled the room with warmth from its glow.

"So, this was your grandmother's recipe for dumplings?"

Cynthia nodded then pointed to something written on the aged index card. "She always left the skin on the onion. Said it added extra coloring to the stock."

"How clever!"

Phineas smiled to himself, for once admiring his best friend's sister. He'd never seen her behave in such a domesticated way before. Of course, he'd known her long enough that even a moment's glimpse into a softer side of Cynthia did not change his opinion of her. Not like *that*, anyway.

No one seemed to notice his appearance in the doorway, so Phineas took in the scene for a moment before the door opened again and Jacob entered the mud room. He stomped his boots on the braided mat, the noise loud enough to catch everyone's attention.

"Ah! There you two are. Phineas, what's the latest with the storm?"

Hearing Christopher's voice, Phineas looked over at his friend. He saw that both Jane and Cynthia were quiet and staring at him. The two women wore completely different expressions. Jane seemed worried, her lips pressed firmly together, while Cynthia had a far different expression on her face. He could only read it as feigned interest. It dawned on him that Christopher's sister had no real desire to be in Blue Mill and, most likely, had only agreed to come because *he* had accompanied her brother. He knew he shouldn't have been surprised...but he was.

Did she truly think that he would fall in love with her in Blue Mill when all her efforts in Clearwater had failed?

Shifting his eyes, Phineas looked directly at Jane. "Jacob and I walked down the road a ways and there's definitely flooding." He gestured over his shoulder at the door. "In that rutted area near the bend. But at least the thunder and lightning has lessened though the wind is still gusting something fierce."

"Oh help!" Jane wrung her hands on her lap.

Jacob walked over to the table and sat down next to Cynthia. "That's on the way to our farm," he said, looking directly at the young woman. "And trees are down, too."

Phineas nodded. "It's safe to say that Jane and Jacob will be staying for supper, I'm afraid."

In stark contrast to Jane's disappointment, Christopher beamed, his reaction clearly not noticed by their visitor, but certainly recognized by Phineas.

"I...I am so sorry to be a burden," Jane said in a soft voice. "We should've left earlier when we saw the storm approaching."

"Oh, stuff and nonsense," Christopher replied quickly, rushing to sit beside her at the table. He moved his chair closer to the young woman, the legs of it grating against the linoleum. With a broad smile on his face, he gazed at her in a way that left little to the imagination. "It only gives us more time to get to know one another."

Phineas raised an eyebrow.

Jane, however, flushed.

Christopher leaned toward her, his shoulder practically brushing her arm. "It's such a shame that the wind picked up so fast. It started out as such a nice day until the storm interrupted our picnic. But now we can use this opportunity to make up for that lost time."

Jane averted her eyes which made Phineas wonder if she was uncomfortable with his friend's eager attention. For the first time in his life, he was having a hard time reading a young woman's reaction to a man.

"It's such a *wunderbaar* idea." He looked at his sister. "Isn't it, Cynthia?" Without waiting for her answer, he looked back at Jane. "Don't you agree?"

Phineas took a deep breath and turned away. Clearly Christopher was completely besotted with the pretty Jane Bender. If only he'd behave like a proper Amish man—not some love-sick puppy!—and show a hint of decorum. After all, just because he fancied Jane did not mean she returned his affections. Phineas would hate to see his friend suffer heartbreak on account of being over eager for her attention.

As for Cynthia, he couldn't quite get a read on her reaction to spending more time with Jacob. He had paid her a fair amount of attention, more than Phineas ever had, but Phineas wasn't certain if the feelings were mutual on Cynthia's part either. Only time would tell, he thought. And now, with the storm still raging, there was more time to find out exactly where everyone stood.

"Anyway," Christopher continued, resting his hand on Jane's arm. "It will be our pleasure to have you here for supper. I'm sure that Cynthia would love the company. Living with two old *buwes* can't be very much fun for her."

Cynthia gave a half smile but offered no comment.

"And after supper, perhaps we can play Scrabble!"

"Christopher," Phineas called out, eager to stop his friend from making a fool of himself even further. "We should go check on the livestock."

Jacob stood up. "I'll help."

Phineas accepted the offer. Christopher, however, clearly had little desire to join them, but the responsibility of a farmer to his animals was more important than visiting in the kitchen, especially during a storm. Slowly, he began to stand, pausing to whisper something to Jane that only she could hear. Color rose to her cheeks and Phineas turned his head away. He wanted to bear no witness to the frivolities of courtship. Besides having no time for it, he also had no desire to see his best friend behave like an enamored fool.

Marriage was not meant to be based on whispered words and coy blushes, the elements of a worldly love. No. Marriage was based on a partnership, the willingness to work alongside each other toward a common goal both in good times and bad. And, in all his years, Phineas had yet to meet a woman who felt the same way. The women who had all but thrown themselves in front of his buggy wanted the attention of someone like Christopher, and that was something that they would never get from Phineas.

Phineas waited in the mudroom for his friend to join him. He said nothing of Christopher's behavior towards the young woman that he'd only met two days prior. He didn't have to. Sometimes words were not necessary. In this situation, Phineas merely gave Christopher a stern look of reproach before he reached for his hat, plopped it on his head, and hurried outside to brave the wind and rain, knowing that Christopher was reluctantly trailing behind him.

Chapter Fifteen

"What will we do about Jacob and Jane?" Lizzie turned her attention away from her nervous mother who had barely left the window in the past thirty minutes. She didn't even help with the cleanup from the supper meal which was so unlike her. Now that the kitchen was back in order, the dishes washed, dried, and put away, Lizzie wasn't certain if she was more anxious about her sister and brother's wellbeing or the tension that was felt in the house.

Amos stood at the counter, a cup of hot coffee in his hands. As he took a sip, the steam fogged his round glasses. He set down the cup, removed his glasses, and began to clean them with the edge of his shirt. "Storm's letting up so I reckon we could ride over there. See how they made out. Last time was on the property, some of those trees lining their drive looked a bit worse for the wear."

Susan perked up at his announcement. Turning from her post, she clasped her hands to her chest. "Oh Amos! Would you?"

An amused expression crossed Amos's face causing Lizzie to stifle a laugh. "Would that make you feel better, Susan?"

The look of relief that crossed Susan's face only added to the comedy playing out in the kitchen. Her mother, however, appeared oblivious to the undercurrent of teasing. "Tremendously!"

"That is all a man can ask for," Amos commented glibly, a tone lost on his wife. "Shall we venture forth, Elizabeth? he asked with a wink, "Save your mother from this agony of fright that has paralyzed her this past half-hour?"

Ten minutes later, Lizzie sat beside her father in the buggy. No sooner had they turned left at the end of their driveway did Lizzie realize that, for once, her mother's fears might not have been unfounded. Across the road, a large tree had fallen onto a neighbor's fence, the giant limbs crushing the no-climb wire and covering the right side of the road.

"I'll have to help fix with that fencing when I return," her father mumbled, more to himself than to her. "Can't have his cows wandering into the road."

The next property fared worse with two trees blocking their driveway. And further down the road, a large stream was overflowing into a pasture. The horse continued trotting, but not for long. Her father pulled on the reins and, abruptly, stopped the buggy.

Lizzie glanced at him, more concerned than ever when she noticed the muscles flex in his jaw. He was nervous and *that* was not like him. Worry was something reserved for Susan, not Amos.

"What is it, Daed?"

He gestured with his chin toward the road. "There's a tree down up ahead. It's blocking the road. We won't be able to continue. Not with the buggy anyway."

For a moment, Lizzie began to fear that they'd have to postpone
 their efforts to fetch Jane and Jacob. The idea of her sister spending the night at the Burkholders did not sit well with her though knowing Jacob was there to act as a proper chaperone made her feel a wee bit better. There was no doubt that tongues would wag throughout the church district once people found out which, undoubtedly, they would.

"What will we do then?"

He pulled on the reins and slowed the horse until it came to a complete stop. "I'm going to head back to the *haus*, but I want you to walk ahead."

"Me?" she practically squeaked.

He nodded. "Burkholders' driveway is only a half-mile past the tree, Lizzie. Around that bend. I'll meet you there, but I don't want to leave the horse on the road. Another wind gust could knock over more trees or break limbs."

Lizzie eyed the sky. It didn't look as if remnants of the storm might creep up on them, but, then again, the sky was getting darker with each passing minute. The first storm had sprung up most unexpectedly, so she understood her father's apprehensions especially since night would soon be upon them.

"Okay." She slid open the door to the buggy and climbed out.

Her father nodded. "That's right. You just check on them and sit tight. I'll be there as soon as I can."

Alone, Lizzie approached the large tree. Like the others, its roots had been ripped from the ground and the full length of its trunk blocked the road. Everywhere she looked, leaves and limbs blanketed the area. Sighing, she hoisted her skirt in one hand as she reached out for a branch to pull herself over the trunk. When her leg brushed against the heavy bark, she felt her skin sting as it dug into her calf.

"Oh help," she muttered, glancing down to see a trickle of blood on her shin.

By the time she'd climbed over the large tree, the sound of her father's horse and buggy had already disappeared. She didn't have reason to travel this road too often and wasn't very familiar with it. When the macadam ended, the dirt road turned to mud and she held up her dress, avoiding the large puddles. At one point, she started walking on the grass to avoid splashing dirt onto her hem.

By the time she'd reached the bend in the road, her nerves were already rattled. She wished that she'd gone back to the house with her father instead of traipsing alone to the Burkholders. And if Jacob and Jane *weren't* there, if they'd left and somehow made it home on foot through the pastures and down that muddy hill, Lizzie just knew that she'd be mortified, especially if she had to face Phineas alone.

There was something about that man that bothered her. More than bothered, she admitted to herself as she walked, hardly paying attention to the road. At first, she had thought him an odd man, definitely too old to be attending a youth gathering, that was for sure and certain. And, when he had spoken, his arrogance and pride, especially when he insulted *her*, had created a sour impression which only validated her impression of him.

And yet, the previous afternoon, when she'd seen him in the buggy, those dark eyes staring at her, she couldn't help but try and steady her nerves. *Barely tolerable,* he'd said. Those flippant words did not match with the curious gaze that studied her while he conversed with her father.

"Hold up there," someone called out to her. There was a grave sense of urgency to his voice and, immediately, she froze.

Startled, Lizzie looked to see none other than Phineas Denner standing on the gravel road ahead. She certainly hoped that he couldn't read minds for, if he could, he'd know that she had been thinking about him.

"What's wrong?"

Phineas pointed to the bridge. "It's too dangerous. Stay right where you are."

Lizzie's eyes shifted to where Phineas pointed. She hadn't been paying attention and hadn't noticed the small foot bridge a few steps ahead. There was a dip in the road and it was almost dark. Sure enough, there was a narrow river that cut under the road, the water rushing over the narrow bridge. There were no railings on it and, with the water flowing so fiercely, one bad step might have caused her to slip. If that had happened, there was no doubt that the current would have swept her away.

"Let me come fetch you."

Fetch her? Perhaps she hadn't heard him correctly. "What?" she called out.

He didn't respond in words, but in action. Slowly, he walked up the embankment along the side of the river. He slipped once on the slick grass but caught himself before falling. There was a tree at the top, not too large in the trunk and she noticed that he was tying something to it. The wind picked up and her kapp flew from her head but she didn't dare chase after it. Within minutes, Phineas was standing beside her.

"Oh!" She caught her breath. "I wasn't expecting that!"

"I jumped over," he said. "From the embankment. But now, I'm afraid we will have to walk across that bridge."

Lizzie frowned. "What's the point of that? Then we'll both be in danger."

He gestured to his waist where the end of a rope was tied. He'd secured himself to the tree at the top of the embankment. "This will prevent us from being swept away should we lose our footing."

She still wasn't understanding how that would help.

Phineas didn't explain with words. Instead, he stood behind her and, to her surprise, pressed his chest against her back. Before she could spin around to ask what he was doing, she felt him tying the rope around her waist so that they were, indeed, tethered together.

"Let's go," he said, his words breathless in her ear, as he wrapped one arm around her waist and pulled her closer to him.

She, too, felt breathless, but she suspected it was for very different reasons. She'd never stood so close to a man before and, despite not caring for Phineas Denner, she felt a bit overwhelmed by his touch.

He held onto the rope and nudged her forward. As soon as she stepped into the water, she caught her breath. It was cold and the current was strong, much stronger than she had anticipated. Phineas tightened his grip on her and, despite not wanting to, Lizzie clung to his arm.

Slowly, one step at a time, they made their way across the flooded bridge.

It was only when they reached the other side that Lizzie managed to catch her breath. She hadn't realized she had been holding it.

Phineas took a moment before he released his hold on her.

"Are you alright then?"

She nodded, unable to find her words. He was standing behind her, so close that she could feel the warmth of his breath when he spoke to her. In that moment, she was glad that he couldn't see her face for she knew that it was flushed red with embarrassment.

"*Gut.*" Once again, his warm breath was felt on her neck. "Let me untie this then."

With deft hands, he untied the rope and stepped back. As soon as she was free of the restraint, Lizzie felt strange. It was almost as if she were disappointed that he was no longer by her side.

Slowly, she turned around and peered up at him. "That was very dangerous."

"It was." His voice held no sense of arrogance or boastfulness at what he'd just done.

"Why didn't you just tell me to turn back?"

He raised one eyebrow, a look of amusement crossing his face. Staring down, his large frame overshadowing her petite one, he merely answered with his own question. "Would you have?"

Lizzie shook her head.

"Hm," he said with a single nod. "That's what I thought."

She didn't know how to respond but, perhaps, it was because her knees suddenly felt weak. Even worse, she noticed that her heart was racing. She knew that she didn't care for this man—he was far too proud. But now, standing before him, just the two of them, she was suddenly feeling a bit differently.

He eyed her with great curiosity. "Are you okay?"

Lizzie pressed her lips together and took a step away from him. "I...I think I'm just woozy from all the excitement."

Once again, he nodded. "Then let's get to the farm. You should dry off, or you'll get sick."

"Did you walk all the way here, then?" he asked, his deep voice calmer and kinder than she remembered.

"*Ja.* I mean, my *daed* drove me part of the way. There's a tree down, blocking the road. He told me to walk ahead and he'd meet me. But he wanted to return the horse and buggy first."

He made a noise, deep in his throat, which she wasn't certain how to interpret.

"How is Jane?"

"I imagine quite fine," Phineas said. "I left her in the kitchen with Cynthia. They were comparing recipes while Jacob's and Christopher are scouting the farm and assessing the damage to the fencing."

The way he said it made Lizzie smile. To the point and nothing more, a lack of emotion on his face that spoke volumes.

"Why am I not surprised?" she said, more to herself than to him. "And to think that we were all so worried at home."

Phineas kept stealing a sideward glance at her as they walked. Lizzie could feel his eyes upon her occasionally. "Worried? Did you think we'd let them travel home in such weather?"

"I'm sure I don't know you or any of the Burkholders well enough to form an opinion about what you would or would not do."

There was a momentary pause before he responded with a simple, "I see."

Lizzie wondered if she had offended him so she quickly added, "But I'm pleased to learn that you did what one *should* do in such a situation."

She thought she heard him give a soft chuckle, but, when she looked over at him, his expression remained unchanged.

They continued walking in silence, Lizzie all too aware of his presence beside her.

Chapter Sixteen

Phineas stood in the doorway, watching as Lizzie hurried across the kitchen floor to the side room where her sister sat on the sofa by the windows. Cynthia and Jane had retired to the sitting room where a small fire was set in the wood burning stove. They were both engrossed in crocheting and didn't noticed that he had returned.

"Jane!" Lizzie rushed forward as soon as she saw her sister.

At the sound of her voice, Jane looked up from her crocheting. "Lizzie! What on earth are you doing here?"

Dropping onto the sofa next to her, they embraced, a look of relief on both their faces. Besides mothers to young children, it was a gesture that Phineas had rarely seen expressed among Amish women he knew. Surely these two young women were extraordinarily close to have no qualms about showing their affection for each other in such a public manner. He found it to be an endearing and sweet gesture.

When Lizzie pulled away, she held her sister at arm's length. "We were so worried about you!"

Jane gave a little nervous laugh. "Nervous? About me? Whatever for? You knew I was here."

"Ja, well, we were afraid you and Jacob might have thought to come home, to beat the storm and then got caught in it." Lizzie peered down into Jane's lap, most likely noticing that her sister had been crocheting. "And yet, here you are, safe like we hoped." She glanced around the room, her eyes pausing for a moment on Cynthia who had barely acknowledged her presence. "Where is Jacob, anyway?"

As Jane told her how they watched the storm from the kitchen and how Christopher and Jacob had gone to check on the fencing and livestock, Phineas leaned against the doorframe, studying Lizzie with renewed interest.

When he'd spotted her walking down the road, something about her determined gait had caught him off-guard. He had suspected that Jane's father would come for his daughter and son; he'd never expected that *Lizzie* would make that journey. Alone. Surely, she possessed a strength of character to venture along the road after such a storm and as night was approaching.

And such a storm it had been. Perhaps because Blue Mill was situated in a valley, hence being called Lower Austen County, the winds had swept in fast and furious. Phineas had almost feared that a tornado might descend upon them. The skies had changed from blue to gray and then black within minutes and the winds ripped across the bare fields with nothing to break their powerful force. The neglected farm had suffered for certain. Roofing had ripped off the barn and limbs from trees crashed to the ground.

After it had weakened enough to venture outside, Christopher and Jacob checked the pasture where the livestock had been grazing while Phineas made his way down the dirt lane to check how the roads had fared. That was when he'd come upon Lizzie. For a few long moments, he'd watched her, seeing her in a different light. Few young women in Clearwater would have undertaken such a journey in such dangerous conditions.

When he realized that she'd taken no notice of the flooded bridge, he'd felt a surge of fear. Had he not been there, she would have certainly walked right into harm's way as it was clear that her thoughts were elsewhere. And, if she had, she would have been swept away, most certainly injured and, quite possibly, killed.

Now, as he watched her sitting next to Jane, her back straight and her lips smiling at her sister, Phineas realized that she was much prettier than he'd initially thought that Sunday morning he saw her walking to church. Perhaps it was because he hadn't *wanted* to be in Blue Mill—he longed for his own farm in Clearwater—or maybe it was because Cynthia had been irritating him with her negative talk about the community. It was almost as if she had been pointing out their flaws to make her feel better about herself. If he'd only been able to travel alone with Christopher, things might have been different and his attitude in much better spirits.

"You came alone?" Jane's eyes widened when she realized that her father was nowhere to be seen.

"Nee, Daed and I drove down the road, but there's a large oak tree blocking the way. I scaled it and walked ahead by myself. He wanted to take the horse and buggy home," Lizzie explained. "He said he'd try crossing through the pasture to fetch us on foot."

Jane caught her breath, her tongue making a short clicking noise. "A tree! Oh my!"

"That's not all," Lizzie continued. "The river's flooded so high it's covering the foot bridge."

"Flooded!"

"Completely impassable."

For a split second, Jane froze as if trying to comprehend what her sister had just told her. "If it's impassable, how did you cross?"

Phineas waited, wondering how Lizzie would explain his help. She paused long enough for the color to rise to her cheeks, a shade of pink that darkened when she glanced at him. Why hadn't he noticed how pretty she was before?

"Oh, well..." Another pause. "Phineas was there. He...he was kind enough to help me cross safely."

Upon hearing this, Cynthia stopped crocheting and Jane's mouth opened a little, her lips pursed in a perfect O. She raised her eyebrows, turning her gaze to look at Phineas.

Finally, it was Cynthia who spoke, her teeth clenched and her eyes blazing. "Is that so?"

Lizzie folded her hand in her lap and looked away. Phineas, however, was not about to stand by idly with Cynthia's tone clearly indicating disdain. For what reason, he couldn't fathom.

"Is it anything more or less than I would do for anyone?" He scowled; his eyebrows knit together in disapproval.

Suddenly, Lizzie looked up, her own eyes appearing to fire back at Cynthia. "Surely you wouldn't have expected him to let me cross on my own, would you now?" She lifted her chin. "Why, I find his good sense to predict someone coming to Jane's aid rather—" Her eyes shifted in his direction. "—admirable, as I'm sure you would agree, ja?"

Cynthia made a face. "Of course," she muttered before returning her attention to her crocheting. "It just sounds dangerous is all."

Phineas stood there, his curiosity slowly piqued, especially when he realized that Lizzie, too, clearly found Cynthia as tedious and wearisome as he did. Was there something more to Lizzie Bender than he'd originally thought? Or would she disappoint him as every other young Amish woman had?

Chapter Seventeen

By the time Amos arrived, it was almost six o'clock. Lizzie still sat next to her sister, half-heartedly listening as Jane and Cynthia talked. They certainly appeared to be getting along well, a fact that Lizzie didn't quite understand. Cynthia spoke in a manner that smacked of self-righteousness, reminding her a little too much of the first time she met Phineas.

Lizzie suspected she'd have to pray for forgiveness, because she knew she did not care for Christopher's sister one bit. And she also suspected that the feeling was mutual, although Lizzie could not imagine why that would be so. She'd barely had any contact with her at all, more because of Cynthia's attitude than for any other reason.

And yet, when Phineas returned to the sitting room, her father and Jacob in tow, Lizzie couldn't help but notice how Cynthia brightened and straightened her shoulders. When she spoke, she often deferred to him as if he might have something to add. Something about the way Cynthia stared at Phineas made her wonder, once again, if they were courting.

A more perfect couple could not exist, she thought wryly.

Still, when she thought back to how Phineas had behaved on the road, she wondered if there might not be something hidden beneath his austere exterior. He'd behaved quite differently than on Sunday. His concern for her safety and the way he had held her as they crossed the water had surprised her. In fact, the memory of being in his arms, pressed against his chest, made her flush and she had to force herself to think of something—anything!—other than that moment.

"Jane! Lizzie!" Amos wiped his boots on the mat by the doorway before he stepped inside the room. "I see you are both in good form." He leveled his eyes at Lizzie. "And I heard about the bridge. How fortunate you were that Denner was there. I never once thought the river would have flooded over it."

Lizzie noticed Cynthia's eyes narrow at the mention of Phineas's brave rescue. She couldn't help herself from adding, "How clever for him to bring that rope."

Jane turned to face her sister. "You said nothing about a rope."

Lizzie shrugged, aware that Phineas still stood in the doorway, watching her. He wore a curious expression as if he were amused. For some reason, seeing his face egged her on. "Had I forgotten to mention it?" She gave a little laugh.

"I guess I hadn't a moment to get a word in edgewise," she teased her sister lightly, even though that wasn't true. She'd had plenty of time to share her story. She just hadn't wanted to share all the details.

"How bad was the river?" Jane asked, concern etched on her face.

"It was nothing, truly." She sighed dramatically. "We managed to get through."

"Thanks to Denner," Amos said. "I'd hate to think what might've happened if he hadn't been there to help you, Lizzie. Surely you would have been swept away." He shuddered as if the thought was more than he could bare.

"Swept away?" Cynthia turned to look at Phineas, her eyes questioning and a slight smile on her lips, one that carried no mirth but only amusement. "How harrowing! Do tell us, Phineas, what happened," she drawled. "I'm sure everyone is anxious to hear about your exciting adventure."

From the corner of her eye, Lizzie noticed Phineas stiffen and turn away, the muscles in his jaws tightening as if he were bothered by her request. In fact, he looked more than uncomfortable; he appeared downright irritated. Suddenly, it dawned on Lizzie that Phineas was not interested in Cynthia. In fact, she wondered if Phineas felt the same way as *she* did about Cynthia.

Clearing her throat, Lizzie saved him the discomfort of answering. "I already told you that Phineas helped me across the flooded bridge."

"But what is this business about a rope?" Cynthia gave a forced little laugh that sounded unkind and sarcastic "It all sounds so dangerous and exciting!"

To Lizzie's surprise, Jane chimed in. "Ja, Lizzie. Tell us what happened."

Lizzie frowned at her sister. "The water was rushing something fierce, so he tied a rope to a tree to keep us from being swept away. It was nothing, really."

Phineas crossed the room and stood in front of the window, staring outside. When Lizzie glanced at him, she noticed he held his hands clasped behind his back, his shoulders stiff and straight. Perhaps it was the unwanted attention that made him uncomfortable, or, she thought, perhaps he wasn't quite as uncomfortable as he had led on. The thought humored her as she returned her attention to her sister who had gasped.

"Oh my! That doesn't sound uneventful at all!"

Lizzie gave her a reassuring smile. "Ah, but his ingenuity made it so."

"How so?" Cynthia asked, a deep layer of contempt dripping from her tongue.

Oh, Lizzie didn't care for Christopher's sister at all! Just the tone of voice that she adopted when she spoke to Lizzie provoked her ire. But, instead of directly confronting Cynthia, Lizzie chose a different tactic. Smiling, she placed her hand on her chest. "Why! He predicted that someone was going to come to see how Jane and my brother fared. And he brought a rope to help that person cross. Tied me to him so tight that I wouldn't get swept away. Considerate *and* clever" She let her eyes move from Cynthia's to Phineas's. "Imagine that."

Irritated, Cynthia clucked her tongue and looked away.

But Lizzie didn't care if the young woman was annoyed by the accolades she'd given Phineas. Despite remembering his harsh words about her at the youth gathering, couldn't deny that he'd impressed her at the river. While she wasn't one to give out compliments too often, she knew when they were deserved and, surely, he had saved her certain injury.

"I suspect the road is still blocked?" Phineas asked, directing the question to Amos.

The abrupt change in conversation eased the tension in the room. Cynthia bent her head over her crocheting, her fingers moving rapidly as if she were anxious to be done with the whole conversation. For some reason, that gave Lizzie a small sense of satisfaction though, realizing that, she quickly prayed for forgiveness. She needed to be more tolerant of others, especially people like Cynthia Burkholder.

"Ja, it is. By horse anyway. But the river's water has receded." Amos glanced at the clock. "Reckon we best go see what can be done about that tree. Jacob's already moving branches. Mayhaps the *Englische* will have arrived to help."

To everyone's surprise, Christopher hurried over and knelt by Jane's side. Gently, he took her hand in his, an overtly intimate gesture that startled Lizzie just as much as it did Jane. "We'll work hard, Jane, to clear the roads so you may return home. While your company here is—" He hesitated and lowered his voice. "—most pleasant, I'm more than certain you would prefer to be home with your family rather than here with two bachelors and a *maedel.*"

Jane blushed, but a hint of a smile crossed her lips.

Lizzie, however, raised an eyebrow at Christopher's words. *Maedel?* Cynthia was considered such? Perhaps Cynthia was not as young as Lizzie had thought and that would certainly explain her sour attitude. It was more than clear that Christopher favored Jane, so *she* was not competition for Phineas's affections. Lizzie, however, was a different story entirely. Of course, those words that Phineas had spoken at the singing haunted Lizzie and her own first impression of him lingered in the back of her mind.

And yet, Lizzie couldn't help but sense that something might have changed—perhaps for them both—to alter their initial impressions of one another.

Quietly, she thought back to those moments crossing the flooded bridge when she'd been in his arms, and she blushed. She thought she heard him give a soft chuckle before he left the room, which only enflamed her cheeks even more. Had he read her mind?

With a deep breath, she glanced at Jane then turned her head to look outside. She could see Jacob and her father heading down the driveway, Phineas leading the way and Christopher jogging to catch up to them. "Jane," she began. "I think I might be of more use helping the men."

Cynthia spun around, a horrified look on her face. "Help the men?"

"*Ja!*" Lizzie replied. By the expression on her face, it was clear that such an idea had never crossed her mind. "Many hands make light the work."

"What can *you* do?" Cynthia scoffed. "Move a tree trunk?"

"While I might not be able to do heavy lifting, I can certainly move brambles and debris. Some help is better than no help at all, I imagine." She didn't wait for a response from Cynthia who sat there, with a sour look. Instead, Lizzie quickly headed toward the side room where she'd left her wet shoes earlier.

Outside, the dark clouds had begun to disappear, and the moon could be seen between the remaining clouds. In the distance, her eyes noticed the faint stars overhead. For a moment, she stood there and stared at them. Stars always lifted her sprits, the not-so-subtle reminder of God's promise to the world. Whenever she saw them, she felt as if God was speaking directly to her.

"You're smiling."

She started at the sound of Phineas' voice behind her. "Oh!"

He held up his hand. "I didn't mean to scare you."

"I was just lost in thought, that's all." She pointed toward the sky. "I love stars."

He made a noise in his throat, acknowledging what she'd said without speaking as if in reverence of the beautiful sight. For a long moment, he stood there in silence.

Feeling awkward, Lizzie glanced toward the road. "Are there many people helping?"

He nodded. "Many. Both Amish and Englischers."

She wondered why he wasn't with them.

As if reading her mind, he gestured toward the barn. "Fetching the chainsaw."

"Oh."

"If you wait a minute, we can walk together. You can help pull some branches, if you don't mind."

"Of course."

Hard work had never been off-putting for Lizzie. There was nothing like rolling up your sleeves and getting dirty as you worked outside. Whether she was working in the field or the barn, she didn't care. She preferred being outside, with her father, rather than inside with her mother and younger sister. Their tendency to gossip irritated Lizzie to no end. She never could understand how, day in and day out, Jane tolerated them with such patience.

Side-by-side, Lizzie and Phineas, carrying the gasoline-powered chainsaw, walked in silence. As they approached the road, Lizzie couldn't believe all the leaves and branches littering the ground. The bridge, however, was no longer flooded. When they turned the corner to where the tree had fallen, she wasn't surprised to see a dozen Amish men working alongside the Englischers.

Chainsaws roared, the noise breaking the post-storm silence. Without waiting for direction, Lizzie began working alongside one of their neighbors, carrying broken branches to the side of the road. With so many men helping, she knew it wouldn't take long until the road was clear. That was the way the Amish worked: together as a community.

Every once in a while, she glanced up, curious to see Phineas wielding the chainsaw. He had a determined expression on his face. It surprised her to see how hard he worked. She wouldn't have thought of him as being so driven. At least not before tonight, anyway.

It was almost eight when her father approached her.

"Lizzie," he said. "The road's almost clear. Go fetch Jane."

"No sense walking." For the second time that afternoon, Phineas surprised her. "I'll go hitch up the horse and take you back," he offered, wiping his dirty hands on his pants. The chainsaw sat on the ground at his feet. Peering over his shoulder, he considered the remnants of the tree. "Not much left to do here, anyway."

"Well, I thank you for the offer," Amos said. "But we don't want to trouble you. You've already been inconvenienced enough for one night."

Phineas raised an eyebrow as if questioning Amos's statement. But rather than argue, he merely shrugged. "It's no bother but suit yourself."

She felt a conflict of emotions at the way he'd so easily given in. As she walked back toward the Burkholders' house to collect her sister, Lizzie realized that she felt a touch disappointed. She'd seen a new side of Phineas Denner, one that was remarkably different than the man she'd heard criticizing her just two days prior. And yet, as soon as she recognized her feelings, she reminded herself that he *had* disparaged her without even spending more than a few minutes getting to know to her.

It was better that he didn't drive them home, she told herself. Regardless of his actions earlier that day, he was not the sort of man she would ever trust. Perhaps, she thought with self-satisfaction, it is *he* who is barely tolerable.

On the walk home, Jane and Lizzie lingered far enough behind their father to share a private conversation.

"He's *wunderbarr gut,* Lizzie," Jane whispered, even though their father and brother were too far ahead to overhear their words.

Lizzie smiled to herself. "Oh?"

"Oh ja. Christopher's so kind and attentive. We had a *wunderbaar* time at the picnic," Jane said with a wistful sigh. "And when the storm came, he was very concerned for my safety."

It was easy to see that Christopher Burkholder was a good-hearted man, just as it was easy to see that Jane was besotted with him.

"I think he's smitten with you," Lizzie said.

Jane linked her arm with Lizzie's. "Do you really think so?"

"I do." Lizzie smiled. "I really, really do."

Clearly Jane felt the same about him.

Sighing, Jane leaned her head against Lizzie's shoulder. At that moment, she felt her heart swell, the happiness she experienced for her eldest sibling—and best friend—beyond description.

"Oh, I hope so, Lizzie." And then, lifting her head, Jane returned her sister's smile. "I really, really do."

They both laughed then picked up their pace to catch up with their father and brother.

Chapter Eighteen

Seeing the lone cow wandering aimlessly in the middle of the road surprised Phineas more than anything he'd seen as of late. It was a cream-colored Jersey cow with an udder full of milk. Undoubtedly, it belonged to one of Christopher's neighbors, for cows weren't known to wander too far from the herd, though Phineas hadn't noticed any Jersey cows in the nearby fields before. Most of the Amish folk in Blue Mill had black and white Holstein cows.

It was Thursday and enough time had passed since the storm that the high rivers had receded, and the damaged property had been tended. No, the cow should not have been wandering. After all, most of the fences along the road had been repaired. He should know because he'd helped most of the neighbors mend them.

"Whoa!" He pulled back on the reins, easing the horse to a full stop. Only then did he step down from the buggy. He grabbed a spare lead rope that he kept under his front seat, then slowly approached the animal.

On his farm in Clearwater, he had a few cows. He liked the idea of fresh milk and cheese, although he rarely partook of the former and never made the latter. With just a small herd, it was easy enough to manage their needs. But he also knew that cows were, as a rule, a great deal of work with little reward. Additionally, unlike horses, cows weren't known to show affection.

This one, however, was friendly enough. It didn't move away from him and even let him rub his hand along its neck. Carefully, he wrapped the rope in such a way that he could lead the cow or, if it didn't cooperate, secure it until he could locate the owner.

He didn't have to look far for, just as he tied the rope around its neck, he saw someone approaching.

Squinting his eyes, Phineas tried to focus on the figure in the distance. When the person neared, he realized it was none other than Lizzie. She was walking fast, her pace suggesting that she was in a hurry. Upon seeing him, she halted and stood in the middle of the road, staring at him from a few hundred yards away.

"Oh," she called out. "It's you."

Phineas held up the end of the lead rope. "Lose something?"

Slower now, Lizzie walked toward him. She wasn't wearing a prayer kapp and several strands of her brown hair had escaped the bun at the nape of her neck. Her feet were dirty, and she clearly wore a work dress for the hem was tattered and torn. Still, to Phineas, he saw through her appearance for what it truly was: the sign of a hard-working young woman.

As she neared, Lizzie glanced at the cow who merely stood there, chewing her cud and staring beyond the road toward the green pasture that beckoned to her. "I'm afraid she escaped," Lizzie said with what he could only describe as an embarrassed sigh.

"I gathered as much," he chuckled, hoping to put her at ease, "when I found the cow in the middle of the road."

She gave him a suspicious look.

"Must've wanted to take a stroll around the neighborhood," he added lightly.

She gave a small laugh. The sound of it struck Phineas as rather pleasant. He'd never paid attention to such things before, but, for some reason, Lizzie's laughter was quite agreeable to him.

"I reckon that's exactly what she thought." She reached for the lead. "Naughty cow," she scolded playfully.

Phineas let her take the rope, but he didn't release it. For the briefest moment, they were both holding the lead. When she realized that he wasn't letting go, she questioned him with her eyes.

"I'll walk her back," he said, "if you don't mind driving the horse."

Lizzie stiffened. "I can take her."

"I'm sure you can." Phineas refused to break eye contact. "But I was raised to help my neighbor and, if you would humor me, I'd prefer to lead the cow home."

Something shifted in her mind. Slowly, she released her hold on the rope. "I...I see."

He thought he noticed her cheeks flush.

"Then by all means," she said, stepping away from the cow. She walked over to the horse and, taking ahold of its bridle, began walking with it down the road toward her house.

"You can drive her," he said.

"Nee, that's all right. I prefer walking with you."

I prefer walking with you.

Something about those five words struck him. He'd never gone walking with a girl before—neither by chance nor by choice.

In Clearwater, the women were far too interested in the size of his farm and his position in the community than the character he possessed. Phineas didn't understand why. A farm was just a farm. It wasn't his fault that his parents had no other children to inherit the land. No Amish children, anyway.

As for his position in his church district, he only did what any good Christian man would: help others, worship daily, and follow the Ordnung. He didn't promote himself as being above others, but the community tended to look to him as an unspoken leader. He'd even learned that, when a new preacher was needed, his name had been put forth by several worshippers to be included in the lot at a future time. However, he wasn't married and that was a requirement to minister to the members of the *g'may.*

He'd adopted a stern exterior, first because he'd been overwhelmed by inheriting his father's farm at such a young age. The responsibility had nearly broken him until he'd taken the load off his shoulders and hired a young, unmarried Amish man to help. And of course, when Christopher had agreed to work his farm, it was as if he were sharing the load with a brother rather than a friend.

Later, he maintained his unyielding mannerisms to discourage the young women from flirting with him. Soon enough, it had become more than a habit; it had become a part of who he was. And yet, deep down, that wasn't who he *truly* was. The only problem was that he was the only one who knew that. Except for Christopher, Phineas kept people at a distance, not wanting to let them get too close. He preferred it that way as there was less risk of being hurt when one put up a protective barrier.

Lizzie Bender was no different, or so he presumed. She knew nothing about him beyond the fact that he was helping Christopher set up his farm in Blue Mill. And yet, she held the horse's reins, quietly walking beside him as he led the cow down the road toward the turn off that led to the Benders' driveway. She didn't try to force conversation like other young women might. She seemed perfectly content to just be in his company.

And he found that he appreciated that more than he would have imagined.

Was it possible that Lizzie could see through his tough exterior or was she merely being polite? The question occupied his thoughts while he walked in the direction of her father's farm with both the cow and Lizzie in tow.

Chapter Nineteen

"Denner! Lizzie! *Wie gehts?*"

Lizzie had been so engrossed in her thoughts that she hadn't realized her father was walking down the road toward them. For the past half mile, she'd been following in silence beside Phineas, the only noise being the sounds of the animal's hooves and the buggy wheels against the pavement.

Startled, she looked up and saw her father waving as he neared. He smiled at Phineas leading the runaway cow back toward the farm.

"I see you're bringing home my two wayward girls," Amos teased as he stopped before them.

"Daed." Lizzie balked at his words. She dared not look at Phineas, fearful of what he must think after hearing her father calling her 'wayward'. Surely his already poor opinion of her must be even lower now. Embarrassed, Lizzie stood by the horse, her hand still upon its bridle. She reached over and stroked its neck, trying to focus on the gleaming shine to the horse's coat and not on her own discomfort. "You shouldn't tease me like that."

To her surprise, however, Phineas chuckled at her father's choice of words. "Wayward girls, eh? That's one way to look at it." He glanced at the cow beside him and tugged at the lead. "At least for this young miss, anyway."

Puzzled, Lizzie looked at him. Had he just defended her?

Unperturbed, Amos reached out and took the lead from Phineas. "That back fencing," he shook his head and clucked his tongue. "It's needed fixing for a while now. Just been putting it off for some no-good reason." He reached up and scratched his forehead, just under the rim of his straw hat. "The rain from Tuesday's storm must have loosened the dirt enough so that a certain wandering cow could escape." He sighed, reaching up to wipe the sweat from his brow with the back of his arm. "I'll have to fetch some cement from town, I reckon, to shore up the posts. No sense putting it off any longer. If one cow found the weak spot, others will surely follow."

To Lizzie's surprise, Phineas gestured toward his buggy. "I was just heading that way—into town for a few supplies—if you'd like me to pick up the cement for you."

Her father's eyes widened. For a moment, Lizzie thought he would decline the offer. Her father wasn't one to accept help from others too often. But he surprised her when he responded with an appreciative smile.

"Why, that would be much appreciated, Denner. I wasn't planning on a trip into town today. Too much to do around here and now, with the cow breaking free..." He let his sentence remain unfinished.

Knowingly, Phineas nodded. "That's the way it happens on a farm. As much as you plan your day, something's always bound to sidetrack you."

Amos laughed. "Ain't that the truth?"

Lizzie shifted her weight, barely listening to the conversation. She had a lot to do herself. The garden needed tending. The soil had been prepared the previous week. She'd spent an entire day weeding it and removing rocks before taking the next afternoon to spread manure, raking it into the soil. Now, she needed to start planting seeds and cover them with hay so that the birds didn't peck at them. If she didn't start soon, they'd have no vegetables in the summertime. It wasn't as if Katie would volunteer to help; she hated to get her hands dirty. Like Jane, Katie preferred working inside the house to working the land.

Suddenly, an uncomfortable feeling overwhelmed her. She shifted her eyes and realized that Phineas was studying her. She wondered for how long he'd been staring. The way he looked at her, his dark eyes so intense, made her feel uneasy. She had no idea what he was thinking and that put her on edge. Quickly, she looked away.

He cleared his throat. "Mayhaps Lizzie might ride along,"

Immediately, she jerked up her head up and met his eyes.

He held her gaze as he spoke. "I mean, I'm still not familiar with these roads and all. I could use someone who knows the area to help guide me."

Her mouth opened, but no words came out. Surely, he knew how to get to town! Why, he'd gone to town the other day with Cynthia. Why on earth would he want her tagging along?

"And, of course, the company would be welcomed," he continued.

Surprised, she shut her mouth and looked away.

Out of the corner of her eye, she thought she saw her father's mouth curl into a small smile. "Well, I reckon I won't need Lizzie for a while. Morning chores are done and all—"

"The cows need milking," she quickly pointed out.

"I believe I'm more than capable of milking a few cows," her father quipped. "Jacob's home, anyway."

"The garden—"

"—can wait until the afternoon." Amos pressed his lips together, a silent hint that she dare not protest further. Her father had spoken. She was to go with Phineas and there was no point in searching for more excuses. "Why don't you run into the *haus* and see if your *maem* needs anything from town while you're there. And fetch my wallet for me, ja?"

She felt frozen in place, her feet refusing to move. Phineas stepped forward to take the horse's bridle from her hand.

"I'll wait here with the buggy."

She didn't look at him. Instead, she nodded then hurried down the driveway, too aware that both Phineas and her father had fallen back into conversation.

Why had Phineas asked her to join him? After all, he was the one who said she was 'barely tolerable.' What could have possibly changed his mind? Her stomach felt queasy and her nerves on fire as she bounded up the porch steps and hurried inside.

"Land's sake, Elizabeth!" Her mother turned away from the counter and put her hand on her hip. "Such a ruckus!"

"Sorry, Maem."

From the looks of it, her mother was busy passing milk curds through the cheese press. Katie was nowhere to be seen and Jane was bent over a pair of their father's pants, mending a tear in the leg.

"Uh...Daed sent me in," Lizzie said. "I'm heading to town, if you need anything."

Her mother's eyes narrowed. "Heading to town?" she squeaked. "Whatever for? You *know* I do my shopping on Fridays. Today's Thursday. Why would you be going to town *today*?"

Lizzie fought the urge to roll her eyes. Her mother had never been one deviate from her schedule. She much preferred order and structure, a routine that did not stray. "It wasn't planned—"

"Of course, it wasn't planned! Just as I haven't planned a list or checked to see what I might need!"

Jane looked up, a curious expression on her face. "Why *are* you going to town, Lizzie? Has something happened?"

Leave it to her sister to ask the logical question. Relieved, Lizzie faced her. "Ja, it did. One of the cows escaped. It knocked down a fence post, I'm afraid."

"Just shore it up for the time being! Your father has far too much to do around here to go traipsing into town today."

"That's just it. Daed's not going." Lizzie took a deep breath. "I am."

Her mother looked confused. "You're going alone?"

While there was no reason that Lizzie *couldn't* go alone with the horse and buggy, she knew that her mother didn't like her daughters driving into town without a chaperone. She always had visions of car accidents or runaway horses. Whenever she worried about such things, no amount of reassurance from anyone could convince her otherwise. "Nee, I'm not."

"Then who, exactly, do you think will be with accompanying you?" Susan turned toward Jane. "Your *schweister*?"

"Uh, nee." Lizzie shifted her weight uncomfortably. Why was her mother making such a big deal about nothing? "Not Jane."

"Then who?"

"Well, when I went to find the cow—" She glanced at her mother. "—I ran into Phineas Denner."

The irritated look on her mother's face vanished and it was immediately replaced with one of interest. "Denner? Christopher Burkholder's friend?" Even the tone of her voice softened. "The one you said was so unpleasant?"

Nodding, Lizzie continued. "He offered to go into town to fetch cement to fix the post, but he wanted me to ride along."

Her mother inhaled.

"I mean, he's not from around here and all," Lizzie quickly added.

"Heavens to Betsy!" She clapped her hands. "Twice the blessings from these new neighbors!"

This time, Lizzie did roll her eyes. "Oh Mother!"

"Hush now, Elizabeth!" Susan held her hands together and pressed them to her chest. "To think, *both* my Jane and my Lizzie have special friends." She exhaled.

"I'm merely riding into town with him," Lizzie pointed out in a flat tone. "I *highly* doubt courting is on his mind, Maem."

"Oh, of course it is!" Susan shot back.

"He's much older than I am."

Her mother dismissed her with a half-hearted wave. "Stuff and nonsense, Elizabeth. He's no more than thirty, I'd guess."

"He lives far away," she countered. "Mayhaps he has his own girl back home, anyway."

Her mother huffed. "Then he's no business asking another girl to ride into town with him."

Lizzie shook her head. Why did her mother have to make so much out of nothing? A simple buggy ride. "Your imagination is running wild, Maem," she said dismissively. "He doesn't know his way to town." Even as the words passed her lips, Lizzie knew how ridiculous they sounded. It wasn't too difficult to navigate the backroads toward Blue Mill's center.

Her mother didn't seem to notice the color that flooded her daughter's cheeks, as her focus was squarely on Phineas's intentions. "Surely that's the *real* reason," she scoffed. "Well, at least you're being neighborly and helpful. A man is bound to appreciate *that*."

Jane, however, was not so easily fooled. She appeared to be staring at Lizzie and the intensity of her sister's gaze made her feel uncomfortable.

"I thought you didn't care for him."

Lizzie made a face at her sister. "Not *you*, too, Jane."

Jane raised an eyebrow.

"He's merely doing a favor for Daed," Lizzie said, her voice thick with frustration. But, despite the words that slipped past her lips, Lizzie couldn't help remembering the way he had gazed at her when he'd ask if she would accompany him. She also couldn't deny that the idea of spending part of the morning in his company, driving to town and learning more about him, was not entirely unpleasant to her. The truth was that, ever since the previous day at the flooded bridge, she hadn't been able to stop thinking about him.

And yet, every time she did think about him, two words echoed in her ears. *Barely tolerable.* Those words continued to haunt her. For a man who had said such terrible things *about* her, he was being rather attentive *now.* The contradiction was bothersome. Clearly, he had formed an opinion of her at the youth gathering and criticized her based on that first impression. Now, however, he was behaving as if he'd never said those words let alone thought them.

After she grabbed her purse and father's wallet, she hurried back outside, telling herself to keep her feelings in check. Part of her was excited that he'd asked her to ride with him even though she was bothered by the memory of his insult. She needed to be openminded. After all, she knew very little about him. Though, growing up, she'd often heard the expression that a cow's spots might fade in the summer, but they never truly changed. While she hadn't understood it then, she certainly did now. People rarely changed.

That, of course, led to Lizzie to ponder the next pressing thought: Who exactly was this Phineas Denner anyway?

Chapter Twenty

For the first few miles, neither one of them spoke. Phineas didn't feel particularly burdened by the silence. In fact, he preferred the quiet. If Lizzie had begun chattering away, like most other young women, Phineas would have been sorely disappointed. She had begun impressing him as far more sensible than that. Words were meant to be sowed carefully, not simply scattered in the wind in the hopes of taking root.

As he approached town, however, he found himself wondering why she hadn't said *anything* yet. It had been almost twenty minutes and not a single word had been spoken. Perhaps he had been wrong to invite her to ride along with him. Had she only agreed because she felt an obligation to her father or worse yet, an obligation to him because he had rescued her from the bridge?

An upcoming stop signed caused Phineas to slow the trotting horse to a walk and then a full stop. He took advantage of the moment to glance at her then decided that maybe she was uncomfortable being alone in his presence in such small quarters.

"You all right then?"

She'd been looking out the window, not paying any attention to him. Now that he'd spoken, she turned her head and her big, chocolate brown eyes met his. He hadn't noticed how large they were. And they appeared to dance as the corners of her mouth bent upward, in the hint of a smile.

"Of course, I'm all right," she replied, her voice soft and even. "Why wouldn't I be?"

"You're awfully quiet."

Lizzie took a deep breath and, slowly, exhaled. "I find unnecessary—" She glanced at him, a sparkle in her eyes. "—forced conversation to be—" She paused and placed a finger to the side of her cheek. "—barely tolerable."

Phineas raised his eyebrow at her chosen words. "Barely tolerable?"

"Ja, that's what I said. Barely tolerable. Don't you agree?" And then she turned her head back toward the window so she could continue gazing at the passing landscape.

Phineas swallowed. Was it possible that she had overheard him that night at the youth singing a few days earlier? He hadn't meant to speak in such a condescending way about the people of Blue Mill; he'd just been in a terrible mood. Between Christopher mooning over Jane and Cynthia always at his elbow, Phineas had found himself seeing everything through dirty lenses. Truth be told, at that very moment, in his eyes there had been nothing redeemable about Blue Mill.

Now, however, Phineas knew that he did not feel that way. In fact, he'd grown used to the small-town mindset. Even more so, as of late, he'd been looking forward to spending more time with a certain young woman. He wondered if his reckless words had ruined his chances to leave a favorable impression upon her memory.

Clearing his throat, he glanced at her. "Sometimes when you try something new," he began slowly, "what you thought was barely tolerable—" He emphasized the word 'tolerable.' "—is surprisingly endurable."

He watched as Lizzie's mouth opened. "Endurable?" she repeated.

"Bearable," he corrected quickly. "Perhaps that's better."

She gave an incredulous laugh. "That's even *worse!*"

Inwardly, Phineas sighed. This wasn't going the way he wanted. "Are we still talking about conversation, Lizzie? Or are we talking about something else?"

Sobering, she straightened her shoulders. "I think you know exactly what I'm talking about, Phineas."

Clearly, she *had* overheard him.

It wasn't often that anyone caught him off-guard. Lizzie Bender, however, had done just that. He stared straight ahead, wondering how, if at all, he could salvage not just the buggy ride but his potential budding friendship with the young woman seated next to him.

"Lizzie, I apologize if you overheard me say—"

"I know I'm supposed to accept that apology," she said, interrupting him. "It's the Christian thing to do, but I'm not certain that I *can* do that, Phineas. Making such a statement about someone you didn't even know indicates that you are very judgmental, unless, of course, you were, in fact, merely judging me on my outer appearance, which speaks poorly of your character."

His eyes widened. "My character?" He sighed. "You are quite wrong, Lizzie. I'm not judgmental at all."

"Then you were commenting on my appearance?" She made a face. "I reckon that's even worse for that would make you shallow."

He took a deep breath and searched his mind for the right words. There were none. How could he explain how he had been feeling that evening? That his comments truly had nothing to do with *her* but with the situation itself. He hadn't been happy about going to the youth gathering that evening. He wasn't even happy about being there, in Blue Mill, with Christopher at that time. He hadn't wanted his friend to move to Lower Austen County. In fact, he'd encouraged him to consider partnering with him on his own farm.

But Christopher had been insistent that he wanted to build something of his own.

Phineas exhaled slowly. "I apologize, Lizzie, for what I said. There is no excuse beyond I was not myself that evening. I've no interest in youth gatherings. I much prefer a quiet evening at home, reading Scripture." He paused, glancing at her. She kept her hands folded on her lap and continued to stare out the window. The serious expression on her face, however, indicated that she was, indeed, listening to him. "Might you give me another chance to prove myself worthy?"

The silence became deafening and Phineas began to worry that she would hold a grudge against him. It wasn't Christian to refuse forgiveness when someone was truly apologetic. Had he misjudged her yet again?

"Turn here," she said at last, pointing to the right. "The hardware store is about a mile down this road."

He followed her direction, still wondering whether she would forgive him or not.

Finally, she sighed and turned toward him. "Phineas, I will permit you that chance to change *my* first impression of you," she said. "Although I've no idea why you'd even bother. It's not as though it matters much, anyway."

As she spoke, Phineas felt as though he had been hit in the gut. *It's not as though it matters much, anyway.*

Oh, he thought to himself, how very wrong you are, Lizzie Bender. Very wrong indeed.

Chapter Twenty-One

His apology had caught her off-guard. She hadn't expected Phineas to speak so candidly. Not only had he admitted that he said those words and had been wrong to speak so harshly about her, but he also requested a chance to prove himself worthy of her friendship.

Asking for the opportunity to prove himself worthy wasn't something she'd been prepared to entertain. And yet, now that he requested it, Lizzie wondered at the source of his motivation. Phineas lived far enough from Blue Mill that Lizzie knew she'd never see him again once he returned home. Judging from his age, she suspected that he was a lifelong bachelor. Surely if he intended to marry, he'd have done it by now, so clearly, he was seeking a friendship at best.

Still, as they walked through the store, Phineas two paces ahead of her, she stared at his back and admired his broad shoulders and confident posture. Even though he had claimed that the store was not familiar to him, he didn't have to ask which aisle housed the supplies needed for fixing her father's fence. Clearly, he'd been there before, and Lizzie wondered at how much work had been done at Christopher's farm. She hadn't a chance to see much of the grounds the night before because by the time the storm had let up, it was well into evening.

It was good for someone to invest in the upkeep of the old family farm. The previous tenants had let it fall further into disrepair.

When Phineas found the cement, he picked up not one or two but three bags as if they weighed nothing.

"You think he'll need that many?" she asked.

He nodded. "Ja, I do. I noticed some other posts that could use reinforcement. Better to be safe than sorry."

"I can carry one," she offered, holding out her hands to lighten his load. Phineas, however, gave her a quizzical look and, politely refused her offer.

At the counter, he set down the bags of cement. A small cloud of white dust rose from the corner of one bag.

"Ah, Phineas!" An older Amish man walked out of the back room and greeted him with a broad smile. "You're becoming quite the regular. Mayhaps you'll move to Blue Mill after all!"

Lizzie looked up and saw Phineas return the greeting with a friendly smile and nod. "Mayhaps, John. But I'd have to find a farm comparable to mine in Clearwater."

John tugged at his whiskery beard. "How many acres did you say it was?"

Phineas leaned his elbow on the top bag of cement and made a face. "I don't reckon I *did* say how many acres it is," he replied and commented no further, a clear indication that he had no intention of disclosing such information. "Now, besides these bags of cement, I'll be needing another box of nails and some more of that barbed wire."

"Barbed wire?" Lizzie's eyes widened. Amish farmers in Blue Mill typically used boards for their fencing, not wire and certainly not *barbed* wire.

Peering down at her, his dark eyes barely visible from beneath the brim of his hat, he nodded. "I prefer putting a strand of wire in-between the fence boards, Lizzie."

"But why?"

She thought she saw the hint of a smile on his lips when he bent down as if to whisper in her ear. "Keeps the cows from itching their rumps against the fence and *that* means less broken boards to fix."

Feeling foolish, Lizzie looked away. Why hadn't she thought of that? In fact, she couldn't help but wonder why more Amish farmers didn't use barbed wire. "Smart," she muttered.

Chuckling at their exchange, the man behind the counter gave a little shake of his head. "Seems like it'd be common sense, don't it now, Lizzie? But I'm with you. Haven't seen many Amish farmers using wire for that purpose. And, unfortunately, I've no more in stock, Phineas." He glanced over his shoulder at a calendar hanging on the back wall. "Should have more arriving on

Monday, though. Feel free to stop back then. I'll set a few rolls aside, if you can wait that long."

Phineas appeared to ponder that for a moment and then he nodded. "Most appreciated. Monday will do fine. The cows can't do too much damage between their arrival on Saturday and Monday, I reckon."

This was news, indeed!

Lizzie couldn't help but wonder if Jane knew that Christopher had purchased cows already. While she shouldn't have been surprised—he had moved to Blue Mill to farm—she hadn't realized that Christopher intended to have livestock. Her father would be interested to hear about this, too.

"I thought he was going to just farm," she said.

Phineas raised an eyebrow in response to her comment. "I did, too, but he insists that a farm isn't complete without a small dairy herd."

She made a face. It wasn't as simple as just buying cows and milking them. There was a lot of equipment to purchase and maintain. "Does he know anything about managing a dairy?"

In response to her question, Phineas laughed. "He'd be quite the fool if he didn't, wouldn't you say, Lizzie?"

Immediately, she looked away, feeling a burning heat rise to her cheeks. Of course, he knew about cows, she thought, scolding herself for having asked such a thoughtless question.

He must have sensed her embarrassment for he quickly sobered. "I'm sorry, Lizzie," he said softly. "I didn't mean to make light of your question. It just caught me off-guard."

She pursed her lips and glanced around the store. Thankfully John had disappeared into the back room to fetch the nails that Phineas needed. She turned toward him and faced him dead on. "While I'm glad that Christopher has rented the farm, I know nothing about the Burkholder family, Phineas, except that they are relations with my daed. Distant relations at that."

With a somber expression, Phineas gave a simple nod. "Duly noted, Lizzie. Again, my apologies. If it helps, I'd be happy to fill in some of those details on our way back to your daed's farm." He glanced over his shoulder at John who had stepped from the back room. "After my other errands, of course."

After paying for the cement and nails, Phineas put the items in the back of his buggy before they walked next door to the small grocery store. Lizzie felt uneasy when she spotted her friend, Emma, driving her horse and buggy down the main road. There was no questioning that she'd seen Lizzie walking beside Phineas for, when she raised her hand to wave at them, there was a broad smile with a knowing expression plastered on Emma's face.

"You know her?"

Startled that he'd been paying attention to the awkward exchange, she looked up at him. It wasn't the first time that she'd noticed how attractive he was. His dark eyes searched hers and his face, tanned from working outside, was chiseled and rugged in a way that made him appear even more handsome.

"My friend, Emma," she replied.

"If she is your friend, why don't you look happier about seeing her?"

Of course, he'd ask such a question, she thought, suspecting that her cheeks flushed pink. Once again, it appeared as if he'd read her mind. "She just likes to gossip, that's all."

Phineas stood before the door of the grocery store and opened it for her. As she walked under his arm, he lowered it, just enough so that she stopped and peered up at him.

"There's nothing to gossip about here, Elizabeth," he said in a soft voice. "Besides, sometimes it's best to let busybodies spread the roots of their idle talk. I've found truth in the Scripture that states the mouths of fools are often their ruin." He kept his eyes on hers, his arm still blocking her way. "Mayhaps you might rethink the extent of your friendship with such a person or risk being judged of wearing the same cloak." With that, he lifted his arm and let her pass.

Speechless, Lizzie entered the store, his words repeating in her head. She'd never thought much about Emma and her propensity for gossip having a negative impact on her own reputation. Certainly, she hoped that Phineas did not think she, too, was one who spread false stories or let curiosity guide her actions.

She lingered at the entrance to the store, waiting for Phineas to complete his shopping. Her mind still reeled at the idea that people might lump her in the same category as Emma. Even worse, she felt a tightness in her chest at the thought that *he* was one of those people.

When he approached her, a plain paper bag in his arms, he paused. "Are you okay or is something wrong?" he asked, a genuine expression of concern on his face.

She lowered her gaze and opened the door, slipping through it. When he followed, she waited until the door had shut before she spoke. "I do not wear that cloak, Phineas."

He appeared baffled by her words. "Excuse me?"

"The cloak of gossip," she explained. "I am not like my friend, Emma."

The hint of a smile crossed his lips and his expression softened. "I'm quite sure you're correct, Elizabeth."

That was the second time he used her proper name that day and she found it rather curious. No one, besides her mother, ever called her 'Elizabeth' and then only when she was in trying to make a point. She found it both curious and comforting.

"Were you concerned I might think otherwise?" he inquired.

Suddenly, she realized that she *had* been concerned about that very thing, but she couldn't understand why. She barely knew this man and, while she found herself mildly intrigued by the variety of thoughts she'd had about him, as well as the conflicting emotions she'd felt, she knew that he was merely a passing acquaintance in her life. Why *should* she care what he thought about her?

"Nee," she said softly. "I reckon not."

But she could tell from the way his lips twitched, as if he were fighting the urge not to grin, and how his eyes sparkled, that Phineas knew she was not being completely honest.

"I see." Slowly, he started walking toward the parking lot where he'd left the horse tied to a hitching post. Lizzie fell in step beside him. "That's *gut* because I'd be unhappy to think that I've given you any reason to feel such concern."

This time, she knew that her cheeks burned red and she wished that she could cover her face. What was it about this man that made her feel so unsettled? Normally she was full of self-confidence and rarely ever behaved in such a fanciful manner. No, she expected behavior like *that* from her mother and younger sister, Katie, not her. In fact, Lizzie had always prided herself on being much more sensible than sensational.

In silence, she sat beside him as they made their way home.

He didn't seem to mind the quiet as he made no attempt to speak. At least not until they arrived in her driveway. When he stopped the horse near the barn, Lizzie could hardly wait to escape into the house where she could gather her thoughts. It had been quite an afternoon with so many mixed emotions and her head was starting to pound.

But the weight of his hand on her arm stopped her from opening the buggy door.

Curious, she looked at him.

"Before you go inside," he began in a somber tone, "I was wondering if, mayhaps, you'd care to join us for Sunday supper."

Her eyes widened. Had Phineas Denner just invited her to supper? The thought of such an invitation left her speechless.

"With Jane and Jacob, too," he added.

"Oh, ja. Jane and Jacob, too," she repeated quickly. "Of course."

He smiled, an amused expression on his face.

"I can only ask," she managed to say, too aware that his hand still rested on her arm. His touch was soft and warm. She found that her skin tingled under his fingers in a warm and wonderful way. And yet, when she remembered her presumptive comment from earlier, she had to pull her arm from his grasp. "Which I shall do in the morning," she mumbled before stepping from the buggy and hurrying into the house.

She paused at the door and turned around, her hand on the doorknob.

He stood there, watching her, that same amused smile playing on his lips.

No, Phineas Denner might not have given her reason to worry about him being concerned, but, as she disappeared inside and away from his inquisitive gaze, she suddenly realized that, deep down, she wished he had.

Chapter Twenty-Two

On Friday evening, Phineas waited until both Christopher and Cynthia were finished with their supper before he made his announcement about having extended an invitation to the three Benders. He hadn't mentioned it before that moment for several reasons, the primary one being that he hadn't wanted Cynthia to find the time to come up with an excuse. Now, less than two days before the scheduled meal, it would be impolite to back out of hosting the small social gathering on such short notice.

The two men were seated in the kitchen, Phineas perusing the day-old newspaper and Christopher writing a letter to his father. Cynthia was at the sink washing the dishes. It had been a long day, preparing the paddock and barn for the arrival of the cows on Saturday morning. As Christopher hadn't been able to figure out the schematics of installing the milk containment system in the back room, Phineas had taken charge. Then, when he tested it, he'd realized that Christopher had accidentally left the valve open for the propane. Due to the erroneous set up, it had all leaked out—although, truth be told, Phineas suspected that the tank hadn't been filled more than a quarter of the way. Still, they'd had to arrange for an emergency delivery. The cows would need to be milked over the weekend, that was for certain. Therefore, they needed to ensure that the cooling system was operable and functional.

Now that the house was quiet, Phineas had figured it would be the best time to share his news. After all, Cynthia would have to plan the meal the following day and, likely, go to the grocery store in the morning. Phineas had already made a mental note that he would defer the task of accompanying her to Christopher.

"Supper? On Sunday?" Cynthia's mouth hung open. The look of surprise etched on her face was priceless. She gave him a blank stare as if she hadn't heard him properly. "The three of them?" she practically squeaked from disbelief.

Indifferent to her reaction, Phineas lifted his coffee cup and took a long sip, avoiding her glare. "Ja, the three of them."

"Jane, Jacob, *and* Lizzie?" she said as if she hadn't heard him the first time.

Phineas gave her a cool look before answering. "Unless you'd fancy me inviting her parents and younger *schweister*, too," he quipped back.

Cynthia scoffed and rolled her eyes. "It certainly wouldn't be any worse, I imagine!"

If Phineas' suspected her dislike of Lizzie before—merely because she presented a threat for his attention—he required no further proof. She made no attempt to hide her dislike of his news.

Unlike his sister, however, Christopher's response was completely contrary. Immediately, his eyes sparkled, and he gushed, "That's a *wunderbarr gut* idea, Phineas!" He glanced at his sister, a hopeful smile on his face. "After all, our picnic was cut short the other day, thanks to that storm. This will certainly give us time to make up for what was lost on Tuesday!"

Cynthia, however, was clearly not convinced that any of this was a good idea. "I don't understand, Phineas, what this is about."

He lifted and dropped his shoulders in a gentle shrug. "Not much to explain. I ran into Elizabeth Bender yesterday while I was helping Amos fix some fencing. She assisted me with a few things—" He neglected to mention that he hadn't truly *needed* her help, not for running the errands. Sometimes less said was better, he thought. "—and, to thank her, I invited them over."

"Whatever for?"

Leveling his gaze at Cynthia, Phineas contemplated trying to hide the truth, but, for once, he decided to not beat too much around the bush. "I find myself wanting to get to know the family better," he started slowly and saw her eyes narrow. While he might have thought to hide the truth just a bit from Cynthia, Phineas decided to not hide his irritation with her. "And you, Cynthia, might do well to spend some time with Jacob."

She caught her breath. The expression on her face spoke of her surprise at Phineas's words. He'd expected as much. But Phineas knew that the time was right for making Cynthia understand the hard truth—and that was the fact that there would never be a future between them. If she was hanging her bonnet on the hopes that he'd court her, she was sorely mistaken. Redirecting her attention to another young Amish man who was better suited for her was, in all honesty, the kindest act he could bestow upon her.

Clearly Cynthia thought otherwise.

"Jacob? Their *bruder*?"

He ignored Christopher's muffled laugh. "Ja, their *bruder*."

"I can't imagine why you'd suggest that." She crossed her arms over her chest. "He's just a boy anyway!"

This time, Christopher spoke up. "I believe he's twenty-four. That's hardly a boy, Schweister."

Dismissively, she waved her hand at him. "Well, he *behaves* like a boy."

Phineas frowned. "I find that a misguided observation, Cynthia. For starters, you barely spoke two words to him at *your* picnic." He stressed the word 'your' which caused her to make a face. "In fact, I'd go so far as to say you were rather ill-mannered."

This time, her eyes widened as if his accusation had insulted her character. "Ill-mannered? I fail to see—"

Phineas held up his hand, stopping her mid-sentence. "What you didn't see, Cynthia, while you were sitting inside crocheting, was that Jacob Bender is a hard-working young man who cares about his neighbors. And from what I can tell, he comes from a decent family. He went out of his way to help your bruder fixing fences and removing limbs. He also worked very hard to help his neighbors, all of whom have nothing but the highest regard for him. Those are not traits of a boy, but of a godly man."

Her face appeared to darken at the reproach.

Phineas, however, merely continued talking. "And, as I will be returning to Clearwater shortly and you will be staying here with *your bruder—*" A not-too-subtle reminder, he thought, that she would *not* be accompanying him on that particular journey. "—it would be wise for you to cultivate some relationships with the young people of Blue Mill."

"I quite agree," Christopher added eagerly.

Phineas glanced at him for a moment before adding "Especially Jacob Bender."

She lifted her chin defiantly and crossed her arms over her chest. "*Especially* Jacob Bender?" she questioned.

He raised an eyebrow. "That's what I said and that's exactly what I meant, Cynthia. Otherwise, you might find yourself alone on Sunday afternoon while Christopher and I get to know Jacob's *schweisters* better." He paused, folding the newspaper and setting it on the table. Slowly, he stood up, eager to retire for the evening. However, he didn't leave without offering a final, parting comment. "You'd do well to open your eyes and your heart a bit more if you ever intend to do more than clean Christopher's kitchen."

The color drained from her cheeks. "I see," she replied.

For that, Phineas was glad. He certainly didn't want to spell it out in more detail. No, nothing good would come if he admitted to Cynthia that, during the remainder of his stay, he intended to spend as much time as possible with Lizzie Bender. She'd impressed him with her work ethic and good nature, her ability to talk with him so easily being a third delightful benefit. He'd never had a relationship with a young woman whom he might consider a friend.

Now that he was getting to know her, Phineas realized that he was looking forward to spending with the next few weeks with her. No one, not even Cynthia, would get in his way of doing just that.

Chapter Twenty-Three

It was early morning on Saturday when Lizzie finally had a chance to catch Jacob and Jane alone in the kitchen. Their mother had left already, having taken Katie to the neighbors to bake cookies. Her absence afforded her older children the rare chance to slow down a bit after the breakfast dishes had been washed and before the outdoor chores needed to be dealt with. It also provided Lizzie with the convenient moment to talk with her siblings, safe from the prying and curious ears of their mother.

The last thing Lizzie wanted was for their mother to get any ideas about the Burkholders, that was for sure and certain. The Amish grapevine spread far and wide with gossip, Susan Bender being more than happy to fertilize it whenever possible.

"I'm not certain what you're plans are for tomorrow," she began slowly, taking her time to speak. She ran her finger along the edge of the table, avoiding looking at Jane. "But, on Thursday, Phineas..." She paused. If she just blurted out what Phineas had asked, they'd surely suspect something. Quickly, she backtracked. "As you know Jane, the cow broke through the fence and then, after he caught it, he offered to fetch cement for Daed from town."

Jacob gave her a strange look.

"The post was broken. From the rain, you know."

"Oh." He returned his attention to the newspaper he'd been reading. Clearly Jacob wasn't interested at all. For the past two days, he'd been working with a friend, helping to build a workshop behind their stable. "I hadn't heard, *nee.*"

"Well, you see, I rode along with Phineas to town He doesn't know his way around the area yet," Lizzie quickly explained to Jacob. "And he *was* doing a favor for Daed so I couldn't rightly say no."

With a delighted gleam in her eyes, Jane tried to hide her smile. Lizzie pressed her lips together and focused her attention on her brother. "Anyway," she said in a long drawn out and exaggerated tone, "Phineas invited the *three*—" She rolled her eyes toward her sister. "—of us to supper at the Burkholders' *haus* on Sunday."

For a moment, neither Jane nor Jacob spoke. Lizzie waited, anticipating their response. Surely Jane would want to attend, but Lizzie wasn't so certain about Jacob. From the looks of things on Tuesday, Cynthia had barely given him the time of day and he'd said nothing about the picnic after they returned that night.

"Why didn't you mention this invitation yesterday?" Jane asked softly.

Lizzie shrugged. The truth was that she didn't know why she hadn't informed her sister and brother about the invitation. For most of Friday, she thought that she might send word to the Burkholder farm that none of them could attend. After all, Phineas would be leaving soon and what was the point of cultivating a friendship with him? she told herself. He was older and lived alone, as far as she knew. Most likely he was a dedicated bachelor or, just as likely, was courting a young woman from Clearwater. There would be no purpose served in befriending him, she repeated to herself throughout the day.

But then, after a long, sleepless night, Lizzie knew that she had to share the news with her siblings. Not only was it unfair to hide it from them, Lizzie also came to terms with the fact that she *wanted* to attend and surely, she should support Jane's chance at getting to know Christopher better, too. Whether it was pointless or not for her to attend, she shouldn't be selfish. Plus, if she was being honest with herself, she found that she was even more curious about Phineas Denner.

And so, she had decided to share the invitation with Jane and Jacob as soon as she woke up.

With a gentle shrug, she tried to appear disinterested. "I just forgot, I reckon."

Jane accepted Lizzie's answer and gave her a soft smile. "I think that would be nice to visit with them again. What about you, Jacob?"

Both Lizzie and Jane watched him as he stood up from the table. Folding the newspaper, he carried it over to the burn pile near the wood-burning stove and plopped it on top of the other papers. For a long moment, he stood with his back facing his sisters. It seemed was taken aback by the invitation and didn't know how to respond.

"If I say I'd prefer not, does that mean neither of you would attend?"

Jane sighed. "It wouldn't be proper, I'm afraid."

Jacob gestured toward Lizzie. "But *she* didn't attend the picnic the other day."

"Why wouldn't you want to go for supper?" Lizzie asked, quick to change the subject.

However, Jacob wasn't about to fall for that trick. "I'll answer that if you tell me why you didn't want to go on the picnic?" he shot back just as quickly.

Always the peacekeeper, Jane held up her hands. "Now Jacob, I thought you knew that *Cynthia* invited me the other day. Not Lizzy. This is a bit different."

"I fail to see how."

Lizzie grew tired of listening to Jacob's arguing. "It just is Jacob."

He made a face at her.

Ignoring him, Lizzie tried to direct him back to the original question. "Besides, it's not that complicated. You either want to attend or you don't." She looked from Jane to Jacob and then back to Jane. "I promised to ask."

186

Jacob pushed off the counter and stood up straight. "Well, I'll go if I must."

Lizzie gave a little laugh. "Such enthusiasm!"

Jane, however, gave him a quizzical look. "Did something happen, Jacob? You were rather eager to attend the picnic earlier this week."

He shrugged and walked over to the counter where a half-eaten loaf of bread sat on the cutting board. He grabbed the serrated knife and sliced off a piece. "*Nothing* happened. That's the problem." Taking a bite of the bread, he chewed it slowly.

"I don't understand," Jane said.

Lizzie, however, thought that *she* understood. It had to do with the way Cynthia had all but ignored him, she imagined. When Phineas had extended the invitation to include both her and Jacob as well, her brother had been rather eager to accept. Lizzie suspected that the pretty young woman seated beside Phineas in the buggy, might have added to the fervor with which he'd agreed. But, after spending some time with the young woman, he'd probably learned what Lizzie had suspected all along: Cynthia Burkholder was *not* the kindest of women.

"Leave him be," Lizzie said softly. "He needn't go if he doesn't want."

Jane sighed. "Then I reckon I can't go, either."

At this comment, Lizzie's mouth dropped. "Why ever not?"

"I can't go alone," she replied. "I wasn't even the one who was originally invited. How would that appear if neither of you went and I attended by myself."

Lizzie frowned. What on earth was she talking about? And then, suddenly, it dawned on her. Jane had automatically assumed that Lizzie would once again find an excuse to not attend the supper. After all, she'd refused the first invitation.

"Well," Lizzie began slowly.

She toyed with the edge of a paper napkin, hoping to appear nonchalant and indifferent. As she responded, she made certain to avoid eye contact lest her sister might see through her charade. While she wasn't a hundred percent certain that she'd been wrong about Phineas, a small voice inside was urging her to give him a second chance. She couldn't be sure why, but she knew that it would be wrong to ignore the inner feelings she was experiencing.

"I reckon I could go along with you. Just this once."

Jane clapped her hands together, clearly delighted with her sister's announcement. "Oh, *danke*, Lizzie!"

With an exaggerated rolling of his eyes, Jacob sighed. "Fine. If Lizzie goes, I'll go, too. No sense sitting home on a Sunday and I might as well drive you so you aren't walking home in the dark." He popped the heel of the bread into his mouth. "But don't let me just sit there like a bump on a log like last time, Jane!" He wagged his finger at her. "If that hoity-toity Cynthia ignores me again, you best include me in the conversation, or I'll just quietly disappear, and you can both walk home for all I care."

"Jacob!"

Lizzie, however, laughed. She'd suspected as much and now her brother confirmed it. He, too, had seen through Cynthia's flirtatious manner when in the presence of Phineas. Clearly, at the picnic, her conduct had must have been another attempt to lure Phineas in. She wasn't surprised. After all, Lizzie had witnessed it herself firsthand.

"Don't worry, Bruder," Lizzie said, her voice thick with sarcasm. "I'll make certain *you're* not the one ignored tonight."

Clearly, he understood her unspoken message, and with a smile, winked at her. "Knew I could count on you."

Jane shook her head, rolling her eyes toward the ceiling, then clucked her tongue. "The two of you are incorrigible!"

Laughing, Jacob slipped from the room, disappearing into the mudroom to change into his work boots. Moments later, Lizzie heard his heavy boots stomping down the porch steps.

Chapter Twenty-Four

The previous day, Phineas had suffered through the trip to town with Cynthia. He had insisted that Christopher take her, but, with the arrival of the dairy herd earlier than expected, his friend was far too preoccupied.

The cows had arrived shortly after dawn—and long before his trip to town with Cynthia. As Christopher was unloading them from the trailer, the excitement in the air was overwhelming. Phineas couldn't help but feel a touch of pride for his friend's enthusiasm. Christopher seemed speechless and couldn't keep himself from grinning and staring at the cows. Whenever one passed manure, Christopher was quick to fetch a rake to pick it up.

Phineas couldn't help but laugh to himself. Such passion would surely fade within a day or two, but he knew better than to say anything to ruin the moment. It wasn't often that a second or third son could find himself in such a fine situation. Farms were hard to come by and only so many sons could inherit property from their family.

Christopher hadn't been one of them. And yet, rather than settle for a profession that didn't interest him, Christopher had found a way to find his own land to farm.

Watching his friend admire the new herd, Phineas suddenly realized the truth: Christopher had known that it was better to rent the farm from the Benders than to work alongside Phineas on *his* property.

Truly, a man needed to make his own way in the world and not feel dependent on others. It was nice to see that Christopher had achieved this through hard work and determination.

Of course, with the way things appeared to be progressing with Jane, he might very well inherit his own farm one day soon. Should he wed Jane, it would make perfect sense for Amos to gift them the old family farm. While not as large as the Bender's, it would certainly sustain a modest Amish family quite nicely.

So, when Cynthia needed to go to the market, Phineas found himself making the journey with her. But, because of the words he spoke to her the previous day, she seemed much less talkative and far less forward. Thankfully, the short trip was uneventful and spent mostly in silence and for that he was grateful.

Once they were home, Cynthia spent the remainder of the afternoon cleaning to prepare for their guests the following day. Clearly having company meant much more work than Phineas had anticipated.

But then, come Sunday morning, Phineas almost wished that he *could* run another errand. Christopher appeared almost as nervous as Cynthia was irritated. She had added too much flour to her dough, and it hadn't risen properly so she had to start over. Then, she lost track of the time and burned the berry pie that was intended for dessert. Between the two of them, Phineas didn't know which one vexed him more!

"Do you think you've made enough potato salad?" Christopher asked as he hovered over Cynthia's shoulder.

"I promise you that I have," she said, exasperated by his endless questions. "For the third time, I make that promise."

Christopher turned around and leaned against the counter. "Oh, I know, I know. I should stop meddling—"

"You should, indeed!"

"—but I want everything just right, especially after the disastrous picnic last week."

Phineas looked up. Disastrous? He'd hardly thought it was *disastrous*. Only God could tame Mother Nature.

"Everything will be just right," Cynthia reassured him as she had not ten minutes earlier.

He pushed away from the counter and began to pace the kitchen floor. Phineas sat at the table, nursing a lukewarm cup of coffee while reading through The Budget newspaper from the previous week.

"Did you read this about Clearwater?" he asked Christopher, hoping to distract his friend and stop him from pacing in circles.

"I don't recall," Christopher said half-heartedly. "Has something happened at home?"

"Ja, John's mother's in hospital. Surgery or something of the sort. Seems she took ill a few days after we left."

This news clearly did not stop his friend from pacing.

"Oh, ja, and church was held at the Schwartz farm the week after we left."

Christopher appeared to not care in the least.

Irritated, Phineas set down the paper and stared at his friend. "If you pace anymore," he said tartly, "you'll wear a track in the middle of the floor."

He stopped. "Why do I feel so nervous?" he asked. "It's supper. Nothing more."

Phineas wanted to tell him the truth, that Christopher was completely smitten with Jane Bender. But he had never been one to pry into private matters with his friend. Just as he'd stayed out of the decision-making process when Christopher had decided to lease this farm and move to Blue Mill, Phineas would not provide an opinion on the matter.

"Mayhaps I should go check on the cows," he mumbled absentmindedly.

Phineas stood up. "A wunderbarr gut idea and I'll join you."

Together, they walked outside and across the turnaround in the driveway to the dairy barn. It was not as large as the Benders' barn, but they'd managed to paint it before the delivery of the cows.

The inside of the barn, too, had been cleaned. They'd scrubbed years of grease from the concrete floor and decades of dirt and cobwebs from the windowpanes, a simple task that improved the lighting tenfold.

The morning milking had been completed and the cows had been sent to pasture before Phineas helped Christopher muck the aisles and clean the equipment. Everything was ready for the evening milking and chores.

"It's a good head of cows," Phineas said as he wandered over to the back gate that overlooked the field. The animals were grazing on the early spring grass and the sun was high in the sky. It was a picture-perfect day.

Most of the cows were Holsteins, black and white cows, but a few were solid black. Phineas felt those were much more handsome. He studied them for a bit, taking pride in them as if they were his own. "Several look pregnant."

"A good investment then," Christopher joked. "Two for the price of one."

Phineas smiled. "That is quite true."

"Do you think," Christopher began slowly, "that Jane might be a worthy investment, too?"

Phineas took a moment to find the right words to assure his friend. This type of question was exactly the sort that he always tried to avoid. Before answering, he cleared his throat, buying more time to say the right thing. "I believe that time will tell, Christopher," he said at last. "You've only just met Jane. Get to know her better and then follow your heart" He laid his hand on Christopher's shoulder and smiled. "And enjoy the moments you are getting to know her. Everything will be fine, but in God's time, not yours."

Chapter Twenty-Five

On Sunday afternoon, Lizzie spent extra time in her bedroom getting ready to depart for their walk to the Burkholders' farm. As she brushed her hair, Lizzie couldn't help but feel apprehensive about supper with Phineas. She felt so torn. While there was a part of her that wanted to go, there was also something about him that made her wish she could *not* attend.

But that was impossible. At least not without serious repercussions.

To simply not attend would be rude. And, if she feigned an illness at the last minute, neither Jane nor Jacob would trust that she was being sincere. Without Lizzie attending, it would be awkward for them, especially since Phineas had shared the invitation with her directly and not her siblings.

She looked in the mirror and scolded herself for second-guessing the visit. It was, after all, just a supper. A supper with neighbors, she reminded herself. Nothing more and nothing less. Besides, the attraction between Christopher and Jane was more than obvious. It wasn't often that a new young—and unmarried!—man moved into the community, and one who rented the adjacent family farm? Surely *that* was an act of God. His hand had to be a part of the developing relationship between her sister and Christopher.

No, she must go and go she will, even if spending the rest of the day at the Burkholders made her a tad nervous.

Ever since Thursday, when Phineas had driven her to town for the cement—a ride that had been filled with quiet pleasantries—she'd found herself daydreaming about him.

All day on Friday and Saturday, she'd look up every time she heard an approaching horse and buggy, wondering if, perhaps, it was Phineas coming to visit. When it wasn't, she'd chastise herself for having entertained such childish fancies, burying her disappointment deep inside. She had to remind herself on more than one occasion that he would be returning to Clearwater soon and, in all likelihood, had a special friend waiting back home.

Over the past few days, she'd convinced herself, without any doubt, that Phineas had extended the invitation for one and only one reason: he knew that Christopher had developed feelings for Jane and he wanted to promote the match by showing his support.

Try as she might, she kept thinking back to the day of the torrential storm and how Phineas had held her tightly as they crossed the flooded bridge. The memory of how his arms felt while holding her made her catch her breath every time she thought about that night. But she also caught her breath every time she recalled those two little words Phineas had uttered at the youth gathering the night of the singing: *barely tolerable.*

"Lizzie? Are you ready yet?"

Hearing her sister calling to her from the bottom of the staircase, Lizzie inhaled then stole a final glimpse in the small oval mirror that hung on the wall over the dresser. Her hair shone in the sunlight that streamed through the window, streaks of reddish gold highlights framing her face. How had she never noticed them before?

"Ja, coming," she called back as she reached for her prayer kapp. Carefully, she placed it on her head and carefully pinned it to her hair.

Reluctantly, she left the safety and security of her bedroom and trudged down the stairs. Her black shoes made soft scraping noises as she descended.

"What's taken you so long, Elizabeth?" Standing near the pantry, Susan gave her a stern look. "You'll make everyone late!"

"This just isn't fair," Katie whined. She sat at the table, leaning her cheek against her hand. "Everyone has something fun to do except me."

Susan clucked her tongue. "Oh, stuff and nonsense, Katie! You will accompany us to visit with the bishop and his family."

Lizzie had to stifle a laugh as Katie rolled her eyes and sank deeper into despair.

"I said *fun,* Maem," she mumbled.

Lizzie leaned over Katie's shoulder and whispered, "Mayhaps his nephew Thomas will be visiting. That would perk you up a bit, don't you think?"

Katie slapped Lizzie's arm, but color rose to her cheeks. Everyone knew that Katie had a small crush on the Bishop's nephew.

"Leave her be, now, Elizabeth!" Susan turned toward the pantry, reaching up to fetch a large plastic container. "And hurry along! Jane and Jacob are outside waiting for you!"

Dutifully, Lizzie hurried out the kitchen door and jogged across the yard to where her brother and sister waited.

"It's about time," Jacob scolded. "We're supposed to be there by now."

Jane placated him by pressing her hand against his arm. "It's alright," she said in a calm, soothing voice. "A few minutes late won't offend anyone, I'm sure."

Now as they walked to the Burkholders' farm, Lizzie did her best to focus on Jane's excitement at seeing Christopher again.

"Do you think they play Scrabble?"

"There will be six of us and Scrabble is only good for four," Lizzie pointed out, shifting the basket she carried from one hand to the other. Not wanting to arrive empty handed, she'd baked an applesauce cake for dessert. Also tucked inside the basket were the deviled eggs that Jane had made. "Even if they do play, I don't think Christopher or Phineas would permit someone to be left out of a game."

Jane nodded. "I hadn't thought of that. I suppose Scrabble's out of the question, then."

No sooner had they rounded the bend when an open-top carriage approached them then slowed to a halt. Phineas waved them over.

"Are you going somewhere?" Lizzie said, a light teasing tone to her voice. "Have you forgotten your invitation?"

"Nee, I haven't." The crease in his brow deepened. "I was on my way to collect you."

Lizzie laughed. "You make us sound like we're eggs in the chicken coop?"

Jane nudged her sharply in the ribs.

"We're perfectly capable of walking," Lizzie added in a somber tone, "but *danke* for thinking of us."

"Well, I'm here now so get in." He gestured to the bench beside him. "No sense in casting me off empty handed."

Lizzie stared at him, curious about his choice of words. But she held her tongue and did as he instructed, setting the basket on the floor of the carriage before climbing up and settling down on the seat beside him. Jane sat next to her and Jacob hopped in the back. Once they were settled, Phineas urged the horse to continue down the road until he could find a safe place to turn around.

"You're very assertive, aren't you?"

Lizzie hesitated to respond, at first not understanding that he had directed the question at her. "Me?"

"Ja, you."

Beside her, Jane lifted her hand to cover her mouth—most likely suppressing a smile—then turned her head to look back at Jacob to see if he had heard the question posed to their sister.

"I reckon I haven't given it much thought," Lizzie replied at last. "But I'm certainly not submissive, if that's what you mean."

Phineas caught his breath. "I did *not* mean that at all!"

"Well, when someone comments on a person's character, pointing out their strengths as if they are flaws, they usually view it negatively. And if being assertive is considered a negative trait, then I could only presume you would prefer the opposite which is definitely submissive."

"And obedient," Jane added softly, practically choking back a laugh.

"Ja, and obedient." Lizzie echoed as she faced Phineas. "Clearly I am neither of those two things."

"To no one?"

She straightened her shoulders and lifted her chin. "Certainly not."

"Hm." He kept his eyes on the road ahead. "Such a shame."

Once again, his choice of words caught her off-guard. *A shame?* "What's that supposed to mean?"

201

"Nothing much, I suppose, but I had thought you'd taken your kneeling vow."

Lizzie's mouth opened, but no words came out. Not at first. She realized that she'd stepped into a trap. *Clever*, she thought. "I see where you're going with this, Phineas Denner." She scowled at him. "And there is a difference between being submissive and obedient to a fellow person as opposed to God."

Did he really chuckle?

"And I most certainly *did* take my kneeling vow!" she said hastily. Crossing her arms over her chest, Lizzie faced her sister, vowing to shut out Phineas for the rest of the day. If she hadn't already been in the buggy, she'd have turned around and walked home. But she didn't want to make a scene. Besides, Jane had been so excited about going that Lizzie didn't want to spoil the afternoon for her sister.

"Well," he said lightly. "That's good to know."

Lizzie's mouth opened, but no words came out. She felt the inconsistency of emotions that was far too familiar when she was in his presence. Part of her was excited by his verbal sparring—she appreciated his intelligence as well as his willingness to share his thoughts and opinions. She couldn't say the same of most Amish men. The majority were too timid to express their feelings. But she was also irritated that he'd so easily corrected her without a thought to her feelings.

Shutting her mouth, she fidgeted in the seat, too aware that his arm brushed against hers every time they hit a rut in the road. What was it about Phineas Denner that brought out the worse in her?

Chapter Twenty-Six

During supper, Phineas couldn't help but notice that Lizzie directed most of her attention to Jane, Jacob, and Christopher. She practically ignored Cynthia—a fact that amused him—but she was also clearly ignoring *him* too.

When they had first arrived at the house, Lizzie spent much of the afternoon talking with Christopher, often deferring to her brother to make him feel as though he were a part of the conversation. With Cynthia left out, a scowl on her face, Phineas had chuckled about how the tides had turned. It was barely a week ago when it was Cynthia who had snubbed Lizzie. But why was Lizzie not paying attention to him? He was truly perplexed. Had he said or done something to upset her?

Still, rather than force himself into the middle of their conversations, he sat back and listened to their exchanges, watching her from the shadows of the chair where he sat.

For the next twenty minutes he studied her. The way she tilted her head to the side when her sister addressed her, the way she lifted her hand to her mouth when she laughed and the soothing sound of her voice, all of which had him mesmerized. There was something about this Lizzie Bender that caught his fancy. She was different than any other woman he'd ever met. The truth was that most other women went out of their way to catch his attention while Lizzie Bender acted as though she couldn't care less if he existed or not.

The challenge was set, that was for sure and certain.

During dessert, he decided to tease her a bit. She would have no choice but to acknowledge his presence.

"Lizzie, might you pass me the peaches?"

She barely looked at him as she slid the bowl across the table.

He spooned some onto his plate and then pushed the bowl back toward her. "Care for any?"

She shook her head.

"You don't like peaches, Lizzie?"

This time, she couldn't ignore him without appearing rude. Sighing, she shifted her eyes toward him. "I like peaches fine, Phineas. I just don't care for any tonight."

Cynthia perked up. "I think I'll have some more."

Indifferently, Lizzie passed the bowl to her without so much as a glance.

"I noticed you didn't have any pie," Phineas said, gesturing toward the peanut butter cream pie.

"I'm not a fan of peanut butter."

Jane made a noise, like the soft intake of breath. "Lizzie!"

Lizzie faced her sister. "What?"

"You love peanut butter!"

"Not tonight, I fear."

Phineas smiled to himself. Cynthia had made the pie and Lizzie most likely didn't try it for that very reason.

"Perhaps after supper, we could play Scrabble," Christopher offered, his eyes lighting up and his voice hopeful.

Phineas noticed that Lizzie glanced at Jane, a silent communication shared between them.

"I've always liked Scrabble," Christopher continued. "Although I don't always pick the best words." He leaned over and touched Jane's arm. "Phineas, however, is rather competitive when it comes to Scrabble. He's far too smart to beat."

"That's a high compliment," Phineas responded. "But undeserved, I'm sure."

Cynthia cleared her throat and spoke up. "Well, Scrabble is only for four people. How can we play? We're six."

A moment of silence filled the room.

Phineas waited, watching as Lizzie's eyes met Jane's for the second time.

"I suppose I could clean up while you all play," she offered.

Christopher frowned. "Nee, Lizzie. That's not fair. I'll sit out."

"But it was your suggestion to play!"

He shook his head. "You're our guests. You should play."

Jacob pushed back his dessert plate. "I can sit out. I'm never fast enough to think of good words."

To everyone's surprise, Cynthia spoke up. "Mayhaps we could be partners, Jacob?"

Phineas watched as Lizzie tried to hide her disbelief then glanced at Jacob to see his reaction. He, too, appeared taken back by this unexpected attention from Cynthia. When he failed to respond, Cynthia's expression softened and she smiled at him.

"I...I reckon we could partner up," he finally offered. "Someone else would have to partner up, too, I suppose. Or, we could *all* partner up and just play with three."

"No need to make it so complicated." Phineas raised his hand. "I'll sit out." He leveled his gaze across the table to stare at Lizzie. "I'll keep Lizzie company." He paused, pushing his chair back from the table and placing his hands on the arms as if he were preparing to stand. "Perhaps a walk outside, Lizzie?"

His suggestion was met silence but then, with all eyes on her, she nodded. "I should clean up first."

Standing at last, Phineas gestured toward the door. "Cleaning can wait for later. I want to show you something in the back paddock while it's still light out. To get your thoughts."

Slowly, Lizzie pushed back her chair and stood up. She glanced down at Jane, another silent communication to which her sister raised an eyebrow and hid a knowing smile.

Once outside, they walked in silence toward the barn. The cows were already in the fenced barnyard, the ground muddy and wet, both from the recent storm and abundance of manure. The pungent aroma of cow dung filled the air with the strong scent of ammonia and sulfur. To Phineas, it smelled like home.

"The cows have made themselves at home," Lizzie said, as if reading his mind.

"Indeed." He paused. "Christopher purchased them from a farmer across town who was culling his herd."

Lizzie exhaled slowly. "Fortunate for Christopher, but I don't like hearing that a farmer is downsizing."

Her words struck him as odd. "Why's that?"

She gave a little shrug. "Too many Amish farmers are abandoning dairy farming. I know it's not as profitable these days, but the work is honest, and honesty keeps one closer to God."

He raised an eyebrow. "That's an interesting perspective."

"Isn't it worth the financial discomfort to work the earth rather than succumb to worldliness?" She stopped at the fencing and watched the cows. Her eyes scanned the barnyard as if studying each cow. "Seems many younger Amish folk prefer the nine-to-five life of the Englische to the fifteen-hour days of farming."

Standing beside her, Phineas followed her gaze. Her comment resonated with him. He'd never looked at it that way. Perhaps that was why so many of the Amish women in Clearwater wanted to court him. It might not have been his wealth that they were after but the promise of a Godlier life *because* of it.

"There's something to be said for—how did you put it?—work that is honest."

For the first time, she tilted her head to look up at him and smiled. "While I'm surprised you agree with me, I must admit that I'm glad of it."

He suddenly became very aware that she was at least half a foot shorter than he and much more petite than he thought. He'd never noticed how small she was before now. And yet, he'd seen her working harder than many of the hired hands on his own farm. Elizabeth Bender was not the typical Amish woman who preferred housework to calloused hands, and a sweaty back. She was also not afraid to share her opinions, even if they might be offensive.

In his case, he was far from offended when she pointed out his flaws. Instead, he was impressed that she spoke her mind.

Chapter Twenty-Seven

Walking beside Phineas down the line of fencing that led away from the barnyard and toward the back pasture, there was a comfortable silence between them. Instead of idle chit chat, Lizzie heard only the crunching of gravel beneath their feet and an occasional bellow from the barnyard. She hadn't brought along her sweater. It was still early enough in spring that, later that evening, she'd surely need it to keep a chill from her shoulders.

Unsure of where Phineas was leading her now, Lizzie merely followed him. He led her behind the barn and toward the paddock, pausing to take her elbow as they climbed over a broken fence.

"Do you mind walking through the grass?"

She gave him a quizzical look. "Why would I mind?"

"Well, there are still muddy spots from the rain last evening."

She couldn't help but laugh. "Truly?"

"Mostly along the streambed and closer to the trees."

Lizzie couldn't help but tease him. He'd thought she'd questioned the muddy spots when, in truth, she'd been laughing that he'd even asked the question at all.

Growing up on a farm, dirt and mud were a part of daily life, especially in the spring. She couldn't imagine that he thought her so delicate as to be opposed to stepping through puddles and mud.

There was something endearing, however, about his having asked her the question. His concern for her welfare, once again, touched her and, yet, she couldn't help herself from responding in jest.

"What would you say if I said that I did mind?"

Phineas stopped walking. For a moment, he stared into the distance, as if he were giving great thought to her question.

"It wasn't a serious question, Phineas," she said at last. "But I appreciate you thinking to ask me."

He raised an eyebrow.

"I mean, most people—especially men—might not think to ask that," she said with a slight shrug. "Mud and dirt are part of farm life, don't you think? Surely I haven't given you the impression that I'm so delicate as to be wary of dirtying my shoes?"

The corners of his mouth twitched as if he suppressed a smile.

"What's so funny?" she asked.

"Your question." He tilted his head as he studied her. "If I admitted that you had given me that impression, you'll take offense that I considered you so fragile. However, if I accept that you have not given me that impression, I risk affronting your sensitivities that I had *not*!"

It took Lizzie a moment to realize the difficult situation she had put him in. Admittedly, it delighted her. "So how shall you respond, then?"

He made an exaggerated serious face. "I shall respond in silence, rather than risk upsetting you."

She laughed and, at last, he permitted the smile to cross his lips.

They continued walking quietly again. Lizzie wondered what on earth he'd wanted to show her so far from the house and barn.

She hadn't been in these fields in years, not since her grandparents had passed away. Ever since their passing, two families had leased the farm. Lizzie had known that her mother encouraged the sale of the farm, but Amos held firm. He'd always felt that land was important to hang onto. At first, Lizzie hadn't understood why. Now, however, she rather appreciated her father's foresight.

From the looks of the attention Christopher and Jane showed one another, Lizzie had no doubt that they were well matched. She hoped an early autumn wedding would be in their future. How convenient it would be for the Bender family to have Jane living on the adjacent farm and how fortunate for Christopher as he would not have to worry about leasing it yearly. The farm would stay in the family for generations to come.

As for Cynthia and Jacob, Lizzie didn't hold out too much hope. Yes, the young woman had been more pleasant with Jacob, but he hadn't seemed to notice, at least not until she'd asked him to partner with her for the Scrabble game.

Lizzie smiled. Perhaps there was a chance, she thought, if only Cynthia would come down from her high horse and realize that she wasn't any better than the good people of Blue Mill.

"Something amuses you?"

Breaking free of her thoughts, Lizzie turned and looked up at him. "I'm sorry?"

"You were smiling."

Ah, she thought. He noticed. The color flooded to her cheeks. "I was just thinking about something."

He nodded but inquired no further.

Lizzie, however, took the opportunity to ask the question that was burning in the back of her mind. "You had mentioned you wanted to discuss something with me?"

Phineas made a noise deep within his throat. "Hm."

Patiently, she waited for him to answer. He *had* said that, hadn't he? That he sought her opinion? For what, she could not imagine. To say her curiosity was piqued was an understatement.

Slowly, he turned around, his eyes scanning the paddock. As he had pointed out, it was, indeed, muddy. A small stream, a tributary from the larger one that had flooded during the storm, flowed south, the banks washed clean of grass.

"This paddock had been earmarked for the cows to graze," he started. He lifted his hand and pointed to the fence line along the back of the property. "It's large enough where it won't become a sandlot." He glanced over his shoulder at her to see if she was paying attention. "But I'm fearful of the rains."

"The rains?"

He nodded and turned to face her. "The way that the stream flooded, the cows would quickly turn it into mire, no grass left at least in this area. And then, with summers being so dry, it would be nothing more than dirt."

Lizzie studied the stream. She saw his point. While the paddock made sense to be used for grazing by the herd, they would, indeed, ruin the ground surrounding the stream. "Perhaps paddock rotation during the spring season?"

Phineas shook his head. "Nee, that's not possible if Christopher intends to grow hay *and* corn."

It was a problem, for sure.

"What do you propose, then?" she asked.

"Damming it," he said then pointed downstream. "There. But only enough to have it backfill into a larger body of water. A pond. When the rains come, the dam can be opened to permit it to flow without spilling over the embankment. And during the summers, the larger pond will serve the cows for water."

Clever, Lizzie thought. She wondered why no one else had ever thought of doing that. "I must admit that it's a right *gut* idea, Phineas."

"I thought so, too," he said without any hint of arrogance. "But I'm fearful of doing so as the stream leads to your father's fields."

"Ah!"

Now she understood his reason for speaking to her. While the solution was obvious, the long-term consequences needed to be considered. Most of the farmers in the area depended on the side streams for irrigation of their crops and water for livestock. If Phineas and Christopher dammed the stream branch, water would still trickle onto her father's property but not as plentiful as before.

Her eyes followed the flow of water. It was hard to see exactly where the one property ended and the other began. However, she knew without seeing it, that the stream ran through her father's back fields. She'd walked beside it many times over the years.

"Daed grows hay back there," she said. "It requires water, of course, but much less than corn. I suspect that you should speak to him about it, Phineas. While your idea is on course, in my humble opinion, I shouldn't take the liberty of authorizing something that is not my place to permit. However, surely the thing to do would be to monitor the stream. Christopher could control the flow down to my father's and it would be less burdensome if the dam were created sooner, rather than later, as spring storms bring more rain before the summer months arrive."

For a long moment, he held her gaze. His eyes did not waiver as he studied her, leaving her conflicted. On the one hand, she found his attention curiously exciting while on the other, she felt mildly uncomfortable. Was this the same man who had quipped that she was *barely tolerable* just a week prior?

"*Danke*, Lizzie," he said at last, averting his eyes. "I will speak with him, as you suggested. I'm confident that we can work something out that benefits both Christopher and your *daed.*"

There was something about the way he stared at her that made her wonder if, indeed, that was what he truly had on his mind. Perhaps there was an ulterior motive to his question. She couldn't imagine why he would have wanted her advice when the answer was so plainly obvious. And yet he clearly valued her opinion and that was something she found compelling. Most Amish men would seek advice from other farmers—and certainly not a farmer's daughter!—when it came to crops, cows, or channels.

Despite her curiosity, as they continued walking, she found herself grateful for his company. No more words needed to be shared as the sound of their shoes on the dirt and gravel broke the silence between them.

Chapter Twenty-Eight

On Tuesday, Phineas had driven his horse and buggy to the hardware store just outside of Blue Mill. While he needed some more supplies for fixing the back-paddock fencing, the truth was that he simply needed time away from the Burkholders' farm.

Ever since Sunday, he hadn't been able to stop thinking about Lizzie. For two days, she'd occupied his mind. What was it about the young woman that made his every thought turn to her? She was pretty—he couldn't deny that. But he'd never been one who let his head turn toward a fair face. No. It was something else. Her wit, perhaps, and strong work ethic. Or maybe her intellect and self-confidence. Most Amish women were quiet and reserved around young men. At least that had been his experience. Jane was a perfect example of the typical Amish women he'd encountered throughout the course of his life. Of course, Cynthia broke the mold, but not in a good way.

"Phineas, isn't it?" The older Amish man behind the counter greeted him with a smile. "You've been in here quite a bit lately."

Phineas leaned against the counter. "Ja, been busy fixing up the Burkholder farm. Running low on nails for the fencing. And I'll need some more black stain."

"Staining the fence then?"

He nodded. "Keeps the wood from drying out."

The man raised an eyebrow. "Not many folks around here stain the wood. Too much work, I reckon."

Phineas had noticed that. He wasn't sure if the community didn't stain fencing because they felt it prideful, like the Swartzentruber Amish or if they just felt it was too much work. But Phineas knew from experience that the time spent staining the wood saved it from drying out and splintering. It was a worthy investment in the long run and, if anyone complained, Christopher could blame him, an outsider from Upper Austen County, for having undertaken the task.

After paying for the items, Phineas was about to leave when the man spoke again.

"Seems you're handy around a farm."

Phineas met his gaze but didn't speak.

"Mayhaps you'd be able to help on Friday at the Riehls' place."

"Oh?"

The man nodded. "It's a bit north of here, just two miles from your friend's place. A smaller farm on Winger

Road." He paused, tilting his head as he waited for Phineas's answer. "Eddie Riehl's been in the hospital—cancer, you know—"

Phineas had not known, which wasn't surprising since he didn't know Eddie Riehl. This fact had apparently slipped the store owner's mind.

"—and his place hasn't been tended to, recently. We're organizing a work party to help his family. Women will be cleaning the *haus* and the men helping in the fields. A bit of crop planning, too."

Phineas knew he couldn't refuse. Even though he didn't know the Riehls, he'd never been one to turn his back on someone in need: whether Amish *or* Englische.

"Friday, eh?" He picked up the large plastic container of nails. "I'll be there."

Once outside, he slipped the nails under the seat then untied the horse from the hitching post. He drove around to the back of the store so the large barrel of stain could be loaded into his buggy. It would be foolish to spend Friday away from Christopher's farm. Phineas knew that he needed to return home soon. His hay would be ready to cut, and he needed to fetch his sister from his cousin's house. It wouldn't sit well with him if she overstayed her welcome

And yet, what was one more day?

"Phineas?"

He looked up, surprised to hear his name. Turning to peer out his open buggy door, he saw Lizzie walking toward him. As she neared, he felt his pulse quicken. She wore a pretty pink dress, a color that made her cheeks glow and set off her brown hair and eyes which sparkled when she smiled at him.

"Waiting for something?"

He glanced over his shoulder. The men were taking a long time fetching his stain. "Just picking up a few things. What about you?"

She held up her hands. He'd been so busy admiring her that he hadn't noticed the two plastic bags she carried. "Fabric. Maem's working on a—" She hesitated before adding, "—project."

Suppressing a smile, Phineas nodded. He suspected she had almost said 'quilt' and he wasn't surprised. The way that Christopher had been mooning over Jane certainly indicated that he would be asking for her hand. Of course, it *had* only been a little over a week and making a quilt seemed a bit presumptuous at such an early stage in their courtship. But, from what little he'd gathered from the gossip Cynthia had shared, it seemed everyone in the community knew that Lizzie's mother was anxious to see her daughters wed.

"I see," he said.

She shrugged her shoulders, as if reading his mind.

"Heading back to the farm, then?" He gestured toward the empty seat beside him. "I'll drop you off, then."

For a moment, she merely stared at him, her eyes narrowing as if thinking as to how she should respond.

Inwardly, he chastised himself. Why had he worded it like that? It hadn't been posed as a question but rather a statement. He hadn't meant to sound so familiar with her. It's not as if *they* were courting.

And then, to his surprise, she gave a soft smile. "Ja, Phineas, I think I'd like that, indeed. But I rode my bicycle so only if there is room," she said while glancing to the left where her bike was leaning against a lamp post.

He hopped out of the buggy and lifted the bike then placed it in the back seat. Then, he took Lizzies hand as she climb into the buggy. Once she was seated next to him, he took the reins in both hands, though a part of him really wanted to keep holding her hand with his other. He'd liked the way it had felt in his own, even if had only been for that moment. Perhaps it was because she hadn't reacted to the intimacy of the gesture which appealed to him. Clearly Lizzie Bender was a confident young woman who didn't worry about such things. Phineas found himself hoping that it was because she, too, felt comfortable with him, welcoming his touch as much as he welcomed hers.

As he urged the horse to move forward, Phineas looked in the rectangular side mirror to make sure no cars were speeding down the road. Only then did he direct the buggy onto the pavement.

Chapter Twenty-Nine

Sitting beside Phineas—again!—Lizzie realized that she didn't feel at all uneasy in his presence. Perhaps she hadn't on Saturday, either. But this time, she *knew*.

When he'd said he would drive her home, his friendly tone had caught her off-guard. Normally Phineas was much more formal. She'd watched his expression, searching for any signs and, for the briefest of moments, she thought she noticed something—a change—to indicate that, perhaps, he, too, was feeling more relaxed around her.

She suspected that relaxing was not something Phineas did often.

For the first few minutes of the ride, Lizzie had merely stared out the window and admired the fields of growing hay. Different farms planted hay at different times. This year, her father had planted his hay earlier than usual. Having cut and baled it the previous week, his fields were bare now. Lizzie much preferred the fields green with waving grass that shimmered in the late spring sun.

Phineas cleared his throat.

"I've taken your advice," he said.

Turning away from the window, she faced him. "Oh? About...?"

"The field layout. You were right, you know. Christopher wanted to put the cows in the front field, but the trees along the back field do provide much better shade in the afternoons. In the summer, they won't get overheated back there." His fingers tightened around the reins and he gently eased the horse to stop at the intersection. "So, I put in another fence along the back to create that chute you suggested."

She'd only mentioned that to him on Saturday. How on earth could he have already put it in? "So quickly?"

He nodded. "I put in a system that I use at my own farm. Fiberglass posts with polytape tied into a solar charged electric system. It'll do for now so that Christopher can plant hay in the front field without the cows charging through it."

Clever, she thought. "Well done, Phineas," she said lightly. "And very efficient."

He laughed. "Efficient?"

"Of course! An efficient use of your time. I'd say Christopher's rather lucky to have such a hard-working and wise friend."

"Ah, I see."

She saw him glance at her, his lips twisted into a hint of a smile. But his laughter still rang in her ears. It was something she wished he'd do more often.

"Speaking of hard-working, by any chance," he started, "do you know a man named Eddie Riehl?"

For a moment, she couldn't make sense of his question. "I fail to see the what that has to do with anything. I fear as he's been in the hospital, so he hasn't been able to work for quite some time now."

"That's the one."

"Do *you* know Eddie Riehl?"

"Nee, I do not. But, apparently, there is a work party on Friday at his family farm. I've been invited to go help."

Lizzie's eyes widened. "Are you going?"

"Of course!"

"But, you don't even know him."

A soft shrug. "Does that matter? A man and his family are in need."

She felt a fleeting sense of pride. "That is rather kind of you, Phineas."

"I thought, perhaps, you might want to join me."

Upon hearing his words, Lizzie's mouth opened but, rather than reply, she sat there dumbfounded. Had he truly just asked her to go with him? To a work party? Only courting couples did that. She remained quiet and thought about it for a moment. Perhaps that was how they did things where he was from? Perhaps it didn't mean anything after all.

When she didn't respond, Phineas continued slowly. "I mean, as I don't know this family, of course, it would be nice to attend with someone who is familiar with them."

Lizzie swallowed her disappointment. "I see."

"Anyway, I was wondering if you might wish to accompany me to the event." He looked out the window, checking to make certain that no one was approaching the intersection.

"Given that you don't know the Riehl's, of course."

"That may be so, but I do believe in helping my neighbors."

She shifted her weight on the seat beside him. "But, technically, they aren't your neighbors," she pointed out. "They are *Christopher's* new neighbors. Shouldn't *he* be going?"

Phineas exhaled. "Elizabeth..."

"Why do you call me that?" she asked suddenly.

The change in subject clearly caught him off guard. He gave her a curious look as if her question was nonsensical. "Elizabeth is your given name, isn't it?"

"Ja, it is," she said. "But everyone calls me Lizzie." She tilted her head, studying his face. "Why don't you call me that, too?"

Taking a deep breath, Phineas exhaled. "Because your name is Elizabeth. So, will you come with me or not?"

She moistened her lips, rubbing them together for a moment. To him, it seemed as if she were considering his question with much more thought than he felt required. Surely it was a simple question that could be answered with a simple yes or no. Why was she making this so complicated?

"Lizzie?"

She hadn't realized he had been staring at her.

"You mean attend the work party with you *and* other people?"

This time, *he* paused. "Well, I imagine there will be plenty of other people lending a hand."

"I meant, will there be other people joining *you*? If she told him she'd prefer others to join them, would she sound as if she weren't interested in spending time with *him*? It was all so complicated.

"I...I reckon I will go with you," she said at last.

Phineas eyed her for a long second. "I think..."

Holding her breath, Lizzie waited.

"...if you don't mind, perhaps..."

He paused as Lizzie waited for him to continue. Certainly, she had presumed too much, and he didn't want to embarrass her.

"...we could go together. Just us."

Immediately she relaxed. "I...I think that would be nice, Phineas," she managed to say, hoping that her cheeks hadn't flushed when she spoke. "So yes, Phineas, I'll go with you to the Riehls' work party—"

"Gut."

She knit her eyebrows together, "—but I am curious as to your intentions."

And there it was, the question that had haunted her for the past two days. She'd finally had the courage to ask and, as soon as the words slipped through her lips, she felt a welcome sense of relief.

"My intentions?"

She nodded. "It seems that you will be returning to Clearwater sooner, rather than later."

"I will, ja. Another week or so, I reckon. The spring planting is well underway, but it will soon be time for our first haying." He paused. "Plus, I must fetch my *schweister* from our cousins. She's missed way too much schooling, I fear."

"It's a wonder you didn't bring her with you to Blue Mill," Lizzie said, more to make conversation than for actual interest.

He shrugged. "I reckon she much rather enjoys her time with her cousins. She makes friends wherever she goes and, in truth, despite the distance, they are more like siblings than extended family."

Lizzie raised an eyebrow. "You say that as if it's a bad thing."

"Did I?" He glanced at her. "Perhaps it is, for she can only see those friends once or twice a year. What is the point?"

Surprised, Lizzie stared at him, her eyes wide and her thoughts confused. "And, yet, you have been rather intent upon developing friendships with numerous people here," she said before quickly adding, "Myself included. I'm just curious as to why."

He pursed his lips and his eyes narrowed—a clear indication that she'd asked a question he was not entirely comfortable answering. Finally, after a far too lengthy silence between them, he cleared his throat. "I suppose you're right, Elizabeth. There's nothing wrong with making new friends, even if they live a bit of distance away, don't you agree?"

His answer stung, just a little. She wasn't certain what she'd hoped he was going to say; she only knew that he hadn't said it. Perhaps it was the whisper of those two hurtful words that still resonated in her memory: *barely tolerable*.

She didn't want to be *barely tolerable* to Phineas. In fact, the thought of becoming more than friends with Phineas had been on her mind as of late.

"Nee, Phineas," she said at last when she realized he was still staring at her, waiting for a response. "There's nothing wrong with making new friends at all."

He appeared content with her answer, despite Lizzie feeling a hollow pit form inside her chest. That momentary glimmer of hope that, perhaps, she had meant something just a little bit more than a mere *friend* to him, faded.

They rode the rest of the way to her parents' farm without saying more. Unlike the previous day when they'd walked and talked about irrigation, the silence no longer felt comfortable but rather, strained. Lizzie peered out the window, her face turned away from his, as she realized that the word *friend* had never sounded so unpleasant to her until now.

Chapter Thirty

Phineas arrived at her father's farm at eight-thirty on Friday morning to fetch her. The sun was already high above the tree-tops, shining brightly onto the fields. The fresh, leaves on the tree branches looked brilliant, a light green color which was a true harbinger to spring, and the sky was deep, turquoise blue. All a welcome contrast to the cold, drab gray of winter.

It was the perfect day for a work party.

Phineas smiled to himself. He'd always enjoyed work parties, more because he felt useful in situations that often made him feel helpless. Last year, a neighbor's barn had burned to the ground in Clearwater. Phineas had been one of the first to donate lumber and his time. And the year before that, an elderly widow had broken her leg just around the time when spring gardens were planted. Without being asked, Phineas had tilled the soil and planted the seeds for her.

Nothing made a day more perfect than the fresh breeze on his face and a community that came together in a time of need. Of course, secretly he admitted to himself, that the day was made even more perfect by the fact that Lizzie had agreed to accompany him.

The previous week, he'd truly appreciated her willingness to help the men remove the tree branches and debris that had clogged the road during the storm. She'd been the only woman who'd volunteered to work alongside them. While that wasn't unusual, of course, Phineas had found it admirable.

And then, she'd surprised him even more on Sunday when they'd walked along the lane, talking about his irrigation idea. For some reason, however, he hadn't been taken back by her knowledge of farming, even though she had truly impressed him.

Now, as he guided the horse and buggy down the hill toward her house, Phineas found himself whistling. She was standing at the mailbox as if anxious for his arrival.

When he pulled up alongside her, she greeted him with a nervous smile then climbed inside, glancing over her shoulder, as if anxious that someone might see her getting into his buggy.

"Everything alright?" he asked before he slapped the reins through the open window to send the horse trotting down the road.

"Oh ja," she replied. "I just didn't want Katie to see me leave."

He raised an eyebrow.

Lizzie leaned over, her shoulder brushing against his. "Surely she'd have wanted to tag along."

"Ah."

Lizzie laughed. "And I wouldn't wish that on anyone, *especially* a new friend."

He stiffened at her words, curious as to why she had said such a thing, but he didn't inquire further. They had, after all, talked about friendship during their last buggy ride.

As they headed toward the Riehl farm, they made small talk, their banter light and effortless. The closer they got to the Riehl's, the more relaxed she appeared. In fact, when they arrived and he helped her down from the buggy, she didn't withdraw her hand from his until she was standing firmly on the ground.

Now, as he worked alongside the men, he found that he was often seeking her out among the women who were setting up an outdoor picnic area for the noon meal. It was easy to spot her because she wore a light green dress that stood out from the other women, most of whom were wearing darker colors.

"You arrived with Lizzie Bender, ja?"

Phineas glanced up at the sound of a man speaking to him. "Excuse me?"

The man gestured with his chin in the direction of where Lizzie stood setting the table. "You brought Lizzie Bender here today, didn't you?"

He frowned. Not knowing the man, Phineas wasn't certain why it mattered to him. However, he didn't want to seem rude, so he merely nodded. "My friend is renting a farm from her family."

"I see. The old Bender farm, ja?" He reached up and tugged at his wiry beard. "Been a while since someone's taken over that place. Be good to have some fresh life over thatta way."

Phineas eyed the man, still curious as to why he had asked about Lizzie.

The man glanced again in her direction. "It's *gut* to see Lizzie out and about. Don't often see her without her *schweister*, Jane."

"And you are?"

The man struck out his hand. "Thomas Bender. A cousin."

Immediately, Phineas relaxed. "Wasn't aware there were more Benders in the area."

Thomas laughed. "Oh ja, there's a ton of Benders in Blue Mill. Related to each other in one way or another. Haven't seen much of Amos's kin in a while, given that we live in the next town. But, like I said, it's nice to see Lizzie out. She's always been a hard worker, that one." He grinned. "As good as a son, Amos always said...at least when Jacob wasn't around."

At that, Thomas winked before he wandered away, joining up with another group of men who were working on a reaper that needed attention.

Curious, Phineas looked toward the women again. He watched as Lizzie scurried back and forth, setting the table for the men to enjoy their meal. Unlike the other women, Lizzie didn't linger in groups, chatting or gossiping. Instead, she stuck to her task at hand, eager to get it done and move on to the next chore.

He smiled to himself. She was a hard worker, indeed. After the storm, she'd been outside working alongside the men. Meanwhile, Cynthia and Jane had remained inside the house. It hadn't struck him at the time why Lizzie had insisted upon helping. Now, however, he saw it for what it truly was: an indication of her strong character.

Not for the first time, he found himself admiring her. When she glanced up, brushing a stray hair from her forehead and her eyes swept the field where the men worked until they settled on him. Phineas quickly dipped his head and got back to work.

It would do no good for her to see him staring at her. Embarrassed that he'd been caught, he busied himself helping the men with loading bales of hay into the barn. Sometimes keeping busy was the best way to keep out of trouble, he reminded himself. With Lizzie, he would be wise to remember that.

Chapter Thirty-One

"So, who's that handsome young man who can't keep his eyes off of you?"

Lizzie had been so busy setting the tables that were arranged under the shade of the white oak tree, that she hadn't seen her friend Emma arrive. After all, knowing that the men would be hungry for their noon mean, especially after working all morning in the fields, Lizzie had been hurrying through the chore and, as a result, was lost in thought.

So, when she heard the whispered question from someone standing behind her, she froze for a long few seconds before she turned around to face Emma.

"You startled me," Lizzie managed to say with a forced smile. "When did you get here? I hadn't seen you earlier."

Emma gave a little laugh. "Don't try that tactic with me, Lizzie Bender. I know you far too well to be fooled by you."

"I have no idea what you're talking about," she fibbed.

Emma put her hands on her hips and gave her a stern once-over. "Seriously, Lizzie," she said. "You're avoiding my question. Who *is* that man? I saw him at worship service last Sunday and then—" Emma paused, resting her finger against her cheek, her gaze shifting toward the heavens, "—in town the other day, I believe." She made a face as she looked back at Lizzie. "With you, Lizzie Bender. Crossing the street."

"Really? I don't recall—"

"Fiddle faddle," Emma shot back. "Is he new to the area? How do you know him?"

Lizzie sighed. There was no use trying to change the subject. Once Emma caught the scent of mouthwatering gossip there was no stopping her. "Well, if you must truly know—"

"I must!"

"—he's helping a friend of his, Christopher Burkholder, who recently leased our old family farm."

Emma's blue eyes widened. "You mean that young man who was sitting beside him at worship last week?"

Lizzie nodded. "Ja, him."

"Interesting," Emma mumbled, her eyes momentarily glazing over, a clear indication that her mind was reeling. Lizzie was sure that she was thinking about all the matchmaking possibilities in her future.

Lizzie decided it was fair game to let Emma find out on her own about Christopher's interest in Jane. Besides the fact that Lizzie didn't want to share Jane's private business with anyone, she also found herself mildly annoyed with Emma's constant tendency to gossip.

"Well, that man sure seems rather taken with you," Emma said at last.

For a second, Lizzie felt herself flush. Why on earth would Emma make such a statement? She didn't even know Phineas!

Quickly, Lizzie tried to think of a way to prevent the inevitable gossip that she imagined Emma would spread. "Oh, don't be ridiculous," she said, waving her hand dismissively. "He lives too far away. In Clearwater, of all places!" she said as if that, alone, was reason enough to stop Emma in her tracks.

Emma, however, didn't seem phased in the least. "Distance means nothing when a young man is in love."

Lizzie scowled and clucked her tongue. "Your fanciful ideas, Emma, are rather odd," she scolded. "You know hide nor hair of the man!"

Clearly, Emma wasn't about to drop the subject. "Why! I don't have to know him at all, Lizzie Bender! Anyone with eyes can see for themselves. I only just arrived here, not even thirty minutes ago—Daed's friend, Gabriel, brought me—and I could see that he couldn't take his eyes off you when I was talking with Louisa on the porch."

Lizzie glanced over her shoulder toward the hay loft. She could hardly make out the identity of *any* man by the barn, so she was highly suspect of Emma's claim. More than likely, Louisa had mentioned that Lizzie had arrived in Phineas's buggy.

"Well, I don't see him now, do you?" Lizzie asked sharply.

Emma stared into the distance. "Nee, I do not." She redirected her attention back to Lizzie. "But he *was* there. Watching you."

Lizzie shrugged. "Mayhaps he was just taking in the farm, Emma. You make far too much of such a silly thing."

"If you say so," Emma conceded at last. But Lizzie could tell that, despite her friend having dropped the subject, she was not convinced. "Well, anyway, shall I help you finish setting the table and you can tell me all about this new fellow..." She paused. "What *is* his name, anyway?"

"Phineas. Phineas Denner."

For some reason, it felt like a personal betrayal to confide this simple fact to Emma. She didn't want to tell her friend anything about Phineas or their budding friendship. She didn't want to be asked questions or reminded that he was, in fact, returning to his farm in Clearwater sooner, rather than later. More than likely, the next time she'd see him would be at Jane's wedding to Christopher, if that blessed event should come to be.

So, Lizzie did the wisest thing she could. She held her tongue and shared as little information as possible with Emma, without being rude. Instead, she talked more about Christopher and Cynthia rather than Phineas.

"His friend, Christopher, seems like a nice enough fellow," Lizzie said as she set down the mix-matched collection of glasses, one at each place setting.

"He's from Clearwater, too?"

"Ja, he was anyway. He's here now."

Emma pursed her lips in a thoughtful way. "And his *schweister* is staying here with him?"

Lizzie gave a little shrug. "I reckon someone has to take care of him."

Emma laughed. "So, mayhaps she's only here to tend to his needs until he finds and marries a special friend?"

Again, Lizzie gave a noncommittal shrug. "I wouldn't know." In her mind, however, she wondered if Cynthia would, indeed, return to Clearwater if or when Christopher married. Or, perhaps she would marry a local man and remain to start her own family?

In the days following the meal they'd shared with the Burkholders' the previous Sunday, Jacob appeared to have a different spring to his step. Lizzie had noticed it right away and Jane confirmed that, twice during the week, Jacob had disappeared on foot, heading across the pasture in the direction of the Burkholders' farm.

Something had surely changed between Cynthia and Jacob, that was for certain.

"Such a shame that Clearwater is so far away," Emma continued. "Too far, I'm sure, for that Phineas's interest to carry on. Certainly, it would be a challenge to court from such a distance, don't you reckon?"

Lizzie kept her back to Emma, but she pressed her lips together, irritated by her friend's comment. Oh! Why did

Emma have to voice the very thing that was pressing on her own mind?

"No matter," she managed to say, "Near or far, it's always right *gut* to make new friends."

The noise of gentle tingling rang out. Lizzie looked up to see Louisa's mother pulling the string to the bell that hung from the porch overhang. The men would hear it and stop what they were doing to return to the house for the noon meal.

Lizzie and Emma hurried back and forth from the kitchen to the table, carrying trays and bowls of food so that, when the men arrived, they could sit down, pray, and enjoy the noon meal. If Lizzie knew anything, she knew that the men had worked up quite an appetite from working so hard all morning.

She had just set the last basket of warm rolls on the table when she noticed him, strolling across the field. His tan pants and light blue suspenders stood out from the other men who wore drabber colors. With his straw hat tipped back on his head, Lizzie could see his dark eyes searching the area as if seeking someone out.

Her heart fluttered and a smile touched her lips.

Surely, he was looking for her!

The realization that, perhaps, Emma had spoken the truth gave her goosebumps that ran up her arms. Why would he have any interest in her, she wondered, when he made it clear that he would be leaving Blue Mill within the next week or so?

When his gaze finally fell on her, he turned in her direction and picked up his pace.

Lizzie pressed her lips together and took him in. There was something unusually rugged about him. Perhaps it was the beads of sweat along his forehead or the smear of dirt on his cheek. As he got closer, her breath came in shallow waves, so much so that she had to reach out her hand to steady herself on the edge of the table.

The hint of a smile brushed his lips as if he knew the effect he was having on her, which made her heart beat even faster. Before he reached her, an older man approached him, clapping Phineas on the shoulder as he passed. The man said something which made Phineas laugh, a sound that carried on the breeze.

Emma walked behind her, poking her in the back. "I saw that," she whispered into Lizzie's ear. "Told you so."

Lizzie whirled around and gave her friend a dark look. "I am, after all, the only person he knows here, Emma!" she snapped.

"Uh huh. If you say so." Emma handed her a pitcher of lemonade. "Mayhaps you might want to fill their cups?" she suggested, a mischievous look in her eyes.

Lizzie took the pitcher and willed herself to calm her pounding heart before heading toward the table where the men were seated. She took her time serving each one, reaching between their shoulders for the cup and then filling it, careful not to spill any this time.

When she reached Phineas's side, she hesitated, just long enough for him to sense her presence.

"Ah, there you are," he said, twisting around to look up at her. He graced her with a relaxed smile. "I thought I saw you earlier today. Clearly you women have been busy." He reached for his own cup and handed it to her. "*Danke*, Elizabeth."

Silently, she filled the cup, hoping that he didn't notice the way her hand was shaking. With the greatest of care, she filled it then handed it back to him.

"We've gotten the back field plowed. Someone must have already started it. Didn't take too long."

Lizzie scanned the table. Why was he telling her this? The other men were watching and listening, amused expressions on their faces.

"Anyway, I know how much you like to garden," he continued. "So, I offered to help you till their garden patch after the meal."

"Oh." Her cheeks burned and she knew if she had a mirror, they would be a brilliant shade of red. Why was he paying so much attention to her in front of all these men? By singling her out for such an exchange, tongues would start wagging before the sun had set! "That would be nice," she managed to say.

"With so many men helping in the fields, figure my hand might be better accompanying yours doing something else useful, ja?"

She nodded before walking down the line of men seated on the bench. She didn't need eyes in the back of her head to know that not only was Phineas watching her, but so were the whole lot of men who had just witnessed their exchange. Likewise, she didn't need an extra pair of ears to hear that several of the older men speaking in German, were most likely commenting on the familiar exchange between them. And, she didn't need to understand German to know that one of them had just called Phineas smitten. She knew what *geschlagen* meant because her grandfather used to say it all the time.

Embarrassed, she kept her head down and hurried about her task. The sooner she finished, the sooner she could retreat to the safety of the house where she could collect her thoughts.

At that moment, Lizzie knew that if she didn't reign in her feelings, she risked a bruised heart.

Chapter Thirty-Two

Something had changed about her.

Phineas couldn't quite put his finger on what it was, but he knew that something surely was different.

Unlike earlier that morning, Lizzie appeared distracted, her head bent over as she worked in the Riehls' garden. She was less talkative, focusing on the hoe to break up the ground, occasionally pausing to kneel and pull out a rock which she tossed into a metal bucket at her side.

Phineas worked alongside her, helping to loosen the soil until they'd cleared at least half of the ground. He excused himself and wandered over to the large manure pit that he'd noticed on the far side of the stable. Using an old, splintery shovel, he took his time filling the wheelbarrow. He knew he had to be careful fertilizing the ground if Louisa Riehl intended to plant seed right away. Too much manure could burn the seeds. But Phineas also knew that a good raking could help spread the dung and enrich the dirt with invaluable nutrients.

She looked up when he neared the garden area.

"Oh." Standing, she wiped her hands on her black apron. "Let me help with that."

He shook his head. "I got this. You just keep hoeing, Elizabeth. We'll finish sooner if we divide and conquer."

Quietly, she turned her attention to the soil, the only noise being the gentle *thunk, thunk* of the hoe blade when it hit the ground.

With careful and deliberate movements, Phineas spread small piles of manure on the dirt. When the wheelbarrow was empty, he went to fetch more. By the time he'd finished the fourth trip to the manure pile, he noticed that Lizzie was already raking the fertilizer into the soil, spreading it in a very thin layer.

He set down the wheelbarrow and reached for his shovel, trying to focus on unloading the last amount of manure. For the life of him, he couldn't understand why she was being so quiet and withdrawn. Had he said or done something to offend her?

"Ouch!"

He dropped the shovel and shook his hand, spinning around in a small circle as he tried to quell the pain in his hand.

Immediately, Lizzie dropped the rake and rushed to his side. "What is it?"

Feeling rather foolish, Phineas shut his eyes and tried to catch his breath. "A splinter or two. Big ones, I fear, in my palm."

Before he could open his eyes, he felt the touch of her fingers against his skin. He looked at her, surprised by how gentle she was as, her head bent over as she studied his open hand.

"Oh ja! Two big ones all right," she said softly. She looked up. "One's fairly deep, I'm afraid."

He scowled. "Should've worn work gloves." He glared at the tossed shovel. "That handle has seen better days, that's for certain."

"Kum, Phineas," she coaxed. "Sit down in the sunlight so I can see better. I'll try to take out those splinters."

She led him to a patch of grass and made him sit. Only then did she kneel beside him. She reached behind her waist and withdrew a straight pin from the belt of her apron. Reaching for his hand, she held it lightly on her lap.

"Try not to move," she said.

Phineas stared at the back of her head as she bent over his hand. It dawned on him that wild horses couldn't have dragged him away from her at that very moment despite the pain he was in.

With the gentlest of touches, she poked the straight pin at the opening where the splinters had slid into his flesh. He could feel the tip of the needle probing as she scoffed and mumbled something under her breath.

"What is it?"

She sighed. "Nothing, Phineas. A piece just broke off, that's all. Means I'll have to poke around to seek it." Her eyes fluttered to meet his. "I'm sorry."

He couldn't help but smile. "I think I can handle it."

She raised an eyebrow at him, but then returned her attention toward his palm.

It took her a few minutes to extract both splinters. When she did, she gave a triumphant—but soft—cheer. Immediately, she started to pull her hand away from his, but Phineas stopped her by closing his fingers around hers.

Her eyes flew to his face.

"*Danke*, Elizabeth," he managed to say.

She gave a little tug of her hand, but he refused to release it from his own.

"Phineas—"

"Elizabeth."

She frowned. "I really wish you wouldn't call me that. It reminds me of my mother scolding me."

"I have no desire to call you anything else," he murmured. "Surely it's one of the most beautiful names."

And then, just like that, something passed over her face, like a dark cloud casting a shadow on a sunny patch of land. Her expression no longer appeared confused but defiant.

"It'll be easy to call me nothing at all," she said in a brisk tone, "all the way from Clearwater, Phineas."

The meaning of her words took a moment to register with him. When they did, he tightened his hold. "I see, Elizabeth. So that's what this is about."

"What '*this*' are you referring to?"

He gestured with his free hand toward the place she'd last hoed. "The silence. Ever since we started in the garden, you've been acting differently toward me—"

"I'm not acting differently!" she countered.

"Then how do you explain your silence? We've been working side-by-side, the perfect opportunity to get to know one another better in private."

She gave him a stern look and then, to his surprise, she tugged her hand free from his grasp and rose to her feet. "There's no point in getting to know one another better," she said through clenched teeth. "You'll be leaving for your *home* and your *life* in Clearwater, Phineas." She placed her hands on her hips, giving him a cool stare. "Besides, it isn't like we *know* one another at all. It's only been—what?—two weeks? Less?"

Scrambling to his feet, Phineas faced her, bewildered by this dark side of Lizzie. "I think people can get to know one another sufficiently in such a short amount of time."

"Do you?"

He gave a short laugh. "Don't *you*?" Reaching up, he removed his straw hat and slapped it against his leg. With his free hand, he ran his fingers through his hair. "Back in my parents' day, they'd have spent less time together over the course of four or five weeks, and most of it chaperoned!"

She slid her gaze away from his.

"My *maem* always told me that the time for getting to know a partner is *after* the wedding, anyway," he continued.

Her mouth opened. "*After* the wedding? What good does that do a person?"

Shaking his head, he plopped his hat back onto his head. He felt exasperated by the conversation, truly not understanding where her frustration came from.

"Elizabeth—"

"Lizzie!" she snapped. "Please call me by my name, Phineas, or I think I'll go mad!"

He rolled his eyes and counted to ten. "I'm not leaving for Clearwater for another week yet," he said at last. "I'd like permission to come call on you until then."

She stood before him, her shoulders squared, and her chin tilted upwards. Yet, as much as she tried to appear stoic and unaffected, he could see a hint of sorrow etched into her face.

"I fail to see the purpose," she replied sharply, "to get used to something—" She pursed her lips. "—someone, rather, only to have to say goodbye." She gave a slight shake of her head. "Nee, Phineas, I don't think that's a very practical or sound idea."

So, he thought, it was the fear of being left with a broken heart that caused her to feel the need to distance herself!

"I'll finish here," she said. "I'm sure the other men could use your help."

And with that, Phineas knew that she was dismissing him.

Thoughts flew through his head, a collage of ideas about what he could say or do to change her mind. However, rather than start an argument with her, Phineas merely backed away.

The time would come, he knew, when she'd recognize what a mistake she'd just made. He clenched his jaw, feeling the muscles tighten toward the back of his cheeks. He only hoped that she'd recognize it before it was too late.

Chapter Thirty-Three

"Well, you're in some sort of mood today, aren't you?"

Lizzie cast a stern look at her younger sister. Unfortunately, however, she knew that Katie was telling the truth.

Normally, Lizzie was in a good mood on Saturdays, a day that meant light chores and, usually, visiting with friends. In the evening, she and Jane might attend a volleyball game or go into town to enjoy a treat at the ice cream store. Every other Sunday, they'd rise early to attend the three-hour worship service—which didn't always feel so long *if* the deacon wasn't preaching. As a rule, Lizzie found that she enjoyed worship service. The location of the service always rotated among the parishioners, being held in the Masts' barn one week and then the Clemens' farmhouse another week and someone else's workshop the service after that.

Twice a year, the Benders' hosted the service. Those were Sundays that Lizzie dreaded for her mother would be frantic for a solid two weeks before. Everything had to be perfect, the floors scoured and oiled, the furniture dusted and polished. No, Susan Bender would never risk anyone gossiping about an ill-kept house on *her* watch.

After worship, the congregation enjoyed a fellowship hour, the people sharing a plain noon meal together., Even though the men and women sat at separate tables, it was always Lizzie's favorite part of the day as there was always so much activity and story-telling.

Finally, later that evening, Lizzie and Jane would either visit family with their parents or attend an evening singing with their friends.

Yes, those were all things that usually put Lizzie in a good mood.

But not today.

Instead of feeling happy and looking forward to doing something with her sister and friends, Lizzie merely wanted to crawl up the stairs and disappear under the warmth and comfort of her quilt.

The previous evening, she'd barely slept at all. Only this time, her sleeplessness wasn't because of her mind racing with thoughts about Phineas. No. Last night, thoughts about her own foolish words had haunted her, holding slumber at bay until the early morning hours. By the time she heard the rooster crow, the sun barely cresting over the tops of the trees on the east side of the farm, she guessed she'd slept for two hours, if that.

"Oh hush, you," Lizzie whispered at Katie. "What would you know, anyway?"

Katie made a face at her before skipping out of the kitchen. A moment later, the screen door hinge creaked, and Lizzie heard Katie's footsteps pounding across the porch and down the three steps to the yard.

Miserable, Lizzie leaned her head against her hand, her elbow on the table, and thought about her irrational behavior the previous day.

Why had she let Emma's words get to her? Phineas had been nothing but polite and proper with her, a true friend in the making. Even if he *was* going home soon, that was no reason for Lizzie to snap at him.

And yet she had.

She could only imagine what Phineas thought of her now. There was no amount of apology that could spill from her lips that would erase the memory of her harsh words. And yet, the reason behind her words bothered her almost as much as the words themselves.

Was it possible, she thought, that she had been developing even deeper feelings for Phineas?

Groaning, she covered her eyes with her hands and bent her head, her forehead pressed against the tabletop.

"What's wrong, Lizzie?"

"Go away," she moaned to Jane.

Laughing, Jane slid onto the bench beside her and forced Lizzie to sit up straight. "That bad, ja?"

"And then some." Lizzie felt her sister's fingers touching her hands, gently prying them loose from her face. Blinking,

Lizzie turned to face Jane. "What a mess I've made of everything."

Jane gave a soft, little sigh, a look of compassion etched on her face. "Sometimes we make things worse by overthinking them, Lizzie. I'm sure that's the case."

"Don't be so sure," Lizzie mumbled. "I've done something terrible."

This time, Jane's expression changed from compassion to concern. "Oh? Mayhaps it will help to talk about it?"

Lizzie sincerely doubted that, but she knew that Jane was persistent enough that she might as well confide in her.

"It was awful, Jane," she began with an exasperated moan. "I hadn't felt so terrible until Emma began saying things. And then, my mood shifted and when Phineas and I were working in the garden—"

When Lizzie paused, Jane reached out and placed her hand on her knee. "What happened then?"

"Oh, I said terrible things to him." Abruptly, Lizzie stood up and began pacing the room. "He asked to call upon me."

Jane caught her breath which Lizzie ignored.

"Ja, he did." She turned and continued crossing the floor, her eyes staring at the wall in front of her. "And I basically told him that there was no point."

"Oh Lizzie," Jane whispered.

"I know. I know." Lizzie lifted both her hands to her forehead and rubbed her temples with her thumbs. "I hadn't meant to say such a thing, but I did."

"Because of Emma?"

Lizzie stopped pacing and lifted her gaze to look at her sister. "Ja, because of Emma. She has that effect on people—"

Jane made a face. "Don't we all know it."

"—and when she commented that his living in Clearwater was too far for a special friendship, well—" Lizzie's shoulders slumped. "—I suppose I listened to her and took it out on Phineas."

Immediately, Jane scrambled to her feet and hurried over to Lizzie's side. She placed her hands upon Lizzie's shoulders and stared her straight in the eye. "Now you listen to me, Elizabeth Bender," she said softly. "If Phineas is half the man that I think he is, he will forgive you for a sharp tongue."

"No man forgives a woman a sharp tongue," Lizzie quipped.

Jane laughed. "Why, Daed forgives Maem her tongue at least twenty times a day!"

Even Lizzie found herself smiling at *that* comment.

But Jane wasn't finished yet. "Just wait until tomorrow. I'm sure that you will find the opportunity to apologize to him. After all, if he *does* care for you, he will certainly understand." She paused, leveling her gaze once again to stare Lizzie straight on. "And forgive."

Oh, if only Lizzie could believe that. She wasn't certain that *she* would be so forgiving if the tables were turned. Still, she would never know if Jane's words were true if she didn't at least try. In the meantime, all she could do was hope and pray that the opportunity to apologize to Phineas would present itself sooner rather than later.

Chapter Thirty-Four

He noticed her as soon as he walked into the worship service at Elmer Troyer's house. Unlike the previous week, worship was held inside the large gathering room and not outside in an empty workshop. Even with the windows open, the room was already warm and threatened to become even more uncomfortable by the time the service had ended.

Lizzie sat at the rear of the room on the right side. She looked pale and tired, dark circles under her eyes and, straightaway, Phineas worried that she might be ill.

He'd learned from Christopher that Lizzie hadn't attended the youth volleyball game the previous evening. On the one hand, Phineas was glad that she *hadn't* attended. The thought of her accepting a ride home from another young man hadn't sat well with him. In fact, he'd fretted all evening while he sat home alone, worrying that, perhaps, he should've gone to the event with Cynthia and Christopher.

But on the other hand, when Christopher returned and mentioned that Lizzie had not been there, Phineas spent the rest of the night tossing and turning, wondering if she had stayed home, like he had, or had she gone somewhere else?

For certain, ever since Friday, Phineas had been in a terrible mood. Clearly something had happened while he'd been working in the fields with the other men to make Lizzie act so cold and standoffish toward him. While he'd never hidden the fact that he would return to Clearwater, he hadn't expected her to behave as if he were moving across the country, never to be seen again. It was, in truth, less than an hour car ride from Blue Mill.

During the sermon, Phineas found himself paying less and less attention to the preachers as his eyes wandered to the other side of the room where Lizzie sat. He needed a moment to speak with her in private, a chance to clear the air with her about his true intentions. Or, at least, his perceived intentions.

If only he could spend more time with her. To get to know her better.

But she'd made it quite clear on Friday that she wanted no part of that plan.

He felt Christopher nudge him. Pulled from his thoughts, Phineas glanced at him.

"Kneel," Christopher whispered and gestured with his head toward the other seated men.

Embarrassed to have been caught not paying attention—something Phineas rarely did during worship!—he turned around, dropped to his knees and pressed his forehead against his folded hands which were rested on the bench.

Had worship truly just finished? It was the quickest three hours he'd remembered during a service in a long time.

After the service ended, Phineas worked alongside Christopher and the other men, converting some of the benches into two long tables for the fellowship hour. Several times, Phineas tried to locate Lizzie, but she was nowhere to be found.

"She left," someone said from behind.

Phineas turned around and faced Jacob. "Excuse me?"

"Lizzie left." Jacob gestured toward the door. "If that's who you're looking for, that is."

Trying to appear indifferent, Phineas made a noise, deep in his throat, that neither confirmed nor denied Jacob's statement.

"I reckon you might catch her walking home still," Jacob added. "If you hurry, anyway."

Phineas hesitated, wondering why her brother was sharing this information with him. As far as he knew, no one knew of his feelings towards Lizzie. He felt strongly about keeping such things private.

"I see," he managed to say, unable to stop himself from looking at the door. "Mayhaps I'll go see if she'd care for a ride."

Jacob smiled at him. "You do that. I'm sure she'd be grateful."

Quietly, Phineas slipped from the house, dodging Christopher who, was paying more attention to Jane than anything else around him. Cynthia was standing with some of the other women, one of them he recognized as Emma from the work party on Friday.

It was good that both Christopher and Cynthia were beginning to settle into their new lives in Blue Mill. Yet, he felt a tug at his heart as he realized that he'd be returning to Clearwater, not only alone, but without the companionship of his good friend.

For the first time since his arrival in Blue Mill, Phineas felt sorrow at the fact that, soon, he'd have to set out for home.

It only took him a few minutes to put the bridle on his horse and back it away from the line tied to the trees. Carefully, he held onto the reins as he climbed inside, then pulled gently on the lines to guide the horse down the driveway.

Sure enough, he hadn't travelled a full two minutes before he saw the small figure of a lone Amish woman walking down the road. With her head bent over and shoulders slumped, she looked distracted and deep in thought.

No wonder she appeared surprised when he slowed down the horse and buggy beside her.

"Phineas!"

He motioned to the empty seat beside him. "*Kum*, Elizabeth. Let me take you home."

She hesitated, her eyes darting from his buggy to the end of the lane and, for the briefest of seconds, Phineas thought she might refuse. But, to his delight, she nodded and hurried around to the side of the buggy and climbed in through the open passenger door.

He waited until the buggy was in motion before he took a moment to look at her. "You are well?"

She pressed her lips together and gave a little lift of her shoulders.

"You appear tired," he said when she didn't answer.

"I...I haven't felt well, to be honest," she admitted.

"Oh?" He gave her a quick study, concern etched on his face. "Mayhaps you need to see a doctor?"

She shook her head. "It's not a doctor I need to see."

He raised an eyebrow. "No?"

"Nee." She moistened her lips and took a quick, deep breath. "It's you, Phineas."

"Me?" Her statement confused him. What on earth could he do to help her feel better? "I fail to see—"

She reached out and touched his arm, stopping him mid-sentence. "I owe you an apology," she whispered. "It's been weighing heavy on my head—" She paused and then added, "—and heart. You've been quite considerate towards me, and I returned your kindheartedness with harsh words on Friday."

"Elizabeth, there's no need to apologize."

"Oh ja, there is. That's not like me, Phineas," she said rather quickly. "I'm not *that* person who said those words. It should make no difference whether you are leaving Blue Mill soon. Friendship doesn't have geographic boundaries, does it now?"

Friendship. She spoke the word innocently with the softest of tones and yet Phineas suddenly realized that *friendship* was not what he had in mind. Surely she knew that, too, didn't she?

And then it dawned on him that maybe she didn't.

"That's good to know," he heard himself say at last. "I feel quite the same way."

"You do?" She stared at him, her eyes wide and unblinking.

He nodded. "Ja. After all, I will be saying good-bye to Christopher soon. When I return to Clearwater, I will still consider him one of my closest friends."

At the mention of Clearwater, she averted her eyes.

"Of course, it's not quite as far as one would think," he continued. "I imagine he'll be visiting his family from time to time and, after the first hay cutting, I'm sure to return to visit him as well."

His words were met with silence.

"Have you ever been?" he asked. "To Clearwater, I mean."

She shook her head. "I've barely left Blue Mill, never mind Lower Austen County."

He chuckled. The innocence of her provincial comment amused him. But he understood what she meant. After all, what reason would she have *to* leave Blue Mill? Many Amish youths rarely traveled, unless it was an organized youth group trip or with their families to visit distant relatives.

"Perhaps it's time for you to explore a bit of the world, see what life has to offer outside of Blue Mill," he said.

She gave him a quizzical look. "Perhaps, although I've no reason to do so. This is my home and I'm quite happy here." She turned her head so that he couldn't see her face as she gazed out the open door. "Where would I go, anyway? And with whom would I travel? I'd surely not want to travel far from home alone."

"You never know," he responded slowly, picking his words carefully. "Mayhaps you'll find yourself in a situation where you can see a bit of the world. My advice is to not be too quick to turn down any such offers."

Slowly, she exhaled. "Should one come, I'll be certain to remember your advice."

The buggy approached the driveway of her father's farm and, reluctantly, Phineas directed the horse to pull into it. He'd have enjoyed spending more time with her, but it would be inappropriate to do so at her home without a family member present. Besides, from her melancholy mood, he suspected she preferred to be alone.

Before she got out of the buggy, she gave him a small smile. "*Danke*, Phineas. I'm glad you stopped to offer me the ride."

"Think nothing of it," he replied.

She made a move to step through the open door but, at the last minute, hesitated. "I feel much better for having apologized."

He gave a single nod of his head. "Again, there was no need, but I'm happy that you feel better."

And then, without another word, she trudged into the house, her shoulders once again sunken and her head bent low. She paused at the door, glancing back at him then waved.

He lifted his hand in response as she disappeared through the door, then clucked his tongue and urged the horse to turn around in a large circle before heading back up the driveway toward the road.

For some reason, his heart felt heavy and he couldn't help but feel that Lizzie had just said her final goodbye.

Chapter Thirty-Five

Lizzie stared at her sister, a look of complete disbelief on her face. "What do you mean he's *gone?*"

It was Tuesday and Jane's sudden news was the last thing Lizzie expected to hear that day. No sooner had she walked through the door after doing her errands did Jane abandon her sewing and hurry to her side.

At first, Lizzie thought something terrible had happened because, Jane's face was ashen, and her eyes were wide with concern. She looked around for her mother and little sister. With a dozen different scenarios crossing Lizzie's mind, she froze then braced herself for the news, expecting the worst but praying for the best.

"What's happened, Jane?"

"Phineas left for home."

Lizzie never expected to hear those four words pass her sister's lips.

Jane gave her a sympathetic look. "I'm sorry, Lizzie. I just learned about it this afternoon from Cynthia."

"I can scarce believe it," Lizzie said, her eyes glazing over as she stared at nothing. Left? For Clearwater? It didn't make any sense. He'd said nothing about leaving so soon. Why they saw each other on Sunday, not two days prior. "When exactly did he go?" Lizzie asked, trying to sound indifferent, but she suspected that Jane saw right through her. She'd never been able to hide much from her sister.

"After the noon meal today, apparently." Jane sighed while tugging at the needle she was using to fix the hem of Katie's dress. "Cynthia came over to return my container from Sunday—I left it in Christopher's buggy—and she told me the news."

"I...I see."

Feeling despondent, Lizzie walked over to the kitchen window. For a long moment, she pressed her fingers against the edge of the sink and peered outside. While her eyes studied the landscape, her mind whirled with this most unexpected news.

All morning, she'd worked in the vegetable garden—the air had been warm and the sun shining bright, perfect conditions for gardening—and then, after the noon meal, she had ridden into town with Jacob. They had stopped at the harness store and then picked up some dry goods for their mother before heading back to the farm. Perhaps if she'd stayed home, Cynthia might have told *her* the news in time for her to walk over to the farm to say goodbye before he set out.

But what difference would *that* have made, she asked herself. It wasn't as if she might have changed his mind. She had known all along that he had to go home to tend to his own farm and sister. She had just thought she had a little more time with him, is all.

"Did you know he intended to leave so soon?" Jane asked.

"I did not." She glanced over her shoulder at her sister. "How could I have known? I only saw him on Sunday, and he hadn't said a word to me."

Two days ago, she thought. Had he known then that he was leaving today? If so, why hadn't he shared his plans with her?

Returning her gaze to the window, she took a deep breath and sighed. Outside, everything was starting to grow. The soil was covered in a fine layer of green, the corn beginning to sprout in the back field. In another month, it would be almost a foot tall and by July, it would have tripled in size. Normally, she felt inspired by the tiny sprouts. There was nothing more beautiful that a tall field of corn, the stalks quivering in an early summer breeze. Today, however, she felt no inspiration at all, just, an overwhelming sense of sadness.

By the time those stalks grew, it would only be a memory of the day Phineas had returned to Clearwater and she would have to stare at them through the entire summer and be reminded of him.

Abruptly, she turned away from the window, hugging herself as she forced a weak smile. "Well, Jane, it isn't really that surprising, I suppose." She tried to give a little laugh. "He's been here almost a month already. Surely, he needed to tend to his own business by now. Besides, what does his departure matter to me anyway?"

Jane studied her for a long moment. "Of course," she said at last. "I'm sure it doesn't matter at all."

Having a hard time catching her breath, Lizzie felt as though she needed some fresh air. She stepped out onto the back porch, the screen door slamming behind her. How was it possible that Phineas left? Without even saying goodbye? Surely, he had *not* forgiven her sharp words the previous Friday. Her apology had not been enough to heal the wounds created by her callous remarks.

She paused in front of the barn and stared out at the corn field. The sky was becoming overcast, the hint of rain lingering in the air, a far contrast to the pleasant weather earlier that morning.

Her thoughts raced as she started pacing back and forth, the wind picking up and blowing her kapp from her head. She chased after it, scooping down to catch it between her fingers, but each time she missed by an inch or so. Finally, it settled against the barn where she knelt to grab it. As she sat, she pinned it to her head, feeling the weight of the world on her shoulders and an emptiness in her heart. Knowing that, with Phineas already gone, she most likely wouldn't see him again anytime soon. At least not unless Jane and Christopher married in the autumn.

Clearly, she had imagined something between them that did not exist or else he would have sought her out to at least say goodbye. For that, she scolded herself. How could she have fallen so hard? How could she have thought that Phineas might—just might!—have been interested in courting her?

Still kneeling, in her mind, she replayed every meeting she'd had with him, from the very first time he'd passed her on the road to their last buggy ride on Sunday. And everything in between. Not for the first—and most likely not the last—time, she scolded herself for having spoken so harshly to him at the work party. If only she could take back those words and replay that day, perhaps he would not have left without so much as a goodbye.

Chapter Thirty-Six

When he arrived in Clearwater on Tuesday mid-afternoon, Phineas felt as if he'd been traveling for days.

The hired driver had been late to fetch him that morning, each delayed minute causing Phineas to consider postponing his journey.

He'd made up his mind just the previous day. Too many sleepless nights had made him anxious for a change, for he knew that he'd go mad if he had to keep running into Elizabeth without her feelings being reciprocated.

She'd clearly dismissed him on Sunday. She'd said her goodbyes. The thought of staying in Blue Mill without being able to court her bothered him far more than he anticipated. While he would have preferred to delay his return a few more days, Phineas was wise enough to know that doing so would serve no purpose. Clearly Lizzie had made up her mind. A friendship was all they would ever have.

Upon his return home, Phineas stood on the porch, his bag resting by his feet. The house seemed colder than usual and even more uninviting since he hadn't fetched his sister yet. Slowly, he reached for the door and, with the greatest of reluctance, entered.

The kitchen was empty but not for lack of company. No, it was empty of the love of a family. While that shouldn't have surprised him, for his sister was still at their cousins' house, Phineas knew that the void depressed him. For the past few weeks, he'd been living with the Burkholders and, despite his lack of affection for Cynthia, he found that he enjoyed the presence of a woman in the kitchen.

In Blue Mill, there had always been the lingering scent of freshly baked bread or hints of a warm supper in the oven. In Clearwater, the house had almost no scent at all. The young woman who cleaned for him hadn't been there since his departure so there wasn't even the scent of the Tung oil she used to polish the hardwood floors.

Slowly, he trudged down the hallway then opened the door to the first-floor bedroom. It used to be his parents' and, for years after their death, he had left it exactly as it was during their marriage. But two years ago, during the winter, he'd finally convinced himself that it was more economical to use it so that he could benefit from the wood burning heater in the kitchen. Now, as he stood in the doorway, staring inside, he felt that the bedroom was too large for one person. Tomorrow he would move back upstairs to the room next to his sister.

As hard as he tried not to, he pictured Lizzie in the kitchen—*his* kitchen—her hands kneading dough, flour splattered on her apron. He'd sneak up on her, catching her off-guard and, when she spun around, he'd be there to catch her in his arms should she stumble.

He smiled at the picture he'd just painted in his mind.

"Stop!" he said out loud.

Quickly, he pushed the image from his mind. Three weeks. That was the total amount of time he'd known her. Now, there were many miles separating them and he wouldn't see her again until autumn *if* Christopher married Jane. By then, anything could happen. Perhaps Lizzie would find a nice Amish man from Blue Mill to marry. Maybe she was already courting someone new, a thought that had tortured him during the past few sleepless nights.

Even if she wasn't courting another man, now or in the future, what difference would that make to him? Lizzie was extremely close to her sister and family; she'd never want to move as far away as Clearwater.

He groaned and pushed himself away from the door frame. What on earth was he thinking? Three weeks of knowing someone and already he was envisioning a future? Complete rubbish, he chastised himself. He'd known women in his own community for years and never once thought in such terms about them!

Outside, he tried to busy himself in the dairy barn. His hired man was already tending to the herd.

"You're back!"

Phineas forced a smile. "Indeed, John."

"How was Blue Mill? Did Christopher get settled in?"

Phineas walked to the stainless-steel sink in the back of the barn. "Ja, he sure did." He washed his hands, the cold water from the faucet splashing against his skin. "He'll do well there, I'm sure."

"Lucky man to have the opportunity to work a farm of his own," John said.

"Indeed." Phineas shook his hands, droplets of water flying into the air. He didn't need to be reminded how fortunate they *both* were. Many men, like John, couldn't afford to lease let alone buy their own farm and had to support their families working another man's land. And, even if they could afford to buy a farm, there weren't many available in the area.

Fortunately for John, Phineas had too much land and a generous hand. During harvest time, he even hired a few other men to help. More than one family in Clearwater thrived because of Phineas Denner, another fact that made him popular among the Amish community.

"What's the news here, then?" he asked.

John gave a slight shrug. "Not much. Bishop's wife returned from her visit to her *dochders*, my *maem's* home from the hospital, and Luke's had a baby." He glanced toward the dairy barn. "And two cows birthed while you were gone."

"Well then, seems like everything's on track," he said, more to himself than to John.

His eyes scanned the barn. Unlike the buildings in Blue Mill, *his* were freshly painted—something he always did when the weather turned from cold winter days to warmer spring ones. Every year he made certain to touch up any sections that appeared weathered. Now, however, he realized the futility of such a task. Perhaps the Amish in Blue Mill had it right: why focus so much on the outer appearances when it was what was housed *within* those buildings that truly mattered.

Phineas sighed. "Best get to milking, I reckon."

With so many cows, he'd be preoccupied for well over an hour, even with John's help. And that was most likely the best way to forget about Blue Mill and Elizabeth Bender.

Chapter Thirty-Seven

"Elizabeth!"

Upon hearing her mother call out her name, Lizzie looked up from where she knelt in the garden. To her surprise, she saw her mother running down the driveway, her bare feet pounding against the dry, dusty lane while she frantically waved a white piece of paper in her air.

"What on earth?" Lizzie wondered. She couldn't remember a time when she'd ever seen her mother run.

Sitting back on her feet, Lizzie wiped her hands on her apron before standing up. It was Saturday and, as she had been doing every afternoon, Lizzie was weeding the garden. Not that there were many weeds anyway, but it gave her something to do without anyone else around to bother her. Her mother and younger sister both avoided gardening so Lizzie often sought solace there, in the safety of the fenced in plot of land.

And, ever since she'd learned that Phineas had returned to Clearwater—without even so much as a goodbye!— that quiet time was not only needed to think and reflect, but also needed to help her forget and heal.

Of course, today's quiet time was clearly over for her mother was most certainly headed in her direction and it seemed with pressing news.

"What is it, Maem?" she called out.

Her mother was all smiles as she neared the garden gate. She tried to catch her breath. Clearly the run down the driveway had winded her.

"Oh, Elizabeth! Such exciting news!"

Lizzie wondered what could possibly have her mother in such a heightened state of joy.

"Do tell," she urged, more than curious by this point.

For a quick moment, Susan scanned the piece of paper in her hand and then, lifting her eyes, she practically glowed. "Do you remember your great *aendi*? Mammi's *schweister*, Leah?"

Lizzie frowned. Her grandmother had many younger sisters. Lizzie couldn't remember all of them, especially because most of them lived quite some distance from Blue Mill. "Barely. And, even if I did, I fail to see what could be so thrilling about a letter from one of them!"

"Oh, never mind that." Her mother gave a light laugh and waved the paper in the air between them. "She's written to me, asking for some help."

Lizzie's frown deepened; her disappointment complete. What was so exciting about *that*, she wondered. "What type of help could she possibly need from us?"

Her mother held the letter before her eyes as if reading it for the first time. "Right here," she said, pointing to a section of the paper "She wants *you* to come stay with her."

"Me?" Lizzie made a face. "What on earth for?"

Her mother held out the letter as if Lizzie could read it from that distance. "She's had knee surgery and will be bedridden for another week or so. She's written to ask if you might come care for her."

Lizzie took the paper from her mother. "Me?" she repeated. "She requested me?" Quickly, her eyes scanned the letter and then, with a rolling of her eyes, she handed it back to her mother. "She didn't ask for *me*. She asked if you'd send one of your *dochders.*"

Dramatically, Susan exhaled and put her hand on her hip, giving Lizzie one of her 'why must you question me' looks. "Well, I can't likely send Jane now, can I? Not with Christopher paying so much attention to her! How unfair to send Jane away when she's so close to getting an offer for marriage!"

Lizzie groaned.

Ignoring her daughter, Susan continued. "And Katie." She gave a little scoff and tossed her hands into the air. "What good would *she* do for Leah?"

Unfortunately, Lizzie knew that to be true.

"So, clearly, it must be *you* who goes." She snatched the letter back from Lizzie's hands. "It's the sensible solution."

"I hardly think so," Lizzie laughed without mirth. "I don't know this woman and I don't really want to be someone's caretaker."

"Oh, Elizabeth!" Clearly, her mother was exasperated. Her brow furrowed and she shook her head disapprovingly. "We can't tell her no one's coming. How would that look? We're her family, after all!"

"I've never met her!"

"Oh, fiddle faddle. What's *that* to do with anything? Besides, it's only for a week." Susan looked back at the letter. "Maybe two."

Lizzie clenched her jaw, grinding her teeth as she quickly counted to ten. "I don't even know where she lives."

"Pinella Park," her mother said. "It's in the north of Lower Austen County."

Pinella Park? Lizzie tried to remember if she'd ever heard of that town before. As she rattled her brain, she suspected that Pinella Park must be a *very* small town for she'd never caught any mention of it before. And yet, it was in Lower Austen County so it couldn't be too far.

"I think it would be good for you, Lizzie," her mother said in a soft, but firm, tone. "You've been so quiet and sulky as of late. A change of scenery will be the perfect remedy for whatever is weighing so heavily on your mind."

Maybe she was right, Lizzie thought. With Christopher calling on Jane almost every evening and Jacob disappearing after supper with the horse and buggy, Lizzie was often alone, sitting on the sidelines as she watched her two older siblings developing special friendships with the Burkholders.

"Fine, Maem," Lizzie said with an exasperated sigh. "But not for more than a week."

"Two." Susan pointed to a line in the letter. "She says two."

Lizzie narrowed her eyes. "Two weeks? Why, when I return home my garden will be overrun with weeds and bugs, for sure and certain!"

Her mother clucked her tongue. "Such nonsense. I *have* tended a garden in my day."

Lizzie gave a little laugh. Just the image of her mother on her knees in the dirt was amusing enough, never mind her pulling weeds and dealing with worms. "I'd love to know when!"

Her mother shot her a stern look. "Elizabeth Bender! I did have a life before you came along. And I've managed my own garden plenty until you decided to take over the task." She fussed with the letter, folding it in three and slipping it back into the opened envelope. "Honestly, Lizzie. I don't know where you get such fanciful ideas from. Sometimes I suspect you think none of us could survive without you!"

Clearing her throat, Lizzie turned her attention back to the garden. "Well, we shall see whether or not that's true when I get back, I suppose."

Susan, however, hadn't heard her comment because she was already heading toward the barn, most likely to phone her aunt Leah to finalize arrangements, all the while mumbling about the matters required to prepare her daughter for an extended trip to Pinella Park.

Chapter Thirty-Eight

There was no denying the fact that it was lonely at the farm.

Besides being quiet—unnaturally so, he thought—there was very little interaction with anyone on a daily basis. Of course, he had workers on the farm during the week, but they were there to work, not socialize. And, of course, Grace Ann had returned from their cousins, but, during the week, she left early for school and, in the afternoon, upon her return, Grace Ann helped the hired woman, Ruth, with chores in the house.

There were times during the day that the loneliness seemed overwhelming and that realization surprised Phineas. He couldn't help but acknowledge that he missed the activity of Christopher's house on more than one occasion.

Even more surprising was the fact that Phineas often caught himself staring off into the distance, wondering what Lizzie was doing and where she might be at that very moment.

It had been almost a week since his return to Clearwater. He'd thrown himself into his work, rising early and working late into the evening. Exhausted, he'd collapse in bed at night, sometimes without even changing from his work clothes.

All of that, however, changed on Sunday.

With no unnecessary work permitted , none of his hired men on hand, Phineas found himself feeling lonely once again. Fortunately, it was a worship Sunday. He fell into step with the other men and listened intently to the sermons by the two preachers. If anything could make him forget, a good douse of Scripture would do it.

During the fellowship hour, he'd talked with the other men, regaling them with stories about Blue Mill and Christopher's farm. When he told several men about the storm, more than one ear eavesdropped on the conversation.

"So, Christopher's settling in quite nicely, eh?"

Phineas lifted his gaze from his plate to the meet the bishop's questioning eyes. "I'd say so. Cynthia, too."

The bishop nodded. "That's *gut*. *Gut* for them both. More opportunity there, I reckon. Jacob will be pleased, I'm sure."

Phineas had yet to speak to Christopher's father and, as far as he could tell, he hadn't attended worship that day. He made a mental note to swing by the Burkholders' farm later that week to update them about Christopher's efforts in Blue Mill.

"I received a letter from their church leaders this week past," the bishop said solemnly. "Appears that letters of recommendation are being asked for. Seems Christopher intends to become a permanent member of their *g'may*."

That didn't surprise Phineas. When a church member moved into a new church district, the leaders of the church always shared commendations of the individuals. And, from the way Christopher had taken to both Blue Mill *and* Jane Bender, it was only natural that he'd join their church district.

"I hear tell that there might be more than a farm that interests Christopher," another man said, a twinkle in his aging eyes as he tugged absentmindedly at his gray whiskers. "A certain young woman, eh?"

Phineas frowned. He wasn't prone to idle gossip and wouldn't let any man trick him into telling a tale out of turn. "Why am I not surprised that the Amish grapevine is alive and well, even at such a distance?"

The older man laughed and clapped Phineas on the back good naturedly. "That it is, *sohn*. That it is."

The bishop gave Phineas a sideways look. "What else do us old men have to look forward to," he said lightly, "but gossip to keep us entertained."

After the fellowship hour, Phineas began the short walk back to his farm, Grace Anne in tow. He noticed several young men driving open topped buggies down the road, undoubtedly going to fetch their girls for a Sunday afternoon drive in the beautiful spring weather. He felt a pang of envy as he watched them pass by.

If he were back in Blue Mill, he told himself, he'd probably have gone over to the Benders' farm to visit with Elizabeth. Perhaps he would have taken her for a drive in Christopher's buggy or for a long walk down the back lane of her father's farm.

He frowned, scolding himself for once again thinking of her.

Walking down the long driveway that led to the farmhouse, Phineas took in the long fencing that bordered both sides. His property was vast enough that he had large pastures on either side of the lane as well as behind the farmhouse and barn.

As they turned the corner of the drive and neared the house, the large windmill greeted them with a loud clanking noise as it spun. He'd never noticed how loud it was. In fact, he'd rarely given much thought to the windmill at all. For his entire life, it had just been there, working in the background, bringing water up from the well.

In the distance, the cows meandered through the pasture, grazing as they walked. Phineas paused by the fence-line and watched them. There was something he'd always loved about cows. Fortunately for him, the size of his farm meant that they almost always had green grass to graze upon. Some of the other farmers in the area weren't as fortunate and the cows often stood ankle deep in mud, especially after a good rain.

From behind the barn, Phineas thought he heard his dog barking—probably chasing a wood rat or squirrel. And in the distance, the sound of buggy wheels rumbling against the macadam grew louder as it approached before quieting as it continued past his farm.

It dawned on Phineas that, indeed, he was alone.

Being alone had never bothered him before, so it startled him that it bothered him now. What was it about the silence of the farm that didn't sit right with him? He couldn't put his finger on it, but he suspected it had plenty to do with Elizabeth.

How was it possible, he wondered, for a stranger to affect him so quickly and unexpectedly? He had left Blue Mill and thought to put Elizabeth out of his mind. And, still, as of today, he was still unsuccessful.

Perhaps, he thought, after so many years of focusing just on farming and not having any sort of personal life, he'd tasted a bit of what life could be like when shared with others. Oh, he always had Grace Ann to care for, that was true. But she was different. She was his younger sister, after all. He'd practically raised her after both of their parents passed away.

No, this was much different, and Phineas realized that he no longer wanted to be alone.

For today, however, he knew he had little choice. Quietly, he entered the house, determined to do what he could to focus on anything but Elizabeth Bender for the rest of the afternoon. Once the morning came, he knew he'd be able to throw himself back into his chores and that would occupy his mind for the entire day. Nights seemed to be the worst time. After supper was cleared and Grace Anne had gone to bed, he found the hours dragged on, thoughts of Elizabeth occupying his mind until he found sleep.

Chapter Thirty-Nine

"There you are!"

Lizzie almost stumbled as she rounded the corner of the plain white ranch house. It wasn't that the greeting startled her. No, it was the fact that the woman sitting in the rocking chair on the front porch could have been Lizzie's grandmothers twin. Lizzie couldn't help but take comfort in the familiar smile from the round and slightly weathered face that greeted her.

"Kum, kum! I was so very happy when Susan called me on Saturday," Leah said, waving her hand frantically toward the wooden rocking chair beside her, indicating that Lizzie should sit down. "Sit, sit, dear girl. Tell me everything! Was your drive unbearable?"

Taking the seat, Lizzie shook her head. "Nee, it was—" She hesitated, almost whispering *barely tolerable*, the thought of which almost made her smile. "—just fine, Leah. Just a tad under an hour or so."

Leah clucked her tongue, her eyes widening as if an hour was an excessive amount of time. "On my! An hour?"

Lizzie laughed at the response from her great-aunt. "*Less* than an hour. Honest."

"Well, thank goodness for those Englischers, willing to drive such a distance." Leah reached over and pressed her hand on Lizzie's arm. The touch of the older woman's skin on Lizzie's felt warm and soft, a comforting gesture that instantly made her feel as if she'd known Leah for her entire life. "And thank goodness for you, dear girl. I'm so tickled that you're here."

"I must admit I was surprised that you'd contacted us," Lizzie admitted. Surprised was an understatement. Her mother insisted that they'd met Leah, but Lizzie suspected it had been many years ago and she'd been far too young to remember. It had felt strange to travel so far at the request of a stranger, regardless of the fact she was related to the Bender family. "Whatever made you think to do so?"

Leah gave a little shrug. "I hadn't thought much about it. But when my *sohn* insisted that I move into his house after the surgery—" She made a face, adding in a low voice "—I may be old but I'm not so old that I can't be independent!—he only agreed that I could stay in my own home if I had some help. That's when someone mentioned your family."

If Leah had a son, Lizzie wondered, why didn't one of *his* children stay with her? The thought lingered on her mind but she didn't speak the words out loud.

"Much better to have a distant niece who won't pry and report back on all my coming and goings, don't you think?" she added with a wink that spoke of secret conspiracy.

Lizzie's eyes widened in surprise. "Coming and going? I was under the impression that you were immobile?"

"Pssh!" She waved her hand at Lizzie in a dismissive way. "Immobile sch-mobile. I'll be up and about in no time, child. You'll see. In fact, I've made plans for us to go visiting later this week. Certainly couldn't do *that* with one of my *sohn's kin* lingering about."

"Oh?"

"Indeed!"

Leah looked as satisfied as a cat having just fed on a barn mouse and, suddenly Lizzie thought she might have a grand time with her great aunt. Clearly Leah wasn't in need of a caretaker so much as a person to keep her company and, from the sound of it, keeping Leah company would be more fun than work.

"Who will we be visiting?"

"Why! There's a young woman who works on a farm nearby that I often visit. She's just the dearest woman. Tends to a young girl, Grace Anne, and her older *bruder*. Their parents passed on quite some time ago. I know the two of you will get on famously. We often sit outside on the porch and piece quilt tops while she's waiting for their supper to cook." Leah leaned over and whispered, "She makes the most delicious lemonade. And banana nut bread. Just you wait and see."

The way Leah's eyes lit up made Lizzie laugh. Her great-aunt had an abundance of energy and life exuding from her tiny frame, that was for sure and certain. "I can hardly wait. But perhaps I should go inside now and see about making you a nice supper, Leah. The sun's beginning to set and I'm sure you'd like something to eat."

"Would I?" Leah grinned, exposing a gaping hole in the side of her top teeth. The missing tooth gave her a comical look that only endeared her even more to Lizzie. "If you make chicken the way your *grossmammi* made, I'll be the happiest person in Pinella Park!"

Rising from her seat, Lizzie started across the porch, heading toward the front door. "Chicken it shall be, then," she said, "although I'm not about to make such a claim. Surely you'll be disappointed if you think my baked chicken could ever rival Mammi's!"

"Oh child, I doubt I'll be disappointed. Having someone else cook for me is such a delightful change that it could be burnt and tasteless and I'd still think it wonderful!"

Once again, Lizzie laughed. "Well, I can promise you it won't be burnt and certainly not tasteless."

Leah clapped her hands, her eyes sparkling. "Then we are off to a fabulous start, wouldn't you say, dear Lizzie?"

Chapter Forty

"Did you hear that Leah has a young woman staying with her?"

Phineas barely glanced up from his newspaper. He sat at the table, nursing a lukewarm coffee, as he read the Budget. There were updates from every Amish community throughout the country including some settlements in Mexico, Costa Rica, and Belize. But there was nothing in the paper about Blue Mill that week.

He found that rather odd.

"Phineas!"

Upon hearing her sharp voice, he set down the paper. "What's that, you say?"

Phineas's sister put her hand on her hip and gave him a look of exasperation. "Honestly, Phineas," she said in a teasing tone, "After being gone for so long, you'd think you might pay a bit more attention to me! The paper can most certainly wait, don't you think?"

Smiling at the well-deserved reprimand, Phineas folded the paper and slid it across the table. "Duly noted, my dear *schweister*. And my apologies." He reached for his coffee cup and lifted it to his lips. "Now, what were you saying?"

"Leah. She has a young girl staying with her until she's better. Ruth told me when I got home from school today."

He raised an eyebrow. "You don't say."

Grace Ann nodded. "Ruth said we should invite them over tomorrow to make cookies, if that's fine by you."

A smile broke the seriousness of his expression. "As if you need to ask. It's a *wunderbarr gut* idea, Grace Ann. You and Ruth always enjoy Leah's company, after all. And I'm sure it would do her good to leave the house after her surgery."

His sister picked up the coffee pot and carried it carefully over to the table, leaning down to top off his cup. "I thought so, too. Plus, it will be nice to meet the girl who's staying with her. Oh, I hope she's close to my age. It sure can get boring around here with no one to talk to."

Phineas watched as his sister returned the coffee pot to the stove. He'd missed her while he was away in Blue Mill. When she'd gone to stay with their cousins in the neighboring town, something she often did during the spring and summer months when he was busy with farm work, he hadn't realized how much he would miss her. Phineas felt that spending time with her aunt and cousins did Grace Ann good, a few weeks of female camaraderie that she lacked on their own farm.

Of course, throughout the year, Grace Ann often visited with John's mother, Leah. She was, in fact, a surrogate mother to the young woman. Phineas knew that young girls needed older women in their lives, just as young men needed older men. He often felt remorse that he could provide little more than shelter and food for his sister. His company was certainly lacking in the area of social graces, at least for the company of a young woman of fourteen years.

"Do you suppose you might go to the market today, then? We need chocolate chips for baking tomorrow."

Phineas tilted his head. "Me? I would think that Ruth and you could go."

Grace Ann laughed. "I suppose we could, but Ruth wants to take care of the laundry as it's a warm day and the sun's shining bright. And I'm not fancying that walk by myself."

"Ah ha." He tried to hide his smirk. "So, you wish me to *take* you, is that it?"

"Please, bruder?"

He feigned annoyance at her request, but the truth was he was secretly delighted that she'd asked. "I reckon that's possible."

"Oh *danke*!"

"We can leave momentarily," he said with a slight sigh as he started to get up from the table. "Besides, I've some errands in town anyway. I can drop you off at the market then fetch you when I'm done at the lumber yard."

She clapped her hands in delight, a broad smile lighting up her face. "Perfect! Then we must swing by Leah's on the way home so I can invite her and her guest to bake cookies tomorrow with us. I just knew this was going to be a right *gut* day when I woke this morning!"

He couldn't help but smile at her enthusiasm. There was always something joyous about Grace Ann. She saw the good in everyone and the light in all circumstances. Her attitude was always contagious, and, for that, he enjoyed being in her company twice as much.

Despite their difference in age, they'd always gotten along quite well, even if he sometimes adopted the role of parent as opposed to sibling. Now, however, he could see that their month apart had contributed to her maturity. Gone was the starry-eyed young teenager that he'd said goodbye to a month ago and, in her place, a budding young woman had returned.

Phineas wasn't certain he was prepared for *that* change, yet.

"And, of course, you can tell me all about Blue Mill on our ride over there," Grace Ann gushed as she hurried to take his coffee cup over to the sink. Quickly, she washed it, the sound of the water from the faucet almost drowning out her words. "And I can tell you all about my time with Aendi Doris. What a lively household that is!"

Phineas chuckled to himself. "I can only imagine," he replied, pleased to see some of her youthful enthusiasm return. Perhaps she hadn't matured *too* much after all.

Quietly, he disappeared into the downstairs bedroom to freshen up. Having done chores earlier, his shirt was soiled so he changed into a plain, short sleeved white shirt. He certainly wouldn't go visiting in anything that wasn't properly clean and fresh. After buttoning the shirt, he ran a brush through his hair and glanced into the small mirror over the dresser. For a moment, he barely recognized himself. Where did his sister get her magnetic nature from? He, himself, was more prone to being stoic and serious. In some ways, his sister reminded him of Lizzie, although Grace Ann was obviously much more youthful and excitable about everything.

Just the thought of Lizzie made Phineas smile.

"Are you ready?" Grace Ann called out from the kitchen.

"Ja, I'm ready." He reached for his straw hat that hung from a peg on the wall next to the dresser. Carefully, he placed it on his head and, with one last look in the mirror, nodded. "That'll do," he mumbled and, with the hint of a smile on his lips, turned toward the door. "Coming, Grace Ann."

Chapter Forty-One

Driving the small cart down the long driveway, Lizzie couldn't help but stare at the enormous fields that flanked the lane. Leah, however, continued to prattle on about this and that, oblivious to Lizzie's shock that such a large farm could be owned by an Amish family.

The mule, an older chestnut with a thinning tail, plodded along, its large hooves plunking down with a loud thud as it walked slowly toward the pristine white farmhouse and large dairy barn.

"Ruth and Grace Ann both love springtime," Leah said. "Sitting on the porch is one of our favorite pastimes." She lifted her hand and pointed. "There! See? They've already set out the rocking chairs and refreshments. Such a darling young girl, Grace Ann is!"

Lizzie didn't care half as much about the lemonade or banana bread as she did about the unbelievable condition of the farm. Not one fence board was broken or chipped. There was barely a hint of any weeds growing along the fence line, too. And it was clear that the many fields were growing acres and acres of corn, hay and alfalfa.

"My word," she mumbled. "How many children do they have to work this land?"

"Oh, no children."

Lizzie gasped. "No children?"

"The man isn't married and Grace Ann is too young yet to court. But they've hired help," Leah said. "One small family cannot manage such a large farm. Ruth helps with the inside chores and there are several young farm hands who help with running such a large place."

Lizzie wanted to ask another question but, before the words could form on her lips, she heard a happy welcome cheer from the open doorway of the house.

"Leah! You've come! I was so worried about you!"

To Lizzie's surprise, it wasn't a young woman at all who bounded through the doorway and down the porch steps. It was a girl, perhaps the same age as her own sister, Katie.

She was a lithe girl, perhaps fourteen or fifteen years of age. Her face was framed with blond hair that gave the impression of a pretty halo beneath her prayer kapp. She wore a turquoise dress that, unlike Lizzie's, was clearly newly made. And yet, she wore no shoes and a small cloud of dust rose from beneath her feet as she ran to greet the visitors. It almost made her appear as if she were floating instead of walking.

"How *are* you feeling?" Grace Ann asked, her attention completely focused on Leah.

"Oh, fine, fine," Leah said. She started to swing her leg down so that she could exit the cart. "Thanks to my great niece, Lizzie here, that is."

Grace Ann glanced at Lizzie and smiled. "Why, I've heard so much about you!"

"You have?"

"Of course! I was terribly upset that I didn't get to meet you yesterday when my *bruder* and I stopped over," the young woman said, a smile still on her face and her eyes glowing. "But I heard all about you."

Lizzie gave a soft laugh. She'd heard about Grace Ann's visit the previous day after she'd returned from bicycling to town to fetch some groceries. While disappointed that she hadn't been there to meet Leah's neighbor, Lizzie had been excited to learn that they'd been invited to bake cookies at Grace Ann's farm the next day.

Grace Ann slipped her arm through Lizzie's. "I just know we will be the fastest of friends," she gushed. "We will make cookies today and then we can talk while they are baking. Ruth and I want to hear everything about Blue Mill and your family."

"I thought you said you heard all about me?" Lizzie teased. "If that is the case, what else is there to know?"

Grace Ann laughed. "I heard you had a witty sense of humor!"

Lizzie frowned. Where would she have heard that?

"Now, *kum*, Lizzie and Leah. Ruth has everything ready for us to get started. I think chocolate chip cookies are in order for today, ja?"

Inside the house, Lizzie let her eyes adjust to the darkness. The dark green window shades were pulled down, creating a dimness in the room that was broken by the thin sliver of light coming through the bottom half.

Ruth turned around from the sink where she was scrubbing potatoes for the evening meal and nodded at them both. "Ah, Leah you look as though your managing well."

"Ja. Thanks to the help of Lizzy, here. She's been *wunderbarr* with me."

Grace Ann hurried over to the one window and raised the shade. "Keeps it cooler, you know," she said as a way of explaining. "The afternoon sun can make the kitchen rather warm."

Lizzie said hello to Ruth then helped Leah over to the table so that she could sit down on the bench. Grace Ann immediately started carrying mixing bowls and baking sheets to the table. She laid out the different ingredients before Leah, chattering away as she worked.

"Oh help!"

Lizzie looked up in time to see Leah stumble, the bowl of eggs she was carrying fell to the floor. She jumped up to fetch a rag from Ruth then started to clean up the shattered eggs, the broken yolks seeping in between the floorboards.

"How clumsy of me," Grace Ann muttered. A frown was etched in her forehead and she shook her head in disbelief. "Everything was so perfect and look at this mess now."

Leah reached over and patted Grace Ann's shoulder. "Now, now, dear. It's just some broken eggs."

"I'll have to fetch more from the coop," she said.

Lizzie stepped toward the door. "I'll do that. If you just point me in the right direction, that is. That way you can spend more time with Leah."

Once outside the house, Lizzie took a deep breath. Ruth seemed very kind and organized. It seemed she had her hands full tending to that large house with only the help of a young girl. And, Grace Ann was a bundle of energy, that was for sure and certain. There was something familiar about her, something that Lizzie couldn't quite put her finger on. It was as if she practiced perfection and chastised herself when she fell short.

Despite Grace Ann's tendency toward perfection, Lizzie found that she liked the young girl. She was refreshingly youthful and enthusiastic. In some ways, she reminded Lizzie of a younger version of herself.

Lizzie crossed the barnyard toward the chicken coop. It was next to the stable and the chickens were scattered in the yard, scratching at the dirt and pecking at bugs. Quietly, so that she wouldn't alert the rooster who, from the looks of his spurs, wouldn't have given a second thought of chasing her away, Lizzie slipped around the back of the coop and lifted the hatch in the laying boxes. Sure enough, there were more eggs nestled in the fresh hay.

She lifted the edge of her apron and tucked the eggs safely in the center. Six eggs, one that appeared to have a double yolk. Carefully, she carried them back into the house, using her shoulder to hold open the screen door so that she could pass through without letting go of the edge of her apron.

Immediately, she froze. There was a voice coming from the kitchen, a voice that she recognized at once.

Phineas.

He must have sensed her presence for he stopped talking and turned toward the door. From where he stood in the shadows, she could barely make out his tall form and broad shoulders. But she'd have known that voice anywhere.

"Elizabeth."

He stepped toward her, a beaming smile on his face.

For a second, she almost dropped the apron and, with it, the eggs, but she caught herself just in time.

"Phineas." His name came out like a small poof of air. She could scarcely believe that he stood before her. "Wh-what are you doing here?"

He gave a soft laugh, the deep sound far more relaxed than it ever sounded in Blue Mill. "Why, I live here."

Stunned, Lizzie blinked her eyes rapidly as she tried to make sense of what he'd just told her. "But you live in Clearwater."

He laughed again and gestured with his hand in a sweeping circle. "This is Clearwater."

Lizzie's eyes darted to Leah. "But you live in Pinella Park."

Leah clucked her tongue and made a face. "Oh child, you really do need to leave Blue Mill a bit more often, I fear. Pinella Park is the village *next* to Clearwater. In fact, my house is on the county line, one of the last in Lower Austen County. When you cross the street to Upper Austen County."

She didn't intend to gasp, but she did. Lizzie could barely comprehend what she'd just heard. Leah lived next to Phineas? With her mouth hanging open, Lizzie couldn't speak, even as Grace Ann hurried over to fetch the eggs from her apron.

"Who did you think told me all about you?" Grace Ann said teasingly. "My *bruder*, that's who. Why, he's the one who suggested that you come stay with Leah."

Lizzie's eyes widened. "What?"

Leah gave a delighted laugh, clearly pleased with Lizzie's reaction and the fact that she hadn't known about Phineas's involvement in the arrangement. "Why! He learned of our relation and suggested that you might be a good caretaker. Did you not know?"

Clearly, she had not.

Phineas crossed the room and stood before Lizzie. It was all she could do to keep from staring up at him, stunned by this turn of events. "I didn't think to forewarn you," he said softly. "For that, I'm sorry."

"Why wouldn't you have said something?" she whispered, too aware that Leah and Grace Ann were pretending to busy themselves with the task of cracking the eggs into the bowl while Ruth was mashing the potatoes for supper.

"Perhaps for fear that you wouldn't have come," he replied in an equally soft voice. His eyes drifted over toward the other three women. "*Kum*, Elizabeth. Let me show you around the farm, ja?" He didn't wait for an answer. Instead, he took her elbow in hand and guided her back to the door she'd just walked through.

Words escaped her and she struggled to regain her composure. It was unfathomable to her that she stood beside Phineas, here and now. And he had not only known about her presence in his town, but he had arranged it.

She wasn't certain if she was irritated by the duplicity or pleased by the surprise.

They walked toward the large dairy barn in silence, the only noise being the gravel of the driveway under their shoes. A large black dog lounged in a sunny patch of grass. It barely lifted its head as they passed by.

"You left without saying goodbye," Lizzie said at last.

"I did."

She peered at him. "Why?"

"Sometimes goodbyes are too hard to say," he admitted.

"That wasn't very kind," she scolded.

"Were you saddened by that, then?" His eyes widened and he appeared genuinely interested in her answer.

Lizzie stopped walking. "I...I will confess that I was saddened, Phineas. I felt rather distraught about how our last time together at the work party turned out. I behaved rather poorly when I spoke so sharply to you."

He stood before her; his hands clasped behind his back. "I'd like to think that your words gave way to some unspoken emotion, Elizabeth."

She raised an eyebrow.

"Perhaps frustration at the circumstances," he continued. "And maybe disappointment that I would be returning to Clearwater." He glanced around, a distant expression on his face. "Of course, I would be dishonorable if I didn't admit to feeling the same sense of loss, Elizabeth." He met her gaze once more. "Perhaps that is why I left without saying goodbye."

"And yet you suggested that I come help Leah."

He nodded. "That is true."

"Why?"

He moistened his lips and gazed up at the sky for a long, drawn out moment. She could tell that he was collecting his thoughts, trying to find the right words to express himself. Finally, he took a deep breath and sighed. "Because I wanted to see you again, Elizabeth. Here. On my territory, without your family around or my having to deal with Christopher and his *schweister*. A new place for us to continue getting to know one another without interruption." He paused before he met her steady eye once again. "I confess that I've found it *barely tolerable* being so far from you."

His words caught her off-guard and she lifted her hand to cover her mouth as she laughed.

"Barely tolerable?"

"Moderately endurable, if that," he replied in a light tone, a gleam in his eyes. "And it would please me greatly if I knew that you might have felt the same way."

She pursed her lips and glanced away from him, feeling shy and coy at the same time. When she'd woken that morning, she'd never have suspected such a delightful surprise as this. Standing before Phineas, on his very farm, and hearing him speak such sweet words to her was truly wonderful.

She swung her hips a bit, feeling young and carefree. It was nervous energy that propelled her to give a quick little nod. "Ja, I own that, Phineas. I, too, felt that it was barely tolerable—" She laughed. "—when I knew you were gone, especially without saying goodbye."

His lips curved into a smile and he reached out, gently brushing his finger across her cheek as if smoothing back a loose strand of hair. The touch of his finger on her skin sent a delightful chill up her spine.

"I apologize for that," he said, dropped his hand and lightly caressing her bare arm. "Let's take a walk a spell, then. I would like nothing more than to show you my farm."

She fell into step beside him. At that moment, she couldn't imagine anything she would have preferred doing more than accompanying Phineas on such a tour. With the sun shining overhead and the birds chirping from the treetops, it had turned into an unexpectedly perfect day.

Chapter Forty-Two

How was it possible that so much could change in such a short order of time?

Almost every day for the rest of the week, Phineas spent his free time with Elizabeth. Whether she was over at the house with Grace Ann and Ruth, baking bread or making desserts, or whether he was dining at Leah's house, Phineas quickly realized that there was a routine developing.

Even more importantly, he noticed that she was far more relaxed in his company than she'd been in Blue Mill.

Perhaps it was the proximity of her family that had made her more reserved, but now that she was away from them, he sensed a whole new side to the young woman.

And he enjoyed getting to know this new Elizabeth Bender as much as he had the previous one.

On the days when he knew she was visiting with his sister, Phineas found himself seeking out her company. He enjoyed sitting in the kitchen and watching Lizzie and Grace Ann. They laughed and teased each other mercilessly, almost like sisters. Sometimes they even did baking competitions and, as a matter of course, Phineas was always the judge.

Of course, he never picked one recipe over the other, too worried about hurting one of their feelings, which made Grace Ann scowl and Lizzie laugh. But it was all in good fun and with the best of intentions.

On Saturday, Phineas managed to sneak away from the farm—and Grace Ann!—to entice Lizzie to leave Leah for a few hours.

"Oh, I'm not so sure," Lizzie fretted, looking over her shoulder at her great aunt. She was resting in a reclining chair, her feet propped up against the footrest. "She's been awfully achy today. I think she overdid it yesterday when I was working in the garden."

Phineas leaned against the kitchen counter. "If you were working in the garden, what could she possibly have overdone?"

"Telling me what to do!" Lizzie said laughingly. "I've never seen anyone so fastidious about their garden." She paused, tapping her finger against the side of her head. "Well, anyone besides me, I reckon."

"I heard that!"

Lizzie blushed at the sound of the older woman's voice behind her.

Leah waved her hand dismissively. "Now you go on, Lizzie. I'll be just fine. Besides, it's a beautiful day for a picnic and, if I know Phineas, he's packed a basket full of goodies."

"Are you sure?"

Phineas didn't wait for Leah to answer. Instead, he grabbed her wrist and gently tugged her toward the door. "She said it was fine," he said in a low voice. "And she's right. I have a *wunderbarr* basket full of goodies!"

He drove her away from Pinella Park and deep into Clearwater. Not far from his farm was a large pond that, indeed, had water so blue that it was, in fact, crystal clear. The banks of the pond were vibrant green, the grass disappearing into the edge of the water. A large weeping willow tree hung over the east side of the pond, its wispy branches barely brushing the surface and causing little ringlets to cascade across the glasslike surface.

He stopped the horse near the hitching post. For a Saturday, there was surprisingly no one at the pond. Usually someone would be fishing, or a couple might walk hand-in-hand around the pond. But today, they were all alone.

"It's beautiful here," she said, her voice breathless. "I don't think we've a park like this in Blue Mill."

"A hidden treasure," he said. "Just one of many in Clearwater."

She gave him a teasing smile. "Oh? And what are the others?"

He shifted the basket on his arm and guided her toward the weeping willow. He'd spread the blanket out under its shade, where they could relax and enjoy their treats. "Well, I'd like to think that my farm was another."

She laughed. "Oh ja? A hidden treasure?"

He shrugged. "Mayhaps not so hidden, but a treasure nonetheless."

She leaned her head against his shoulder as they walked. "I will agree to that," she admitted. "Your farm is definitely a pearl when compared to others."

Phineas stopped walking. "Do you really think so, Elizabeth?"

She turned to face him. "I do. It's clear that you take great care of your farm. It's an admirable quality."

He wondered if she thought about her own father's farm with the unpainted buildings and broken fences.

"So, you like it here?" he asked as they stopped under the shade of the tree where he had spread the blanket. "Let's sit awhile." Phineas opened the basket and pulled out a thermos of meadow tea and a smaller basket of muffins.

"Oh, ja! How could anyone not like it here? Leah is delightful. Grace Ann is loads of fun. And you..." She paused, tilting her head as she studied him.

"What about me?" he asked, his breath catching in his throat.

"You're different, Phineas." She pursed her lips as if deep in thought. "More relaxed. More..." She frowned. "More you."

"More me," he repeated softly. "I've never been described as being 'more me' before."

She laughed. "I mean, it's just nice to see this side of you. It's pleasant."

"Pleasant," he repeated her words again.

She swatted at his arm as she crossed her legs and leaned against the trunk of the tree. "You mock me." The color flooded to her cheeks and she averted her gaze.

He delighted in teasing her, in making her blush. And, while he watched her cheeks slowly return to their normal tone, he knew that making her flush like that was something he wanted to do more often.

Chapter Forty-Three

"I suppose I'm feeling well enough for you to return to Blue Mill," Leah said with a sigh. "But oh! How I wish that wasn't so. These have been the most pleasant two weeks in recent memory."

Lizzie looked up from the sampler she was quilting and stared at Leah, startled by her announcement.

It was Saturday evening, one week after the picnic she'd had with Phineas. Every day since had brought her new surprises and all of them wonderfully executed by Phineas. Flowers left on the seat of a rocking chair one morning greeted her when she went outside to feed the horse. Another day, she found a new bird feeder hanging from a shepherd's hook outside the kitchen window, an addition that delighted both Leah and Lizzie.

With every day bringing the most romantic and thoughtful of gestures, leaving Pinella Park had been the furthest thing from Lizzie's mind. And yet, she knew that she couldn't avoid the inevitable. Leah *was* improving and Lizzie *needed* to return to Blue Mill.

"Oh." She bent her head back to focus on her quilting. "I see."

Leah reached over and patted Lizzie's arm. "I suspect you'll miss more than just me when you leave."

Lizzie blushed and tried to maintain her composure. "I'm sure I don't know what you are talking about."

Laughing, Leah leaned back in her chair. "Oh Child! I'm old enough to have seen the melting of two hearts many times over." She wagged her finger at Lizzie. "You can't fool me."

Clearly, she was referring to the attentions Phineas was bestowing on her and the fact that Lizzie was obviously enjoying every moment of them.

Feeling uncomfortable, Lizzie averted her eyes. The bright smile on Leah's face spoke of her pleasure in witnessing the budding romance. But, for Lizzie, the situation felt too intimate to share with anyone, especially her great-aunt.

It was as if Leah could read her mind. "Now, Elizabeth, did you really think I didn't know his intentions from the moment Phineas suggested that I contact Susan about her *dochders*—"

Immediately, Lizzie frowned and looked up. "You knew?"

The expression on Lizzie's face must have delighted Leah for she clapped her hands together, an apparent expression of joy at the secret she had just uncovered.

"Why of course, Lizzie," Leah continued. "He'd just returned from Blue Mill and, when my John mentioned I needed help at home, it was your Phineas who suggested I contact Susan. I knew he had to be sweet on one of you girls."

"I...I had no idea," Lizzie managed to sputter, still surprised that Leah had been able to figure out that he had an ulterior motive. The good fortune of Clearwater being the neighboring town of Pinella Park was obviously God's hand at work.

Unbeknownst by her, he must have already known there was a distant connection between Leah and Lizzie when he'd encouraged her to take the opportunity travel to other parts of the State? Had he already formed this plan before he left for home?

She moved away from Leah and walked toward the large window that looked over the back of the property. Not far in the distance, the border of Phineas's property could be viewed, the crisp freshness of new fencing cutting across another neighbor's field.

When he hadn't appeared surprised to see her in his kitchen, she couldn't help but wonder why he had gone to such great lengths when he could have stayed in Blue Mill a bit longer to court her. It was more than obvious that he had enough helpers at his own farm to stay away a bit longer.

And yet, Lizzie realized that he may have had an ulterior motive after all.

Being in Clearwater, away from her family and obligations, Lizzie had been able to spend uninterrupted time with Phineas in a much more casual setting.

"My, my," Lizzie said softly. "What a thoughtful suggestion for Phineas to make."

"I do agree," Leah said. "But now what will happen? With my knee better, you'll be returning to Blue Mill." She gave a forlorn sigh. "Whatever will Phineas do now?"

Hearing those words from her great-aunt's lips made Lizzie feel as if her stomach flip-flopped. It hadn't sunk in yet that, indeed, she'd be leaving Clearwater with no excuse to return.

Swallowing, Lizzie nodded slowly. "That is true."

"Soon, I imagine?" Leah made a fuss looking at her calendar. "I reckon we could call a car for Monday afternoon or Tuesday morning."

Something in the distance caught Lizzie's eye. It was the movement of a long figure wearing a dark brown coat and brown hat. She squinted, trying to force her eyes to focus, but the person was too far away to make out who it was.

The sun was setting over the western tree line, the sky already turning a brilliant dark orange that was fading to red and purple. Dusk was setting in. Surely that was Phineas inspecting his fence line as his workers would have returned home for the evening. After all, tomorrow was a church Sunday which meant rising early to hurry through chores before worship service.

Without tearing her eyes from the figure in the distance, Lizzie could barely speak. "Aendi, will you excuse me for a few minutes?" she breathed.

"Why of course," Leah said, an expression of curiosity mixed with concern etched on her weathered face. "Go, if you must. I'm fine here by myself."

Lizzie tore herself from the window and managed to pause long enough to smile at her great-aunt. "Danke, Leah."

And then, without further delay, she hurried to the hallway, paused for her shawl which she carelessly threw over her shoulders, then raced out the door.

She needed to talk to Phineas, to tell him that nothing was driven by fate but by his own doing and by the grace of God. Oh, how the knowledge that Phineas had arranged all of this way back when—and hadn't wanted her to know!—warmed her heart. And she couldn't let one more minute pass without letting him know that.

Chapter Forty-Four

Walking along the fence line, he eyed the wire with barely any concern. He'd always made it a habit of walking the property line on Saturday evenings, checking to ensure that no cows could stray away when he was shorthanded. Tomorrow would be a day of worship so no hired hands would be able to help should a cow or two get through.

Rarely were there any breaks in the wire and tonight was no different.

But he'd needed to take that walk, to escape the house, so that he could collect his thoughts.

Earlier that afternoon, Grace Ann had lamented that Leah's condition had improved enough that Lizzie would surely return to Blue Mill within days. It wasn't something he'd considered, especially after spending so much time in her presence over the past week.

Something had changed at the picnic a few days prior. It was as if they had become one person, Phineas uncertain where he ended, and she began. Days became endless until he was in her company again, and when they were apart, her memory never strayed more than a few seconds from his mind.

At night, he couldn't sleep. At meals, he couldn't eat. The only time he felt remotely alive was when she was beside him.

He paused at the back gate, his hand on the wood as his eyes trailed across the field in the direction of Leah's house.

Barely, in the distance, could he make out the small form walking in his direction. At first, it was all he could do to hold his breath, hopeful that, perhaps, it might be her.

When he realized that his hope might turn to fruition, he was quick to unlatch the gate and start walking in her direction.

Overhead, the sky was a painter's mix of colors—red, orange, purple, and blue. The lone figure that approached him appeared larger with each step. Not once did he remove his eyes from that form.

And then, at last, she stood before him.

"Elizabeth."

She peered at him from soft eyes. "Phineas."

Hesitantly, he reached out his hand and pushed the white string of her prayer kapp over her shoulder. In her rush to get to him, she must have forgotten to tie them. He smiled at her negligence which hinted that, mayhaps, she was feeling as anxious as he.

"I...I'll be returning to Blue Mill this week," she said quietly.

"You don't appear to be keen about that," he replied softly.

Her lips parted and she stared up at him. For a moment, it appeared as though she would say something but, then, she seemed to reconsider her words. She swallowed and looked away. "How could I be, Phineas?"

"Your family—"

"My family," she cut him off and gave a little laugh. "Family is where your heart is and my heart—" She shifted her gaze to him once again. "—is not in Blue Mill any longer."

Oh! How his heart rejoiced upon hearing those words. Once again, he reached out, but this time, he brushed his thumb along her cheek, noticing that she shut her eyes and leaned her head against his hand as if demanding that he keep his fingers on her flesh.

"It's not?" he questioned hesitantly.

"Nee, it's not."

This time, it was Phineas who had to swallow. The words lingered on his tongue, but he felt hard-pressed to say them. How many times had he repeated them to himself? Practicing within his head?

"I...I suppose I should ask where your heart resides," he started. "But I suspect I already know the answer."

She made a soft sound that caused him to flush.

"Then I suppose, Elizabeth, there is only one thing left to discuss."

Her eyes fluttered up and she gazed up at him. "And what would that be, Phineas?"

What would you think about—" He stopped midsentence, feeling unnerved under her steady gaze. How could she be so composed at a moment when he felt so out of control? "Well, perhaps this is too forward—"

"Go on," she coaxed.

"—but I would like to know if you might—"

"If I might what?" she said softly.

He jerked his hand away from her face and clutched his hands behind his back as he began to pace. "I can't do this. It's just too difficult."

"What's too difficult?"

"You. Me." He dropped his arms to his side. "Oh Elizabeth, from the very day I first saw you, walking along the road toward the church, I was struck by your poise and beauty. And even though I claimed you were nothing more than barely tolerable—"

Lizzie grimaced.

"—I can assure you that now the only thing I find intolerable is not having you in my life." He stopped pacing and sighed. "There. I have said it," he said, exasperation thick in his voice. "Now it is up to you to wound me with your rejection or save me with your consent."

For a long moment, Lizzie sat there, staring up at him as if contemplating his words. Neither spoke, the delay only agonizing Phineas even more. But, at long last, she reached out and took his hand in hers, her head tilted so that she could peer up into his face, he felt complete.

"Phineas, if that is your way of asking me to marry you," she said softly, "then I save you with my consent." She squeezed his hand then gently ran her thumb across the back of his knuckles, her eyes searching his face. "I, too, find the thought of being without you barely tolerable," she whispered before leaning forward to brush her lips against his fingers. "It seems we are quite the pair; don't you think?"

Something in her voice cracked and he was surprised to see tears welling in her eyes. He reached up and lightly brushed them away.

"Honest and true?" he asked.

"Honest and true."

Once again, he swallowed and then, after a quick glance around to ensure that they were alone, he leaned down and let his lips meet hers for a moment.

Epilogue

Fall arrived late in Clearwater that year. Lizzie didn't much mind for she enjoyed the changing colors of the trees far more than she did the bare gray skeletons of winter that dotted the horizon after the last leaves fell.

She could scarcely believe that it had already been six months since she'd married Phineas. Just the week before, they'd returned to Blue Mill for another wedding, that of Jane and Christopher. It had been held at the Bender farm and would not be the only wedding of the autumn season for, in two more weeks, the Burkholders would host a wedding of their own to celebrate Cynthia's marriage to Jacob.

Oh, how everything had worked itself out!

Now, as Lizzie stood by the fence, leaning her arms against it, she watched Phineas approaching her, his straw hat tipped back on his head and a wide smile on his face.

"*Wie gehts?*" he asked, standing opposite her. He leaned against the top board and let his hand cover hers. "Feeling well?"

She nodded. "Well enough, ja."

Phineas glanced down at her growing stomach. "Is the boppli still so active, then?"

Lizzie flushed and rested her free hand on her belly. At five months, the growing baby was, indeed, keeping her on her toes. "*Ja*, he sure is. I tried to nap earlier but he was of a different mindset."

Phineas laughed. "I never was one for napping."

"So, I blame you then," she teased.

He reached up and stroked the growing beard that covered his chin. "I reckon you must," Phineas said softly. "He's clearly taking after his *daed*. Unless, of course, he's a she."

"Oh, *nee!*" she said with a shake of her head. "No girl could move about as much as this *boppli*! It's definitely a son, for sure and certain."

He laughed, and glancing around to make certain no one was watching, leaned forward to tenderly kiss her lips. "A boy is *gut*," he whispered, his breath sweet and warm on her face. "But I'd welcome a girl just as well."

Dropping his hand, he let his fingers brush against the front of her dress. She shivered and smiled, delighted that Phineas took such interest in the unborn child. His attention to her comfort was only second to her desire to please him.

"I've made your favorite meal," she said. "Grace Ann is setting the table already if you're hungry soon."

"Chicken fried steak and mashed potatoes?"

Lizzie beamed at his pleasure. "And homemade buttermilk biscuits with creamed green beans."

Quickly, he climbed the fence and jumped down beside her. "Why, Elizabeth, I fear you'll fatten me like a veal calf for market!" He held her hand for a few steps and then, casually, took a step further apart from her in case any of the working men were lingering about.

"Oh, I think not," she countered. "The way you work, I could feed you six meals a day and I suspect you'd barely gain a pound!" Her hand fell back to her stomach. "I think I gain them all for you, anyway."

They fell into step together, Phineas occasionally brushing his arm against hers. It was hard for him to keep distance from her, but the anticipation of them being alone later, of holding her in his arms in the darkness of their room, quenched his desire. Oh, if he could wrap his arms around her and breathe in the sweet scent of lavender from her skin all day and night long, he would. She made him feel as close to heaven on earth as any man could be.

He followed her up the porch steps and held open the door. Before she slipped under his arm, he reached for her hand once again and, gently, pulled her back toward him. Slowly, he leaned down and let his lips touch hers once more.

"I love you, Elizabeth Denner."

She smiled. "And I you, Phineas Denner."

Together, they passed through the doorway, the screen door quietly shutting behind them. In the distance, a yellow bird landed atop the bird feeder just beyond the kitchen window. It jumped from perch to perch, pausing to chirp before dipping its beak into the feeder for some seed.

The sun lowered further behind the trees and the sky began to fade to a darker shade of red, the hint of a bright orange glow piercing through sections of the woods that had already lost most of their leaves.

The loveliness of the evening air on the farm was only surpassed by the love within the Denner household, a hint of which could be seen through the kitchen window in the glow of the propane lantern that lit up the room within.

Esther's Quilt

Book Five of the Amish Quilts of Indiana Series

Releasing June 2020
Preorder now on Amazon.com.

Chapter One

If there was one thing that Esther Raber couldn't tolerate, it was being late.

As a child, she hated being late for school. As a teenager, she despised being late for youth gatherings. But the number one thing she absolutely could not stomach, besides being tardy for church, was being late for work.

In the mornings, she rose at five-thirty so she could be in the kitchen helping her mother prepare breakfast by ten minutes to six. On worship Sundays, she made certain she was ready to leave the house by seven-fifteen sharp. And when it came to her job on the outskirts of Shipshewana, she *always* arrived ten minutes early.

Well, almost always.

In the three years that she'd been working at her uncle's grocery store just north of town, she could count on one hand how many times she'd arrived after her official starting time. Today, however, would make it her *sixth* time and that meant she now needed two hands to count the days that she had been tardy. And that wasn't *any* way to start a Monday.

"Mamm! I really need to get going," she called out. She stood in the kitchen with her arms crossed over the front of her royal blue dress. It wasn't like her mother to have waited until the last minute to tell her something as important as this. If anything, her mother *knew* how fastidious Esther was about being on time. But, for whatever reason, Miriam had forgotten, or worse yet, didn't care, and now she seemed to be moving in slow motion on purpose.

In her mind, Esther tried calculating how long this unexpected errand would *truly* take her. An extra fifteen minutes? Maybe twenty? Swallowing, she pushed her glasses back on the bridge of her nose and glanced at the clock. Maybe if she rode her bicycle extra fast, she thought, she could make up for lost time and wouldn't be as late after all.

"Just a minute, Esther," her mother replied from the basement, her voice muffled by the stone walls of the cellar.

Esther could hear her mother pushing aside boxes from the deep shelves that lined the storage room as if she were looking for something. What on earth could be taking her so long? The way her mother kept everything so organized and tidy, whatever she needed should've been right at her fingertips.

Come on, come on, Esther thought, tapping the toe of her black shoe against the wide boarded floor. Her eyes shifted from the open door that led down to the basement pantry to the clock that hung on the far wall. It was almost seven-forty-five. She was supposed to be at the store by eight-thirty and, with her mother insisting that she stop by her aunt's house beforehand, *that* would never happen.

"I'm going to be late. Really late," she called out, emphasizing the word 'really.'

Her mother didn't respond. Esther wasn't sure if she'd even heard her. But, thankfully, a few seconds later, the sound of footsteps on the old wooden stairs meant that her mother was finally finished fishing around for whatever she sought.

Emerging from the darkness, her mother carried two Tupperware containers. "There. That didn't take so long, now, did it? And Mary will be so appreciative. You know how she is."

Inwardly, Esther groaned. Did her aunt really need those containers returned *today*? It wasn't as if her aunt didn't have *other* containers or, while not as practical, plastic storage bags. "*Ja*, I know. But what I don't know is why this has to be done *before* work. Can't it wait until later this evening?"

Her mother shuffled across the floor, her bare feet making a soft scraping noise as she walked. "I told you before, Esther. Mary's attending a quilting party this afternoon."

Esther shut her eyes, trying to keep her heart from pounding so fast. Already her hands were sweaty and her breath labored. She'd forgotten that her mother had mentioned this the previous week. It had been a comment in passing, nothing that Esther had even thought to register as important, but she had told her none the less. Her elderly aunt was known for being very social in the community, so it wasn't a surprise. At least not to Esther.

But what her mother had failed to mention, was that old aunt Mary needed those two Tupperware containers for the quilting party. Today.

"I certainly didn't *think* it was a big deal. And, it's not as though she needs these containers with all the plastic baggies and paper bags she has stuffed under her kitchen cabinet, anyway."

"Esther Raber!" Her mother gave her a shocked look. "I don't approve of that tone. She's family!"

"Sorry, Mamm." Well. *That* comment helped refocus her a bit. She wasn't usually short or sassy with her mother...or anyone for that matter. "I just hate being late for work, is all."

A quick smile from her mother told Esther that her apology was accepted.

"I know, Esther. It is a bit inconvenient for you. But Mary only called me last night about those containers." She leveled her gaze at Esther. "You know how she forgets things so easily and she was in quite a panic."

Like I am now, Esther wanted to say, but she didn't want to push her luck with her mother. "Panicked about two plastic Tupperware containers?"

Her mother smiled. "*Ja,* for two Tupperware containers. You know how she gets."

Anxious, Esther thought. *Like me.*

With every nerve in her body at attention, Esther watched as her mother moved over to the sink and began to wash the dust off the containers. For some reason, her mother seemed to be moving slower than usual this morning.

"Want me to do that?"

Her mother shook her head without turning around to look at Esther. "*Nee*, Dochder. But *danke* for the offer." Shutting off the faucet, her mother reached for a hand towel and wiped the little beads of water from the outside of each container. "There. Now you can take them over."

Esther hurried across the floor, but before she could grab them, her mother gave her a stern look.

"Don't be rushing out of Mary's without spending a few minutes visiting with her," her mother said slowly. "You know how lonely she is."

Esther took a deep breath—she found *that* hard to believe. "Mary? Lonely? She's the first one to volunteer to help anyone and everyone."

Her mother put her hand on her hip. "That's *not* what I meant, Esther. She lives all alone and she misses visiting with people."

While she wondered how her mother actually knew that to be true, she remained silent on the matter. Instead, she nodded. "Okay. I promise I won't rush, Mamm."

Two years ago, Mary's husband had died. With all of her children grown and married—and all but one of them living in other counties—Mary was definitely alone more often than not. The previous autumn, Esther's parents had encouraged her to move into the empty *dawdihaus* on their property, but Mary refused. She wanted to remain independent, or so she told everyone.

Last winter, Esther had overheard her parents talking about Mary's determination to live alone. They thought she simply didn't want to be a burden to anyone. Besides, Esther had lived in that small house for almost twenty years with her husband. It was, after all, her home.

But Esther certainly felt that she was being burdened today. Her entire schedule would be disrupted, simply because Mary wanted not only to live alone but wanted the immediate return of her Tupperware.

As if reading her mind, her mother handed over the containers. "I just wish she'd move here. Our *dawdihaus* is perfect for her and just sitting there empty ever since Dawdi John David passed on."

Esther couldn't remember when her grandfather had died. She was nineteen now—almost twenty—but she'd been much younger when he passed away. She supposed it was at least ten or more years now. He'd lived with them ever since Esther was born, in the small attached *dawdihaus* behind the main house. And then, he died and the little house remained vacant for quite a long time.

That is until, just a few years ago, one of Esther's older brothers had moved into the *dawdihaus*. They lived there for a while, but his new bride had convinced him to buy a small farm just last year. It had remained empty ever since.

Esther suspected that Johnny's wife didn't like the idea of being so far away from *her* family or, perhaps, she didn't fancy the idea of being so close to *his* family. Either way, Johnny and Beth now lived in Elkhart County and rarely came home to visit. Beth came from a more conservative church district and had never really fit into the Raber family. In fact, Esther had overheard her parents talk more than once about why Johnny had chosen a wife from such a strict Amish community.

"It'll do Mary some good if you can visit a spell with her," her mother continued, walking behind Esther as she hurried to the door.

Inwardly, Esther groaned. She hadn't calculated visiting in her previous tally for total tardiness. "I have work, Mamm," she reminded her.

"I know that, Esther. But this is important."

"So's my work." Esther reached for her black coat and, after setting down the containers, slipped her arms into it. When she looked up, she noticed that her mother was staring at her. With a sigh, Esther relented. "But I promise I won't rush the visit."

Her mother gave her another warm smile. "That's my girl."

Esther hurried outside and grabbed her bicycle. The air was cool, even though spring had officially arrived just a few weeks ago. She placed the containers into the basket and secured them with a piece of twine then started pushing the bicycle down the driveway before placing her foot on the pedal and boosting herself onto the seat.

While she didn't live too far from the grocery store, Mary lived in the opposite direction. Quickly, Esther tried to calculate the fastest route to get there without having to back track too much. Fortunately, the roads were void of traffic due to the early hour. The Englischers who lived nearby didn't usually set out for work until after eight since it took them less time to get there in their automobiles. The only time the roads were congested were in the summer when tourists explored the backroads outside Shipshewana.

Made in the USA
Monee, IL
01 June 2020